MOST SECRET

NAME: Finn Gunnersen

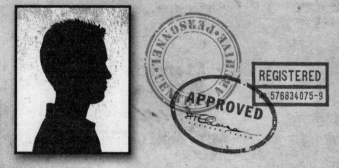

REGISTERED
576834075-9

APPROVED

AGE: 16

BACKGROUND: Born Trondheim, Norway. Father RAF
  Spitfire pilot (killed in action). Mother and
  sister arrested by Gestapo. Escaped from occupied
  Norway by stealing Heinkel 115 float plane.

ASSESSMENT: Outwardly unremarkable.
  Taught to fly by father. Physically fit though not
  strong. Quick to learn and resourceful. Responds
  well under pressure though tendency to be rather
  reckless. Inseparable from Mr Larson and Miss
  Haukelid. A decent, honest lad. Brave but
  vulnerable. Far more courageous than he realises.
  Keen to follow in father's footsteps.

RECOMMENDED
FOR ACTIVE SERVICE
IN THE FIELD
0619-3199-46

MOST SECRET

NAME: Loki Larson

APPROVED

REGISTERED
NO. 576834084-6

AGE: 16

BACKGROUND: Born Trondheim, Norway. Father
commercial pilot and member of local resistance.
Escaped with Mr Gunnersen.

ASSESSMENT: A large lad and as strong as an elk.
Taught to fly by father. Good with his fists. Might
be prone to shoot first and ask questions later. A
loyal and courageous chap who can be relied on in a
crisis. Loki and Finn are lifelong friends and work
well as a team. Loki also close to Miss Haukelid
(potential problem?)

RECOMMENDED
FOR ACTIVE SERVICE
IN THE FIELD
0619-3199-62

MOST SECRET

NAME: Freya Haukelid

AGE: 16

BACKGROUND: Born in remote part of Norway. Father arrested for actively resisting occupation. Mother deceased.

ASSESSMENT: An intelligent girl with tremendous talents. Taught by her father, Freya is an outstanding marksman (rifle) — the best we've come across. Gifted at coding and Morse code, and learns languages quickly. Physically far tougher than her appearance suggests. Despite reservations about sending girls into the field, Freya has the determination and quick-wittedness to succeed.

Also available by Craig Simpson:

SPECIAL OPERATIONS: DOGFIGHT

'A fast-paced thriller' *THE TIMES*
'A full-throttle adventure'
SUNDAY EXPRESS

RESISTANCE

'A terrific romp . . . fans of films
starring Bruce Willis (or David Niven)
should love it' *TES*

A FINN GUNNERSEN ADVENTURE

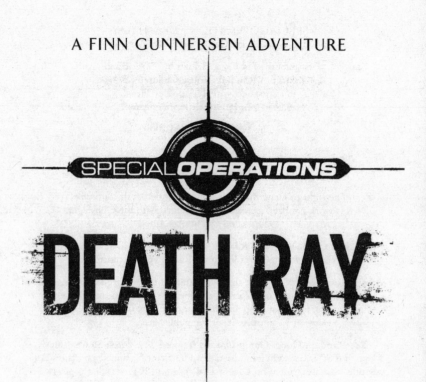

SPECIALOPERATIONS

DEATH RAY

CRAIG SIMPSON

CORGI BOOKS

SPECIAL OPERATIONS: DEATH RAY
A CORGI BOOK 978 0 552 55675 0

First published in Great Britain by Corgi Books,
an imprint of Random House Children's Books,
in association with The Bodley Head,
A Random House Group Company

This edition published 2009

1 3 5 7 9 10 8 6 4 2

The Random House Group Limited supports The Forest Stewardship
Council (FSC), the leading international forest certification organisation. All
our titles that are printed on Greenpeace approved FSC certified paper carry
the FSC logo. Our paper procurement policy can be found at
www.rbooks.co.uk/environment

Set in Bembo

Corgi Books are published by Random House Children's Books,
61–63 Uxbridge Road, London W5 5SA

www.rbooks.co.uk

Addresses for companies within The Random House Group Limited can be
found at: www.randomhouse.co.uk/offices.htm

THE RANDOM HOUSE GROUP Limited Reg. No. 954009

A CIP catalogue record for this book is available from the British Library.

Printed and bound in Great Britain by
CPI Bookmarque, Croydon, CR0 4TD

*For the young men and women who bravely
carried their heavy suitcases into battle*

A big thank you to Mum and Dad, Charlie Sheppard, Harriet Wilson and Carolyn Whitaker for all their encouragement, guidance and support.

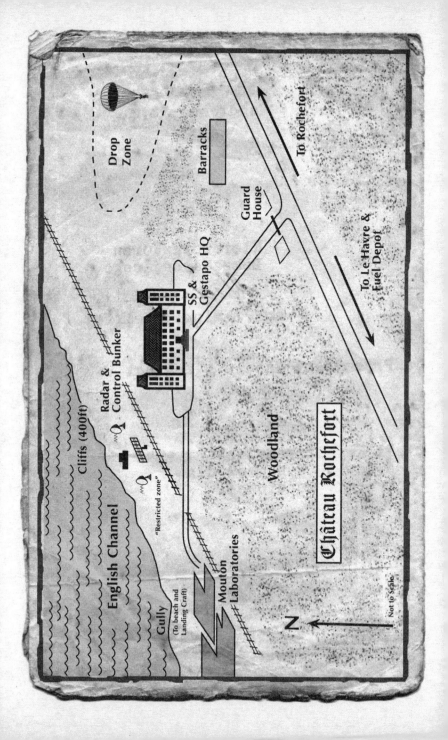

During a war many people have no choice but to fight. Others volunteer out of a sense of duty to King and Country, claiming they are fighting for freedom or to protect their way of life. Some, however, go to war for much more personal reasons – for revenge, or to protect those they love. These are the most powerful reasons of all – and the most dangerous. To protect those you love is a basic instinct and you will stop at nothing to defend them, even if it means betraying others who have entrusted their lives to you. As a member of Special Operations I have learned to question why my fellow agents volunteered. If it was for love or revenge, then it is time for me to start worrying and to watch out for the enemy within.

Finn Gunnersen
1941

Chapter One
Heading South

January 1941

Major Baxter's parting words on the platform of Glasgow station gave me the shivers. 'Well, we've taught you all we can in the precious little time available to us. In God's name I just pray it's enough,' he declared as he reached out and shook each of our hands in turn. His crushing grip said *Good luck, give them hell*, and *Be safe*, all in one. I think he wanted to salute us too, but that wouldn't have looked right, a soldier saluting three sixteen-year-olds. People would have thought that rather strange. Of course, Major Baxter knew what *they* didn't – he knew who and what we were.

A horrible truth dawned on me. To all intents and purposes we didn't exist, not officially, except to the leaders of Special Operations who had our details filed away under lock and key in folders marked MOST SECRET. It was odd knowing that passers-by would barely give us a second glance, not guessing in a million years that we were rapidly becoming pawns in the fight against Hitler's Germany. Without uniforms we looked ordinary, like any other civilians, and that was exactly the point. Ordinary was good, perfect in fact, because that's exactly how secret agents should appear.

A shrill whistle and the frantic slamming of carriage doors heralded our departure. The train jolted forward, slowly gathering pace. I could hear the massive steam locomotive puffing and straining, her huge wheels screeching as they struggled for grip. I spent a moment looking out the misted window. Faces floated past like ghosts. Arms waved. Then it all became a blur. Suddenly the station was gone.

We were heading to London, where we'd change trains before completing our journey. Our final destination was 'classified'. I tried asking, of course, but got the standard reply, a rather worrying 'You'll find out soon enough.'

The corridors of our train were jam-packed with troops and their rifles and kit bags. The floor was slippery, and the stale oppressive air full of cigarette smoke, idle chatter, sneezes and hacking coughs, and the odours of damp cloth and leather. I suspected many of these men had been among the troops heroically plucked from the beaches at Dunkirk the previous summer, in what optimists were calling 'the most successful escape in history'. The word 'retreat' was taboo.

Captain Nils Jacobsen slid shut the door to our compartment and pulled down the blind. Nils was accompanying us on our journey into the unknown. Like Freya, Loki and me, he was Norwegian too. In an unfamiliar foreign country it was good having him around. He knew the ropes. He was in his late twenties, but he looked older: the wrinkles around his tired eyes – eyes that had witnessed many dreadful things – were hallmarks of the stresses and strains of being a fighter pilot. Yet he was cheerful and always grinning and joking.

Gathering up our damp coats and gas masks Nils piled them up on an empty seat. Everyone had to carry their smelly rubber *nosebags* at all times. I often wondered if they really worked but hoped I'd never find out.

Loki and Freya slumped down opposite me, Loki occupying the window seat. Resting her head on his shoulder, Freya closed her eyes and let out a weary sigh. In truth we were all exhausted. For the previous three weeks we'd been hidden away in an isolated Scottish hunting lodge near a place called Arisaig on the west coast. The spectacular Highlands, with its many craggy mountains and deep lochs, reminded me of our home-land. The area was 'Restricted', the War Department banning everyone except those involved with Special Operations from stepping foot inside the zone. We'd got to know the area well while being taught the clandestine arts of reconnaissance, concealment and sabotage by Major Baxter and his men.

Nils unfolded his damp newspaper and handed it to me. 'OK, Finn, get reading out loud.'

I groaned, but seized the paper anyway. We had to practise our English every day, to try and lose our native Norwegian accents. I began with the front page. London had been bombed for the fourth night running. The Blitz had claimed another dozen lives. It was grim reading. As I searched the pages for something lighter, I slipped into my native Norwegian and asked, 'How come the Luftwaffe's still pounding us to oblivion? I thought we'd won the battle of the skies.'

Nils grimaced. 'Winning the Battle of Britain was only a partial victory, Finn. It hasn't stopped the bombing, but on the plus side, we've forced the Luftwaffe to limit most of its raids to the hours of darkness. Their losses would be unsustainable otherwise. And it has almost certainly delayed an invasion: Hitler won't risk crossing the Channel unless he has absolute air superiority.'

'Is there any way of stopping them once and for all?' I asked.

'Doubt it,' Nils replied with a little shrug. 'Our RDF system's good, but not that good.'

Freya briefly opened her eyes. 'What's RDF?'

'Radio Direction Finding,' Nils replied. 'Some call it *radar*.'

We'd never heard of it but wanted to know more.

Nils explained. 'The system uses radio waves, just like wireless sets, only much more powerful. Transmitters along the coastline send out pulses. These pulses bounce off anything solid – like aircraft – and get reflected back. Sensitive receivers pick up the return signals. The aerials are directional and, using the time it takes for the pulses to return, it's possible to work out how far away the aircraft are. The radar operators relay the information to us pilots and then it's down to us to intercept the enemy.'

Nils reached out and took my paper from me. Removing a pen from his pocket, he drew a diagram to illustrate. 'The aerials are huge, Finn, about three hundred feet tall. You can't miss them. I've seen them myself while flying coastal patrols.'

Loki leaned forward for a better look at Nils' picture. 'If they're that big, surely Fritz has seen them too? Why haven't they just bombed the hell out of them?'

Scratching his chin, Nils pulled a face. 'Good point, Loki. If I was Fritz and knew what these aerials were for, I'd make destroying them my first priority. Blow them to smithereens. The fact that hasn't happened suggests that Fritz doesn't know what they are. Maybe he just thinks they're ordinary radio transmitters.'

Nils had taken part in many frenetic dogfights. He'd flown alongside my father, who'd travelled to England and joined the RAF when war broke out. Father had been determined to play his part. And his wish was fulfilled, although ultimately it cost him his life. I was proud of him. People had begun calling Pilots like him *the few*, men to whom so much was owed. Of course *the few* had become *fewer*. Britain was desperately short of pilots. 'Was radar much use to you during the Battle of Britain?' I asked.

After a little thought Nils answered my question. 'Yes. Without radar our fighter squadrons wouldn't have been scrambled in time. It gave us a few precious minutes to get airborne, achieve sufficient altitude and locate the enemy.' He paused before continuing. 'Even now they pick up the incoming night bombers while they're still out over the sea. Our lads try their best to intercept them but darkness gives the enemy the edge.' He began chewing the end of his pen. 'What we really need is to have some sort of radar inside our cockpits. Then we'd effectively be able to see in the dark.'

Loki stretched out a leg and gave Nils a friendly kick. 'Why don't you just eat more carrots?' he joked.

We laughed. It was said that British pilots ate lots of carrots because they thought it helped them to see in the dark.

'Do the Germans have this *radar* as well?' asked Freya.

Nils nodded. 'We believe so. In fact, there's a nasty rumour that they have developed a new long-range system, one which gives them even more time to get their fighters airborne.'

'Do you think it's true?'

'It would make sense. Bomber Command has been experiencing horrendous losses recently. No sooner do they reach the French coast than the enemy swarms about them like flies around a rotting carcass. It's one hell of a problem.'

'Well, if they do have it, it must look very different,' Loki observed.

'What do you mean?' I asked.

'If their system's like ours with all those weird tall aerials, our fighter patrols would have spotted them, wouldn't they? Presumably they haven't or we'd know about it. So Fritz's radar system must look different.'

'I expect you're right,' said Nils.

I resumed reading for about twenty minutes before

noticing that everyone else looked as though they were dozing off. Loki, Freya and me were bound together by more than just a lifetime's friendship. Loki's parents, Freya's father, and my mother and sister all languished back home in the dark, dank prison cells of Trondheim's Kristiansten Fortress – all guests of the infamous Gestapo. The fate of our loved ones was as uncertain as our own and the three of us were united by the dream of their safe release, or of one day returning to free them. With Germany seemingly winning the war, a happy outcome felt far, far away – way beyond our reach.

Our helplessness frequently bubbled to the surface as anger and frustration. We leaned heavily on each other for support. Nils played his part too, reminding us that as far as we knew they were still alive. 'Where there's life, there's hope,' he'd say. Often, *hope* on its own just didn't seem enough.

Loki started to snore. I pressed my head against the back of the seat and closed my eyes too. At Arisaig we'd been up before dawn every day, out running in all weathers over gruelling terrain, then ordered to swim back and forth in the icy waters of the lochs. That was part one of our training. It was no holiday, or like any school I'd ever been to before. It was tough. No allowances were made for the fact we were just kids. We all knew that should we fail or display weakness, our time in Special Ops would be over. We'd learned a lot. Stuff like how to camouflage ourselves in the wilderness, how to avoid detection when crossing open ground, how to build shelters, blow up railway lines – basically how to hit the enemy hard and survive on the run.

Although we'd now left the Highlands behind, our training was far from over. There was a second phase, a second school, somewhere incredibly secret, where we were to be taught spycraft and Lord knows what else. That's where we were heading now. It was a daunting prospect not least because it brought us a step closer to active service, to our first real Special Operation.

Chapter Two
London's Burning, Fire Fire!

It was early evening when we arrived in London. The blackout meant there were few lights to see by. The air was thick with steam and soot, and my nose itched like mad.

'There should be a car waiting outside the station,' Nils announced as we all jumped down onto the platform. 'We have to go across the city to catch the next train from Waterloo. But we've got plenty of time.'

Ambling alongside waiting trains, I watched women on tiptoe hug their men, refusing to let go. There were tears and handkerchiefs, sobs and laughter, smiles and frowns – a whole kaleidoscope of emotions. I realized it was their last desperate moment before parting and I knew that for some there'd be no return. There were lines of small children too, their raincoats buttoned up, their hats and caps pulled down over their ears. Each wore a name tag as though they were an item of luggage, and each carried their gas mask in a little box with shoulder straps. At their feet rested small bags and suitcases, just one each, as though they were off on a short holiday. Some looked excited, a few bewildered, but a good many were crying their eyes out. Women with clipboards were clucking round them, keeping them in line and doing their best to be cheerful. 'What's going on?' I asked.

'They're being evacuated. Should have gone months ago,' Nils replied.

'Evacuated where?'

'All over the place. Basically, anywhere outside the city. Families will take them in and look after them until it's safe for them to return.'

Many of the children were incredibly young. Poor blighters. I smiled as I passed two small grinning boys with cheap-looking toy tin helmets on their heads and wooden rifles in their hands. I saluted them and laughed when they stood to attention and saluted me back. We had something in common – we were all going on an adventure. I just hoped theirs would be less dangerous than ours.

Exiting the station, Nils set about searching for our transport. I'd never been to London before and I soaked up the atmosphere: the hectic streets, the buses, the men on street corners selling newspapers. The city was bustling, frantic, alive. I took a deep breath. After hours of being cooped up on the train it felt good to stretch my legs. There were posters everywhere. One showed a soldier pointing at us and bore the words, '*Is your journey really necessary?*' *Yes!* I found myself thinking. Another showed a sinking ship with the caption, '*A few careless words may end in this*'. It was a reminder to avoid discussing the movements of ships or troops. Not all were so threatening though. One showed a boy clutching a spade and said '*Dig for Victory*'.

'Look at those!' Loki announced excitedly, pointing upwards.

'What?' Following his outstretched arm, I gazed to the heavens and saw shapes in the moonlight. They resembled flabby inflatable elephants and were rapidly rising into the night sky – barrage balloons. I'd read about them. They were huge, over sixty feet long and thirty feet tall, and were filled with hydrogen. Tethered to the ground by a long steel cable, they could be winched up or down thousands of feet in just minutes. I felt alarmed by the sight of them and the inevitable question that sprang to mind. Did they always raise them after dusk, or was trouble heading our way?

Loki yawned. 'At least they'll force the Luftwaffe to keep to higher altitudes.'

'Uh-huh. I'd hate to fly into the supporting cables. They'd cut an aircraft in half.' We both peered up a while. 'I wonder what would happen if one exploded? I wouldn't want to be standing beneath it!'

'Yeah, imagine thousands of feet of cable falling out of the sky.'

Nils ran from one parked car to another, tapping on windows and asking the drivers if they were under orders to escort us across town. Finally, he reached the last vehicle, looked back towards us and shrugged apologetically.

'Oh great!' Freya cursed. 'What do we do now?'

Suddenly something cut through the air. It began as a low-pitched hum but rapidly rose into a screaming whine before oscillating between the two extremes – an air-raid siren! The wailing horror put the fear of God into me. Raising the barrage balloons was no exercise, I realized. Someone knew the enemy was coming! People stopped whatever they were doing and scurried for cover. Nils hurried back and shouted, 'Just what we didn't need. We'll head for the nearest shelter.'

We quickly found ourselves amid a huddle making for the entrance to an underground station. Caught up in the mêlée, we descended the steps. It felt as if we were being carried along on a tidal wave. People pushed and shoved, swore and complained. 'Get a bleedin' move on!' yelled a tall fellow impatiently.

'Faff off!' someone else replied angrily.

I was amazed people didn't trip and fall and disappear beneath a hundred trampling feet. Then again, I supposed Londoners were used to the drill. Eventually we found ourselves in a long corridor close to the subterranean platform, at least fifty feet below ground level. I heard someone shout, 'Mind the gap', and moments later caught a glimpse of a train slowly snaking its way towards the black of a tunnel. We didn't have underground railways back home, except those that ran through the mountains. Gradually panic was replaced by a sense of relief sweeping through the crowds. We'd made it! We were safe.

'How long will we have to stay down here?' asked Freya. 'It's awful. It stinks.'

'As long as it takes,' Nils replied. 'Until we get the all clear.'

The station filled rapidly. I noticed that most came

prepared, some with books, games and blankets under their arms, others weighed down with bags of food. Some looked as if they'd been here for hours already.

The atmosphere was humid and heavy, the air smelling stale, full of dirt and grime. But the people of London seemed a cheery lot, and I heard laughter as well as babies crying. I watched four men play cards and one of them lose half a crown to the others. To my right an elderly chap began a tune on his mouth organ while tapping his feet. Young children sat in a circle and amused themselves with games.

The first bomb fell. It sounded little more than a dull, distant thud. It was strangely reassuring – sounding so far away it surely meant we were safe. But it was quickly followed by more vibrating thumps and bangs: the detonations arrived in clusters, and they grew louder. And louder!

The chatter ceased. Only the cries of griping toddlers broke the hush. It was as if everyone was holding their breath. I tried to imagine what the crews of the German bombers were thinking as they reached out and flipped their bomb-release toggles, their planes lurching upwards, their heavy load of munitions tumbling from the belly of their metallic death machines. Did they care about the horror they'd unleashed? Or was it all too far away, too unreal, *too unimaginable*?

A bomb fell nearby. I flinched as the lights flickered. Another struck. The lights went out for a few seconds and then came back on. People lifted newspapers to shield their heads from the dust and dirt falling from cracks between the bricks in the ceiling. Then more bombs arrived. The place shook. I shook. Loki seized Freya and held her tightly. I heard people praying aloud. We all knew the truth: our place of refuge was safe – unless it suffered a direct hit. Then we might be killed or buried alive. The thunder above us seemed unrelenting, as if an angry giant's boot was stamping down on us. The lights went out, and this time they didn't come back on. People switched on their torches. I felt a hand reach out and grasp mine. It was Freya's. I squeezed it tightly. Another bomb struck and our underground world shook. To my left a woman cried out.

Then it stopped. There were no more bombs.

Eventually the siren wailed the all clear.

Slowly people made their way to the surface. What greeted us made me swallow hard. We'd emerged into a very different London. The evening was lit by an awful, flickering, orange glow. It was hot too. Buildings were ablaze, ferocious flames roaring and spitting. The air was thick with the strange odours of cordite and petroleum, reminding me of spent fireworks. Twisted pieces of shrapnel lay on the pavement amid the rubble; the chunks of bomb casings possessed edges that looked sharp enough to slice through human flesh. We spun on our heels and tried to take it all in.

'They dropped incendiaries,' Nils shouted. 'That's why the fires are so fierce. In some ways they're worse than the bombs. And it looks like the main station has taken some direct hits.'

I saw a crater in the road. Twenty feet wide and ten feet deep, a burst water main inside it spouted high into the night air. It looked like a fountain. Falling droplets sparkled. They almost looked beautiful. To my right a car was on fire. It burned brightly. As flames consumed it, acrid black smoke lifted into the sky. Then I saw that the driver was still sitting behind the steering wheel. I felt the contents of my stomach rise up and looked the other away.

'Jesus, Finn!' Loki placed a comforting arm around Freya's shoulder and held her close. 'This is hell on earth.'

'I've never seen anything like it,' I yelled, shielding my face from the searing heat. My palms were shiny with sweat. 'Even when they bombed Trondheim back home, it wasn't on this scale.'

Wriggling free of Loki's grasp, Freya declared, 'We should try to help.'

'Best leave it to others,' said Nils, anxiously looking round. 'We've got to get across the city. It could take hours in all this chaos.'

'No,' Freya replied firmly. 'There were hundreds of people in the station. Maybe some of them didn't get out. We've got to help.'

'She's right,' I said. 'At least until the fire service gets here.'

Reluctantly Nils agreed. We ran back into the station. Part of the roof had collapsed. The ticket office was now a pile of bricks. A group of men were frantically grabbing fragments of masonry, chunks of wood and metal, and flinging them to one side of a smoking mound. We got to work beside them, pausing every minute or two to see if anyone could hear the muffled voices of those trapped. Fifteen minutes' hard graft yielded nothing more than a shoe, an umbrella and a rag doll. All the while buildings around the station glowed, the air filled with spitting and crackling flames as the roaring fire storms tore through one storey after another. Hearing the bells of ambulances, I stopped for a second to wipe the sweat from my brow.

A fire tender with a dozen more men arrived. Unable to manoeuvre the vehicle onto the platform, instead they unrolled their hoses and set about connecting them to a large, camouflaged water tank and to nearby hydrants. As they began dousing the flames the mass of white hose pipes jerked and wriggled like intertwined snakes. The pressure caused water to spray from poorly sealed connections and form small streams which became waterfalls as they cascaded over the edge of the platform. Wardens wearing helmets and armbands began trying to bring order to the streets outside, telling people to keep back, yelling that it was too dangerous and that buildings might collapse at any moment. It was mayhem.

Defeated, having not saved a soul, we eventually gave up. We headed for the exit, or rather what was left of it – mangled iron railings and gates, and smouldering wood. After a few paces I stopped dead. By my right boot was a small tin helmet. Further to my right was another mountain of rubble. The others kept going but

I was glued to the spot. Those evacuees, I thought. Surely they'd heeded the air-raid warning. Surely one of those small boys had simply dropped his tin helmet in the rush to get to the shelters. Surely . . .

I thought I heard a whimper. It came from the mound. 'Hey!' I called out. 'There's someone under here. Quick, come and help.'

The others returned and we were joined by three young men in uniform. One spoke with a French accent, another sounded Polish. We grabbed, yanked, pulled and heaved, chucking rubble to one side. Others came to help. I found myself gasping for breath, sweat dripping from my nose, my heart pounding. We didn't stop. We kept digging.

'Here!' someone shouted.

I could see a small foot. It was buried deep and we'd have to be careful lifting stuff off in case everything slipped and crushed whoever was beneath. Feverishly we continued clearing a way down. Then, far to my right, Loki called out, 'I can see an arm.'

There were two bodies! We divided ourselves into teams. It became a race. Eventually Nils and I grasped each end of a long heavy plank. On the count of three, we slowly lifted it and flung it aside. I gasped. We'd revealed a small, pale face, all covered in dust and grime. The child looked calm, peaceful, as if he was just taking a nap. I reached down, cleared away some more bricks, grabbed hold of the boy's coat collar and pulled. His eyes flashed open. I let out a cry of surprise. 'He's alive!' I shouted. The boy took a small gasp of air. Then his eyes rolled back into his head. 'He doesn't look good.' I pulled him free. Nils snatched the child from me and rushed him into the arms of the ambulance men. We crowded round as they set to work. And we let out a cheer when, moments later, the lad coughed and spluttered, colour returned to his cheeks and he began sobbing loudly for his mother.

I turned and spotted Loki crouching next to Freya by the mountain of wreckage we'd been dismantling by hand, brick by brick. Half a dozen others were standing round them. I charged back. 'Hey, he's still alive!' I shouted, skidding to a halt. 'How are you doing? Can I help? You OK?'

Freya looked up at me and shook her head. I saw both fury and tears in her eyes. Another small boy was cradled in her arms. I recognized him. He was one of the lads I'd seen earlier. He couldn't have been more than six years old. His lifeless brown eyes stared straight up into mine. I felt sick. Britain was at war, and this was what war looked like.

Loki raised his head and gazed to the heavens. 'You bastards!' he shouted at the top of his voice. 'You *bloody, bloody bastards*!'

Chapter Three
Far from Prying Eyes

It was almost midnight when our train finally pulled into the tiny station. We were the only passengers left in our carriage. I shook Loki and Freya awake and Nils gathered up our gas masks. Wearily we stepped out into the cool night air.

'Where the hell are we?' Loki asked irritably, stretching his arms above his head and yawning. We glanced about for signs. There weren't any. The station was unlit, the small ticket office deserted. In the moonlight I saw half a dozen ponies huddled together for warmth at the far end of the platform. *Ponies?* Confused, I scratched my head.

'There should be a truck waiting,' said Nils. 'Not far to go now. And with any luck there'll be steaming mugs of cocoa waiting for us.' He led the way towards the exit.

'This place is weird,' I observed, noticing that apart from the ticket office and a couple of small cottages there were no other buildings to be seen. All I could make out in the darkness were distant trees in an otherwise flat, open terrain. Surely stations were normally close to cities, towns and villages, I thought. Close to people. Not this one. This one lay at the heart of nowhere.

Our transport, a battered old army truck, was indeed waiting, parked on an area of hard standing outside the station. A rather scruffy soldier leaped out of the cab, ran up to us and saluted Nils half-heartedly, his hand barely reaching his own chin. 'Welcome, sir,' he said cheerfully. 'Do you have any luggage?'

'No,' said Nils. 'It was sent on ahead.'

The soldier looked surprised. 'What, not even a delivery for us?'

Nils shrugged. 'No. Sorry.'

'Damn. The buggers said it would be on your train. Wait here a minute. Shan't be a tick.' The soldier ran off into the station, returning a few seconds later with a broad grin, lugging a heavy-looking sack. 'Phew! They'd have my ruddy guts for garters if I'd left this here.'

'What's in it?' I asked.

'Nazi uniforms!' He laughed heartily. 'Last delivery got left here for days. Right mix-up. Some old dear took a peek and fainted on the spot. Thought Jerry had arrived on our shores and left his dirty laundry out. Daft old bat. Right-o, hop aboard. It's only a ten-minute ride to Mulberry House. Brigadier Devlin is eagerly awaiting your arrival. I'm Corporal Smith, by the way. Smithy to my friends.'

We clambered into the back of the truck and sat down on small benches. The diesel engine started up, and with a hefty jolt we rattled off on the final leg of our journey.

★ ★ ★

Mulberry House lay at the end of a long track that wound through dense woodland. At the gated entrance, complete with cattle grid, our truck stopped and more soldiers inspected our papers by torch light before allowing us to proceed. The vehicle drew to a halt again outside the main entrance. Jumping down onto the gravel drive, we all stared at our new home, a large brick house with tall chimney stacks reaching up into the night sky. In the moonlight, the word bleak sprang to mind as a chill wind whipped about my neck. I shivered and my hair prickled as if full of nits. Looking round, I noticed that there was a small cottage at the side of the main house, partially hidden in the trees.

The door to Mulberry opened and light spilled out. A figure appeared. 'I know an army marches on its stomach,' he bellowed, before adding, 'Well if you don't like it, you can lump it!' It took me a few seconds to realize he was talking to someone inside the house. He turned and quickly surveyed the four of us, his eyes settling on Nils. 'Ah, Captain Jacobsen. Glad to see you all made it in one piece. Splendid. Come in, come in.' He stepped to one side and beckoned us across the threshold. 'I'm Brigadier Devlin. Sorry about all that just now. Mrs Saunders made mock hare soup – a special treat, apparently. Didn't go down too well I'm afraid.'

'What's mock hare soup?' asked Freya.

'Well, miss, mock hare soup is exactly the same as real hare soup except it's made without any hare.'

Freya frowned. We all frowned.

'That's rationing for you, I'm afraid,' the brigadier added, shrugging. 'Cook likes to experiment! You'll soon get used to it.'

The four of us were told to wait in the large drawing room. Freya warmed her hands in front of a roaring log fire while Nils slumped in a leather chair and began impatiently drumming his fingers on its arm. Loki and I wandered around the room inspecting the various paintings and maps hung on the walls and the many tatty books wedged in equally tatty bookcases.

The door opened and the man we knew only as 'X' breezed in. He still had his raincoat and trilby on and he was clutching a thin leather document bag. He was followed by three others: the brigadier, another man in army uniform and a woman carrying a tray.

'Welcome,' said X, making a point of greeting each of us with a warm smile and vice-like handshake. Then he removed his hat and coat and fiddled with the clasp of his bag. 'Help yourselves to cocoa,' he said. 'Oh, and this is Mrs Saunders. She'll be looking after you here – cooking, washing, that sort of thing.'

Mrs Saunders struck me as the homely sort. She was a large lady with rosy cheeks and a smile that was probably comforting if you were five years old and suffering from toothache. She banged down the tray, wiped her hands on her floral apron and left the room, closing the door behind her.

'Right,' said X, clearing his throat. He'd removed some papers from his bag and straightened up. He was ready to begin. We took our seats.

'Welcome to Special Operations, STS Mulberry. That stands for Special Training School, by the way,' he began. 'I'd like to formally introduce you to Brigadier Devlin, who will be your commanding officer.'

I guessed the brigadier to be in his late fifties. Standing rather stiffly, his chest stuck out and shoulders pushed back, he struck me as a career soldier, but one clearly too old now for confronting the enemy eye to eye on the battlefield. He nodded at each of us in turn and managed only the faintest of smiles.

'And the other chap here is Sergeant Walker, your senior training instructor. He's a hard taskmaster and doesn't suffer fools gladly. But do as he says and you may just learn something useful. Isn't that right, Sergeant?'

'Yes, sir,' Walker replied with a sly grin. He was much younger than the brigadier, taller too, and had a mop of ginger hair.

'I've prepared a short opening address,' said X. 'Just to highlight the key points about your time here. It won't take long. As you already know, I am in charge of Special Operations. Last time we met you'd just escaped from Norway and successfully delivered into our hands vital intelligence revealing the location of a hidden German battleship. You might be keen to know that a team of commandos have landed in your homeland. As we speak they are making final preparations to scuttle the ship before she sets sail. The German navy, the Kriegsmarine, are about to be dealt a heavy blow, and maybe, just maybe, Allied Atlantic convoys will be safe from attack, and thousands of sailors spared a watery grave. At least for now.'

Loki punched the air and shouted with delight.

'Pipe down, Mr Larson. The war's not over yet!' X barked sharply.

I felt proud. Many people had risked their lives to bring the fistful of photographs and maps to England safely. Loki, Freya and I had been part of it. We'd got caught up in the dangerous work of the local Resistance and, when everything began to go wrong, I'd found myself lumbered with the priceless intelligence. The Germans were onto us, though, and quickly closed in, arresting our families. Our time was up. As fugitives, we'd run out of friends to turn to and places to hide. And we'd still had the blasted documents!

As Loki and I had grown up flying alongside our fathers, who were pilots, we'd decided we had only one way out – to steal a plane and pray that we knew enough to get her up and down safely. We did – just! The Heinkel 115 float plane had just been sitting there in the fjord, almost as if it was waiting to be nicked.

Following our landing and debriefing in Scotland, X turned up and made us an offer. Would we like the opportunity to hit back at the enemy? Would we mind going back to school? No ordinary school, but a rather special one where we'd be trained as secret agents. X was a shadowy figure, sharp-featured, with cold, hungry, steel-grey eyes. Perfect for his clandestine job. He received his orders directly from the British prime

minister, Mr Winston Churchill, and I think that meant
no one dared question his authority.

'First, I guess you're all wondering where you are.' X
turned and inspected a large map pinned to the wall.
'This map shows southern England.' He tapped a finger
against it. 'London's here.'

'What's left of it,' Loki muttered.

X frowned. Nils explained, 'We were delayed by an
air raid.'

'Ah!' X grimaced. 'Glad you're all in one piece. Now
you are right down here,' he continued, sliding his finger
down towards the middle of the map, close to the coast.
We all leaned forward in our chairs for a better look. 'It's
called the New Forest. The whole area around Mulberry
House is a mix of woodland, open heath, and small
farmsteads. Importantly, it is a *restricted area*. The army is
using much of it for training purposes, and the navy has
a number of sites located on the coast and rivers. I
should also tell you that Mulberry is only one part of
our school. There are other houses in the forest in which
groups are undergoing training just like you.' Turning
away from the map, he began pacing back and forth. 'We
discourage contact with the locals. That's not to say you
can't visit the nearby villages, but you should either
be accompanied by someone in uniform or take
extreme care not to reveal who you are or what you're
doing here.'

'Sounds more like a prison camp,' Freya whispered
under her breath.

X glared at her for a moment before proceeding.

'There are three other students here at Mulberry House. You will get the chance to say hello first thing tomorrow morning. Sergeant Walker shall arrange for various instructors to visit you here. They are from all walks of life, so don't be surprised if some strike you as rather odd or shady characters. After all, who better to teach you about blowing open a safe than a top safe-cracker, or about breaking and entering than a proficient cat burglar?

'Can I ask a question?' I interrupted.

'Yes, Finn, of course.'

'How long will we be here?'

'As long as necessary.' He resumed pacing the room. 'For now, my orders to you are simple. Listen and learn. Soak up everything. Practise hard. Ask questions. Use your time here productively. Waste not one minute. All too soon, frighteningly so in fact, you will find your-selves in enemy territory with minimal equipment. You will have to rely on your wits and your training. You will have to survive undetected amid the enemy for maybe months on end. One slip and you'll be caught. And if you're caught no one will come running to rescue you. You'll be alone.'

I gulped.

X leaned against the back of a chair. 'Unfortunately, there are influential men in high places who think this whole exercise is foolhardy, that training civilians to work behind enemy lines will prove disastrous, and that training boys and girls of your tender age to do the work of soldiers is simply madness.'

'The official Secret Intelligence Services, the SIS, and in particular MI6 are the loudest objectors to our very existence,' the brigadier interrupted sharply. 'But the buggers are wrong. They fail to appreciate the advantages.'

'Advantages?' Freya asked.

'Well, Miss Haukelid, not least the fact that children raise fewer suspicions than adults. And in some occupied countries, particularly France, many of the men have been forced to go and work in Germany. That means there are fewer about on the streets. Those who are often attract attention and get stopped and questioned. It's a big problem. Hopefully you can all slip under the net.'

'Quite so,' X continued. 'Suffice it to say, however, that there's more than a little healthy competition between us and the SIS. I fought tooth and nail to get the Special Operations group up and running, scrounging what I could, begging, borrowing and stealing the rest. Thankfully, Mr Churchill is a firm supporter of my grand plan. Without his backing, the SIS would have us shut down inside a week. Of course, even Mr Churchill's support will not last for ever if we don't deliver. So, we have to be successful. We have to hit the enemy hard.' X glared at each of us in turn to drive the point home. 'Much rests on your shoulders but I'm sure you won't let me down.'

'We will teach you many things here,' Sergeant Walker added. 'Your weapons practice will be stepped up, and you'll learn how to set explosives and detonators, and use timing devices to disrupt the enemy's machinery of war. Naturally, while here you shall also continue the fitness training you began up in Scotland, and further hone your Morse code and cipher skills.'

X gripped the back of the chair tightly with both hands. 'You are all embarking on a most unusual journey – towards a career not far removed from that of the common criminal. But let us all face a stark truth – this war is vile, dirty, nasty and downright underhand. There are no rules. Think of it as nothing less than a battle of good versus evil. And right now the outcome lies precariously in the balance. Put simply, our backs are against the wall.'

Loki raised a hand.

'Yes, Mr Larson. What is it?'

'You mean we're losing?'

'Yes, Mr Larson, things are going badly for us. After the fall of France and the Low Countries, not to mention your own homeland, the Nazis effectively control most of Europe, all the way east to the Baltic and Black Sea. However, all is not lost. Britain remains an island of defiance. We are a painful boil on Hitler's back-side and we don't intend to let him forget it. When we think of war, we often imagine great battles involving thousands of men and machinery such as tanks and artillery, fighter aircraft engaged in frantic dogfights in the skies above us. But there are other aspects to warfare – aspects hidden from the public gaze, rarely reported in newspapers, never spoken of in radio broadcasts and denied by men in authority. I believe it will be these that will decide the outcome of this war. Maybe it will be the breaking of a secret code, or perhaps the destruction of a factory or other vital installation. We just have to make sure it is us who deal that defining blow.' X straightened up stiffly. 'So, lady and gentlemen, having said all that, it just leaves me with the task of wishing you good luck, happy hunting and, as Mr Churchill said to me, "Go forth and set Europe ablaze"!'

Silence filled the room. I don't know about the others, but all I could picture was the horrors we'd witnessed in London – is that what he wanted? For Europe to become one massive bonfire? I shuddered at the idea.

'Any further questions?' asked X.

The silence was broken by the brigadier. 'Sergeant Walker will show you to your rooms now. Try and get a good night's sleep as you'll be up at the crack of dawn.'

X began putting on his coat. 'One thing I forgot to say,' he said. 'If at any time you change your minds, if you can't go through with what we ask of you, then you must tell us. There'll be no shame in it. We can make alternative arrangements. It would be better all round if you dropped out before we sent you behind enemy lines. Safer for everyone.'

'That won't be necessary,' I said. 'You know what we went through to get here.'

'Yes.' He smiled at me. 'I thought you'd say that, Finn Gunnersen. Oh, and another thing. You need to fill these forms in. I'll leave them with you. No rush.

The brigadier or Sergeant Walker will help you if necessary. Sorry, but we can never seem to get away from paperwork completely.'

Loki picked them up and examined them. 'What are they?'

'One you have to sign to say that you'll never tell a living soul about Special Ops – we call it the Official Secrets Act. The other is your last will and testament . . . Just in case.'

Chapter Four
Basic Spycraft

Upstairs, I was relieved to discover we each had our own room. In Scotland, Loki and I shared and he'd snored like an elk suffering from a bad case of flu. I barely got a wink of sleep all the time we were there. My room here was small and sparsely furnished. It smelled dusty and slightly odd, kind of rotten, as if a dead mouse lay hidden beneath the floorboards. The bed was metal-framed with squeaky springs and a thin mattress, and there was a rickety bedside table and cupboard. Our luggage had been sent on ahead – one military issue khaki-coloured canvas kitbag each, containing the standard set of clothes issued to students at Arisaig. I opened it and tipped the contents onto the bed: socks, cotton shirts, ill-fitting trousers, itchy sweaters made from coarse wool and spare grey underpants with weak elastic in the waistband – the sum total of my worldly possessions. Our own clothes, the ones we were wearing when we'd arrived from Norway, had been confiscated along with everything else. My precious leather flying jacket, a gift from Father, and his medals and photographs had all been taken by the authorities for *safekeeping*.

Wearily I undressed and slipped beneath the cold, clammy quilt. It took ages to warm up. Just as I finally got comfortable and was close to drifting off to sleep, I heard the distant drone of aircraft engines. It sounded like there were loads of them. I leaped up and ran to the small bedroom window. Unfastening the latch, I threw it wide open and stuck my head out. Peering up into the night, I saw a scatter of dark specks moving slowly south.

'*The enemy, Finn!*' To my left, Loki was leaning out of his window too.

Dozens of planes in arrow-like formations were flying home after their night-time raids. 'They remind me of birds migrating for the winter,' I called out. 'It's hard to identify their silhouettes, but they're probably Dornier Seventeens.'

'Expect you're right. They call them "flying pencils", don't they?'

'Uh-huh.'

Dorniers were heavy-duty bombers, the pride of the Luftwaffe. They were nicknamed 'flying pencils' because of their unusually long noses and fuselage.

Without warning the night suddenly turned alternately white, then black and then white again, the heavens lit by blinding flashes. The noise was deafening too. It was as if great hammers were beating the sky, or somebody was bashing together two giant dustbin lids.

'Anti-aircraft fire,' Loki shouted across to me. 'Doubt they'll hit anything, though.'

He was probably right. I'd heard that a gunner's task was rather tricky. Shells had to be preset to detonate at a particular altitude, hopefully matching that of the enemy planes. Get it wrong and the enemy would laugh all the way home. Get it right and they would be blown out of the sky. As far as I could tell, luck that night was with the Luftwaffe.

'I've seen enough. Goodnight, Finn.'

'Goodnight, Loki.'

Returning to bed, I lay staring at the chipped paint and cracked plaster ceiling that was intermittently lit by the flashes outside. What had we let ourselves in for? Nowhere was safe any more. Death and destruction hung over the world like a dense fog. It was impossible to see what the future held. Where would we be heading? Would we even live to tell others of our adventures? Would anyone bother to read my last will and testament? I turned over onto my stomach and buried my head in the pillow. I thought of home – to before the war, of my small village on the shores of the Trondheimfjord, and the protective embrace of tall snow-capped mountains within full view of the house I'd been born in. Although it seemed far away, almost another world, by concentrating really hard I could see it all vividly. I could hear familiar voices and laughter. On cold winter nights Father would sit by the fire and dream of making his fortune flying passengers and freight from one end of our rugged country to the other, of moving to a big house in the city. Mother would curse at him and vow never to leave our village, and my sister, Anna, would argue with them both before storming off to her room to sulk. So much had changed. I wanted my old life back. I wanted the impossible.

★ ★ ★

I was woken at six-thirty the next morning by Sergeant Walker thumping a fist on my door and yelling, 'Be up and dressed in five minutes, *or else!*'

At breakfast, Mrs Saunders busied herself making pots of tea and toast. In possession of a fine pair of lungs, she sang along with tunes blaring out of a wireless, merely greeting us with a glance and a nod.

Our fellow students descended the stairs and joined us in the kitchen. We introduced ourselves. Brother and sister Jacques and Amélie Lefebvre were French. Jacques was seventeen and very studious looking, his thick glasses frequently needing to be pushed back up the bridge of his nose with a bony index finger. He struck me as pretty humourless too, his brow permanently creased with worry lines. At just fourteen, Amélie was the youngest among us. In truth I was quite shocked that someone of her age was a member of Special Ops, and wondered whether others, maybe even younger than her, were being trained in the other houses X had mentioned. How old did you have to be to qualify? I wondered. Ten? Twelve? Fourteen? Old enough to pick up a gun? Quite pretty, with a wide smile and warm chestnut eyes, Amélie was tiny for her age. She was the sort of person that once you'd met you were unlikely to forget. I wondered if that was a disadvantage in a secret agent – not easily being able to blend into a crowd.

The third of our new acquaintances was one hell of a surprise. Max Stein was a tall sixteen-year-old German! From Düsseldorf, apparently. On seeing the look of shock on our faces, he held up his hands and grinned, telling us, 'Don't worry, I'm on your side. Honestly!'

One of the rules of Special Operations was that English had to be spoken at all times during training unless we were specifically having lessons in another language. Now I understood why. We were quite a mix. I just hoped that we'd be able to understand each other properly as we were all speaking in a second language. From what I could gather, we were all pretty fluent, except Amélie. She seemed to struggle with anything beyond simple phrases.

Our first lesson at Mulberry was held in the dining room, converted to a makeshift classroom by adding a few desks and chairs. Entering with a large leather bag clutched close to his chest, Dr Milton Witherspoon proudly informed us that he was a lecturer in chemistry at Imperial College, London. He was six foot five, skinny as a rake, and wore circular, silver-framed spectacles. Carefully placing his bag on a table at the front of the room, he removed from it a series of glass bottles and jars and set them out neatly in a row. He then turned, grabbed a piece of chalk and scratched out a single word on the large blackboard screwed to the wall – *Invisibility*.

'There are many ways of concealing messages,' Witherspoon began. 'Who can give me some examples?'

Max raised a hand. 'Codes and ciphers,' he suggested.

'Yes,' Witherspoon replied. 'What else?' He rubbed

out the word he'd written on the blackboard and then pointed to the blank space. 'A clue?'

'Some sort of invisible writing?' said Freya.

Witherspoon smiled. 'Yes. Well done.' He picked up one of his jars and examined it. It was empty. 'I'd like a volunteer, please.'

Loki threw a hand up enthusiastically.

'Ah, thank you. Mr Larson, isn't it? So kind. Please take this jar outside and pee into it.'

'*What?*' Loki was shocked. For a split second I think he assumed he'd misheard and eagerly awaited confirmation of his error from Witherspoon's lips. Unfortunately he was to be disappointed.

'Pee into it. You don't need to fill it up. Half will do. Less, if that's all you can manage.'

I couldn't help but snigger.

'Mr . . . Gunnersen, I presume? Something amusing you?' There was a stern frown on his brow.

'No!' I lied, struggling to keep a straight face.

'Chop chop, Mr Larson, we haven't got all day.'

Loki grabbed the jar and left the room, returning five minutes later. Somewhat embarrassed, he handed the jar to Witherspoon, who smiled again and thanked him profusely. 'Excellent, nice and pale. Not too yellow. Now,' he said, 'all we need is paper and a suitable pen and nib.' He reached into his bag and produced some paper and pens. Dipping a nib into the jar, he quickly removed it and began scratching out a message on a sheet of paper. 'There!' he declared. 'Just let that dry a minute.'

He then held up the piece of paper in front of him. 'Can anybody tell me what I've written? Come closer. Have a proper look.'

We got up and crowded round Witherspoon's desk. I couldn't read anything. The paper looked blank to me. Freya and Amélie reckoned they could see something but were unable to read it. Loki said nothing but remained red-faced.

'Excellent!' Witherspoon declared. 'Someone fetch me that lamp over there, will you, and plug it in. Best if you remove the shade.'

Witherspoon allowed the naked bulb to heat up for a few minutes and then held the paper over the top of it. Slowly he moved it back and forth. We all watched closely. 'Need to try and get an even heat,' he informed us. 'Gently does it.' Slowly words began to form, faint brown words.

'*You can . . .*' Freya began reading aloud.

'*. . . also use egg white or . . .*' Max continued.

'*. . . lemon juice,*' I said, completing the sentence.

'All of them work to a degree,' Witherspoon explained, screwing up the page and lobbing it into a wastepaper basket at the back of the room. 'You could even try *blood serum* if really desperate. Acceptable in an emergency. In my laboratory at the university I have been developing some rather more efficient secret inks.'

For the next half-hour he demonstrated with liquids which left no visible trace on drying but which, when exposed to heat or a spray of some sort, quickly revealed clear print. Others were only revealed under ultraviolet light, mercury vapour or ammonia fumes. 'This is my finest to date,' he declared, holding up a small bottle triumphantly. 'Its beauty is that you can impregnate it into material – a sock for example. An agent can wear the sock into enemy territory, and when the ink is needed, simply take it off and place it in water to soak. Must say, I'm rather chuffed with that one. I'll try and get some socks for you to try out in a week or two.'

Socks? I looked at Loki and pulled a face.

'Now, enough alchemy for one morning,' said our teacher. 'Supposing you don't have access to secret inks, how else might you conceal a message?'

'A book or newspaper, erm . . . words, erm . . .' Amélie suggested. Waving her arms in frustration, she struggled to find the right English phrase. Failing to do so, she looked to Jacques and added, '*Souligner.*'

'Ah, *oui*, Amélie. She means *underlining* the words,' he said.

'Yes. Excellent, Miss Lefebvre. But maybe a little too obvious,' Witherspoon replied. 'Remember, if a message is discovered in your possession it will land you in great trouble. It needs to be better hidden. Try using a pin to make tiny holes through each word or letter instead.' He demonstrated with a piece of newspaper and the point of a safety pin. 'See? Far less visible to the eye, unless—' He held the page up to the light and we saw the little dots appear like stars on a clear night. 'Now they're visible.'

Witherspoon taught us to take great care about where we concealed messages on ourselves. Stitching them into the seams of clothing seemed an obvious idea. What I hadn't considered, though, was the import-ance of using only clothing that can be readily discarded, like a scarf, rather than the hem of a dress or cuff of a shirt. 'If you're caught, you can hardly remove your shirt or trousers, can you?' he pointed out. 'It sounds obvious, but many agents have given themselves away by not taking such simple precautions.'

I made notes as Witherspoon proceeded to put all his jars and paraphernalia back into his bag. 'Well, that's all for now. I'll be back in a few weeks, when I'll explain how you can use a wonderful substance called carborundum to make a train or lorry quite literally grind to a halt. Simply splendid stuff, and very effective too. Cheerio, all!'

No sooner had Witherspoon departed than our next teacher arrived. Stanley Briggs was short, plump and completely bald. With a flourish he wrote the word *Disguises* on the blackboard. 'Any suggestions?'

Loki called out, 'Wig or false moustache.'

'Like this perhaps?' Briggs delved into his bag, produced a long blond hairpiece and placed it on his head. Flicking the fringe out of his eyes, he said, 'Well?'

We all laughed. 'You look ridiculous,' said Freya.

'Yes, I do, don't I,' he said. He tore off the wig. '*And* I'm a professional actor! You're not. And yet' – he paused, suddenly looking incredibly serious – 'being able to quickly change the way you look might just save your lives. Suppose you are walking down a crowded street and you think you are being followed. What might you do? Certainly there's no time to put on wigs and moustaches or apply make-up.'

'Change our clothes in some way?' Freya offered.

'*Yes!*' Briggs thrust up his hands in mock joy. 'Well done, Miss Haukelid. Often the simplest things are the most effective. The tiniest changes to how you look may be enough to throw the enemy off your scent. Simply removing a raincoat or hat, taking or discarding an umbrella, combing one's hair a different way – all have been known to work a treat.' He stopped talking and surveyed the room. 'Good, I think you are all keeping up with me. To summarize, be clever and quick thinking. Use your imagination. Use whatever is to hand.'

'Like what?' I asked.

'Well, maybe you could seize a bicycle and push it along the pavement, or ride off on it. If a dog is tied up outside a shop, perhaps you could take it for a walk. Offer to carry an old lady's shopping for her. Talk to her like she's your grandmother. Confuse the enemy. Such techniques might save your skin. Be confident. *Be daring!*'

I scribbled a few notes. Meanwhile, Briggs turned and scratched the words *Body language* onto the blackboard. I wrote them down as well.

'We're all creatures of habit,' he continued. 'And the enemy knows it. They are trained to spot things, little details. For example, think about how you carry a newspaper – folded under your arm, or in your hand? Which arm or hand? Left or right? Set out to confuse the enemy. Be prepared to change the way you do it at a moment's notice.'

While Jacques got Briggs to repeat most of what he'd just said for Amélie's benefit – she looked completely lost – I wrote down *paper* and then added *slouching* and *hands in pockets*. I had a habit of keeping my hands stuffed in my pockets. It might make a difference, I supposed.

Briggs continued, 'Now let's examine the way we walk. You might be surprised to learn that we all do it differently. It can give you away, so try changing the way you swing your arms, or the way you throw each foot forward.' He demonstrated for us. 'Maybe hunch your shoulders a little.' He stopped, put down his chalk and rubbed his hands together. 'A very convincing limp can be achieved by placing a small stone in one's shoe. Try it out.' He leaned on his desk and peered at us. 'Practise, practise, practise, practise, practise,' he said, to each of us in turn. 'And when you're tired of it, practise some more. Make such things second nature, natural looking. But be careful not to exaggerate. They must be convincing yet not draw attention to you.'

We spent half an hour practising our different walks and nervous tics, and trying to do everything with the wrong hand. Briggs's enthusiasm proved infectious. He seemed to know an awful lot about his subject. By the time he called us to order and got us sat back down I was beginning to wonder whether there was rather more to Stanley Briggs than met the eye. Was he simply a professional actor, or was he an experienced member of the secret services as well?

'Of course, there may be a few situations where more drastic measures are needed,' Briggs added. 'Maybe you're on a mission and a proper disguise is essential.' He reached into his bag and took out some small sponges. He placed them in his mouth, pushing them into his cheeks. 'See the difference? So much the better if you can get hold of some iodine. It can be used to discolour your teeth. You can also try darkening your hair with charcoal or lightening it with talcum powder or hair bleach.' He walked to where Loki was sitting. 'You, Mr Larson, have a pronounced chin cleft. That could be disguised with melted wax.' Loki pulled a face, and then ran a finger along his chin. Briggs returned to the front of the class. 'If you have wrinkles, accentuate them using the lead from soft black pencils. In minutes you'll look five, maybe ten years older.'

There was a snort of derision from the back of the room. I turned and saw Amélie shaking her head. 'Something wrong, *mademoiselle*?' Briggs enquired, tutting and looking to the heavens as if her request for clarification or repetition were a wearisome inevitability.

She spoke slowly, stumbling slightly, but managed to get her point across. 'If you get stopped, you have to give your papers to soldiers – yes? Big problem. You don't look like your photograph. They will arrest you. Then they will take you away. In truck. You'll never be seen again.' She drew a finger across her throat. '*Mort et enterré!*'

We looked at Jacques. 'She means you'll be *dead and buried*,' he said. 'Amélie, you must try and stick to English. I know it's hard but you really must try.'

'Yes, well . . .' Briggs balked uncomfortably. It was the first time I'd seen him look anything other than supremely confident. 'You must choose your disguises carefully. And if at all possible, have false papers made, *including new photographs*.' He glanced sharply at Amélie. 'The art of evading capture is like a game of cat-and-mouse. What I'm teaching you may just give you the edge. But to be blunt, you are the mouse and sometimes the mouse gets caught!'

A bewildered Amélie leaned across to her brother and muttered, '*Chat et souris?* Did he say cat and mouse? Is he crazy?' Jacques explained in French what Briggs had just said. 'Oh!' She nodded and pulled a face. 'You are right!'

It was Jacques' turn to speak up. Rocking back in his chair, he observed, 'You're both right, surely. If you can, it's better to lie low. Don't take risks unless you have no choice. If you can't hide, if you have to escape, or think you're being followed, head for somewhere crowded. Try to lose yourself. Move back and forth. Go in one door and leave by another. Walk quickly but calmly. Don't keep looking over your shoulder. It is a real give-away. Use your eyes. Use the reflections in shop windows.'

Loki pulled a face. He was probably thinking the same as I was. Our French colleagues had clearly already gained practical experience.

'Yes, yes, good advice,' said Briggs. 'Thank you, Mr Lefebvre.'

Loki twisted round and said to Jacques, 'And what if there isn't a crowd?'

'Run like hell!'

Chapter Five
Night of Broken Glass

After Briggs had packed up and left, Loki and I wandered out through the front door of Mulberry House for a little fresh air, and spotted Jacques, sleeves rolled up, peering under the opened bonnet of a car. The soldier who'd driven us from the station the previous night was standing next to him, hands on hips, looking rather impatient. Seeing him in the daylight, I realized just how short he was and, although not exactly skinny, he struck me as quite wiry in a tough sort of way. He was also as ugly as sin, his nose bent from a break at some time in the past. It gave him a curiously unbalanced, lopsided appearance.

'Hand me a screwdriver, Smithy,' said Jacques, holding out a hand while still leaning over the engine.

Smithy obliged and then, seeing Loki and me, called out, 'All right, lads? Jacques here's a bloody marvel. He can fix anything with a motor in it.'

Jacques emerged from beneath the bonnet. 'There is damp in the distributor,' he announced. He held up the distributor cap as proof. 'See! That's why she wasn't running properly.' Jacques took a handkerchief from his pocket and wiped the inside of the cap, then the small rotor under the bonnet. 'There. Perfect. Now try her again.'

The engine started first time.

'What did I tell you? He's a bloody marvel,' Smithy said, beaming.

'Where did you learn about engines, Jacques?' I asked.

'I've always been interested in them,' he replied, cleaning his hands with his hanky. 'And I'd just started studying engineering at university when France was invaded.'

'Corporal Smith! You still here?' We turned and saw Sergeant Walker leaning out of a window. 'Stop yakking and go and fetch those supplies. This isn't a ruddy holiday camp!'

Smithy lazily stiffened to attention and saluted, though it was more of a wave than a salute. 'Yes, Sarge. Right away, Sarge. I'll be there and back in a jiffy. Have those detonators for you by tea time.'

'And tidy yourself up, man. I thought I told you to get your hair cut. You look a ruddy disgrace.'

Smithy waited until Walker disappeared back inside before muttering, 'Flipping slave-driver. "Do this! Do that!" Walker loves barking orders. No peace for the wicked, that's what my old man says. Still, better be off. Like I said to Jacques here when he arrived, if you need anything, just shout. I have contacts.' He tapped the side of his crooked nose and winked. 'There's nothing I can't lay my hands on for a favour or two. See you lads later.' He slammed down the bonnet, jumped into the car and sped off.

Jacques sparked up a match and lit a cigarette while

watching Smithy disappear at speed down the long gravel drive amid clouds of black exhaust fumes. 'That engine needs a lot of work.'

'So, how long have you and Amélie been here?' Loki asked.

'Too long.'

'From what you said earlier about avoiding capture, it sounds like you were involved with the Resistance back home,' I said.

Jacques ignored me.

Loki continued, 'We were too. In Norway. We escaped—'

'Enough!' Jacques interrupted sharply. 'You shouldn't talk about such things.'

'Why?' I said.

'What I don't know, I can't tell. Loose tongues cost lives. Remember that, and remember it well!'

'Sorry,' I said, a bit taken aback at Jacques' abruptness. Feeling embarrassed, I peered at the trees surrounding Mulberry. 'This place is in the middle of nowhere.'

Jacques puffed hard on his cigarette. 'Yes, Finn. Take a good look around.' He pointed to where the driveway disappeared into the trees. 'Even the guards at the gate don't know what we're doing here. Apart from X, only Sergeant Walker, the brigadier, and Corporal Smith know everything.'

'What about Mrs Saunders?' Loki pointed out.

Jacques snorted, 'Oh, yes, how could I forget her? And she dares to call herself a cook. Preposterous!' He snorted again.

'So we're going to be training together,' Loki said, trying to sound enthusiastic. 'Any idea where we'll end up?'

'You'll find out soon enough.'

I didn't like the sound of that. Was Jacques pretending to know something we didn't, or did he know for real?

'Tell me,' he said. 'Your English is very good. How good is your French?'

I shrugged. 'Not bad. Studied it at school like everyone else.'

'Were you top of your class?'

Loki laughed. 'God, no!'

Jacques looked unimpressed. 'What about Freya?'

'Her French is good. Better than ours,' Loki replied. 'She was nearly top of her class . . . once or twice. We can all speak pretty good German though. That was the one upside of living in a country occupied by the Nazis!'

'You and Freya seem pretty close,' Jacques said to my best friend.

Loki's cheeks reddened. Jacques was right, of course. Loki was smitten with Freya. It had started back in Norway, and blossomed since we'd arrived in Britain. Jacques was clearly quick to pick up on such things. 'Yes, we are,' Loki replied defensively.

'Interesting,' Jacques said, thoughtfully. He took the cigarette from his mouth and tapped the ash away.

'How did you and Amélie get recruited into Special Ops?' I asked.

He stared straight ahead. 'You ask too many questions,

Finn. Let's get things straight. I don't ask you about your past, and you don't ask me. That's it. *Compris?* All that matters is the here and now. Stick to that and we'll get along just fine.'

I didn't like Jacques' manner – he was too dismissive of my attempts to get acquainted. 'The way I see it,' I said, wanting to make a point, 'one day we will have to rely on each other, to trust each other with our lives. That might be hard if we don't know one another very well.'

Jacques shook his head at me as if I were really annoying and stupid. I couldn't make up my mind whether he was simply being unfriendly, whether he just had a lot on his mind, or whether he thought us 'new recruits' inexperienced amateurs unworthy of his attention. There was a pompous, arrogant air about him. Then again, I thought, maybe all Frenchmen were like that! Just as I was about to give up on him, he finally said something interesting.

'I hear Freya has excellent radio skills. Is that right?'

'Where did you hear that?' said Loki.

'Oh, a little bird told me.'

A little bird? What did he mean? Loki gave Jacques a long hard stare.

Max wandered out to join us. He nodded hello to me and smiled. Jacques flashed him a cold glance, tossed away his cigarette and briskly walked off back into Mulberry House, deliberately knocking shoulders with Max as he went, muttering something under his breath.

Max stared after him. 'He's hardly spoken to me since

I arrived. He has a thing against Germans. *All Germans!* We're not *all* the same, you know.' His tone was bitter.

'I don't think he's particularly fond of Norwegians either,' Loki replied light-heartedly.

I guessed life had to be especially hard for Max. Anyone learning he was German would immediately feel deep distrust and dislike, possibly even hatred. On meeting Max that morning I'd felt all those things, albeit momentarily, but I'd quickly realized that if he was in Special Ops then he was on our side, and that had to make him all right. *Didn't it?* Well, that's what I'd told myself. 'How come you're part of all this?' I asked, hoping my question didn't get the same brush-off that Jacques had given me. 'It is rather surprising – a German in Special Ops.'

'I'm not the only one, Finn,' Max revealed. 'My family left Germany at the end of nineteen thirty-eight. Along with many others. Things got rather difficult for people like us. You ever heard of *Kristallnacht*?'

I shook my head.

'In English it means *Night of Broken Glass*. That was the night our world changed, when we saw Herr Hitler's true feelings about us Jews,' Max said hatefully. 'My family owned a bookshop in the old part of Düsseldorf. It was the ninth of November: after dark members of the Nazi Sturmabteilung – that's Herr Hitler's Storm Troopers – tried to destroy anything belonging to Jews. My parents' shop had its windows smashed, and all their books were flung into the street and burned. But they counted themselves lucky. I think had they been there at the time, they would have been dealt with in the same way.'

'Maybe you shouldn't be telling us all this?' I said, recalling Jacques' warning. 'What we don't know we can't tell.'

He appeared unconcerned. In fact I got the impression he actually wanted to talk, as if it helped him in some way.

'Why did it happen?' Loki asked.

'A German official in Paris was murdered by a Polish man, who just happened to be a Jew. It gave Herr Hitler the perfect excuse to seek revenge. But it was only the beginning.'

We strolled along the paths that wound around the house. At the back lay a small area of lawn, empty flower beds, some wooden sheds, one distinctly rotten looking, the others more or less brand new, and a brick stable block. 'They keep the weapons and ammunition under lock and key in there,' Max said, nodding towards the stables. The door bore an impressive padlock. 'The practice range is that way,' he added, pointing towards the woods. Then he laughed. 'Jacques couldn't hit a *bus* at more than ten yards. His eyesight's terrible. Seen those thick glasses of his?'

'What about you, Max?' asked Loki.

'I'm not bad. I can hit a target at fifty yards,' he replied, suddenly adopting a slight swagger.

I said nothing but I felt a surge of confidence. Loki, Freya and I had grown up in a nation of hunters, where most kids belonged to one of the many rifle clubs.

Having been taught by her father, Heimar, Freya was a crack shot and had won trophies back home to prove it. She could hit a target at four, maybe five hundred yards. Loki and I weren't far behind her – a hundred or so yards less proficient, perhaps, but still clearly way ahead of Max and Jacques. 'What about Amélie?' I asked.

'She can barely lift a rifle, let alone fire it straight. Although . . .' He paused. 'She's not bad with a pistol. Pretty quick as a matter of fact. Quite impressive.' Then, changing the subject, he said, 'Before you arrived, I heard Walker and the brigadier talking about your escape from Norway. Did you really steal a German seaplane and fly her to Scotland?'

'Yes. A Heinkel 115. Our fathers are pilots,' I replied, and then swallowed hard before correcting myself, 'At least my father was a pilot.'

Max nodded. 'I'm sorry. What did he fly?'

'Spitfire.'

'Where did he—?'

'Not sure,' I interrupted, looking up at the sky. 'Maybe even right up there. I've not seen the official report.'

'I'd love to learn to fly,' said Max enthusiastically. He peered upwards too. 'Up there you must feel truly free. *Phantastisch!*'

'Jacques seems to know something about what we're training for and where we'll be going once we're ready,' said Loki.

Max nodded vigorously. 'I think he knows a great deal. Walker and the brigadier are keeping, erm . . . how do the English say . . . *tight-lipped*. I've been trying to work it out. Jacques spends much time inside the brigadier's office. And Corporal Smith sometimes drives them both somewhere he tells me is very *hush-hush*. They're often gone for hours. Once they didn't even return until the next day. But Corporal Smith won't tell me where he takes them. I've even tried bribing him! I've also seen Walker clutching maps of northern France. That's where Jacques and Amélie come from. A town called Rochefort. I think it's a few miles from the coast.'

'Well, that probably explains why Jacques just asked us if we could speak French,' I said.

Max raised his eyebrows. 'Seems I may be right. I'd put my money on us all heading off to France. To do what, though?' He looked thoughtful a moment. 'Of course, I could be wrong. We might end up all going our separate ways, you back to Norway, Jacques and Amélie back to France, and as for me, well God knows where they'll send me.'

'Where would you *like* to be sent?' Loki asked.

'Berlin would be good. Wouldn't mind having a go at Herr Hitler.' He formed a pistol shape with his fingers. 'Pop, pop, and the war's over. Easy as that!'

We laughed. 'You'd be famous,' I said.

'No, Finn, seriously, I think X has big plans for us. And unfortunately I think whatever the mission is, Jacques is going to be in charge.' Max grimaced. 'And that gives me a bad feeling inside. A *very* bad feeling.'

Chapter Six
The French Connection

Life at Mulberry House quickly settled into a routine and the long days gradually blurred into weeks of intense activity. Discipline was strict. Sergeant Walker insisted we ran every morning before breakfast, taking us on increasingly lengthy forays into the forest. 'Good for blowing the cobwebs away!' he'd yell at us over his shoulder as he set an exhausting pace along narrow paths. These dawn runs turned out to be the only times we ventured beyond the grounds of the house – except for Jacques' secretive trips with the brigadier. And we never spoke to anyone else despite frequently seeing convoys of trucks on the roads and stumbling across platoons of soldiers marching across the heath. Mulberry House, we realized, was very isolated.

Our lessons were a strange mix. One afternoon Walker taught us how to make impressions of keys using matchboxes filled with plasticine, then fashion duplicates by filing down strips of zinc. And I was flabbergasted at how easy it proved to pick simple locks with bent wire. In the evenings we had French lessons. Jacques and Amélie took part too, our teacher insisting that we practise with them. I paired up with Amélie and was soon glad: she showed great patience and gave me loads of encouragement every time I struggled to find the right words. Our teacher, Madame Dupuis, an elderly woman with jet-black hair tied in a tight bun and hideous-looking varicose veins, taught us with an unnerving sense of urgency. Was that because we had much to learn, or was it because we had very little time? When questioned, she refused to say, but her expression suggested both!

We also learned about different identity papers, and the special permits needed to travel in occupied countries. It seemed Max was right about our first mission because much emphasis was placed on the latest intelligence received from occupied France.

There was a lot to take in and my brain ached from it all. We worked hard – except Jacques. He frequently lost concentration and spent much of the day either gazing blankly out of the dining-room window or doodling. During one of our short breaks I took a look at what he'd scribbled. His artistic efforts struck me as strange. The paper on his desk was filled with towers and boxes and what looked like wires strung between them. And then there were dish-like objects from which emerged long zigzagging lines. 'What are these?' I asked him when he returned from the lavatory. 'And what does this mean?' I added, pointing to the numerous repetitions of the phrase *Rayon de la mort* he'd scrawled down the margin of the page.

'None of your business, Finn,' he snapped, scrunching up the paper and putting it in his pocket.

Later, I mentioned it to Freya and Loki, adding that Jacques' doodles bore some similarity to the tall aerial towers Nils had drawn for us while explaining about Britain's radar system. Freya wasn't interested in that. She was struck by the phrase Jacques had written repeatedly as if he'd been given a hundred lines in a detention.

'*Mort* – that means *death*, doesn't it?' she said.

We looked at each other in consternation. Loki finally came up with a good suggestion. 'We should keep a close eye on Jacques. For all our sakes. Agreed? I'm beginning to understand that bad feeling Max was talking about.'

There were visitors to Mulberry House in addition to our various instructors. They came and went day and night, some in uniform, others in civvies. All disappeared into the brigadier's office on arrival and sometimes Jacques would be summoned to join them. As with most things in Special Ops, the reasons behind all this activity remained a mystery to the rest of us; our questions met by a wall of silence.

In the small, strange, closed world of Mulberry House, Mrs Saunders was a rare creature – an ordinary person, a welcome dose of normality. She didn't say much and seemed reluctant to enter into conversation beyond a chirpy good morning, or asking how we were. I suspected she was under orders not to pry, to ignore all that was going on around her, to remember that *officially* none of it existed as far as the outside world was concerned. Her job was simple – feed us and wash our clothes. But I think she understood all too well why we were there, and it had a profound effect on her. I would occasionally see her gazing through the kitchen window while we trained outside. Often her focus settled on Freya or Amélie. She seemed sad. I think she knew it was highly likely that some of us wouldn't live to see the end of the war. Maybe none of us would. We were all young enough to be her sons or daughters and I think she feared getting too close, too familiar.

Complaining bitterly at the inconvenience, Mrs Saunders spent half her life delivering trays of tea and biscuits to the brigadier's office. The other half she spent creating such delicacies as potato scones, curried carrots, nettle soup, and a hideously awful steamed pudding called mealie, which apparently contained leeks, oatmeal and suet. Worryingly it was also affectionately known as 'donkey', although Mrs Saunders couldn't remember why. She insisted that it didn't really contain donkey meat but Loki wasn't so sure! She went about her work as best she could, although feeding us was difficult. Meat, tea, cheese and butter were all strictly rationed, our weekly allowances being a measly few ounces. Thank God for Smithy then! Once a week he'd slip into the kitchen at Mulberry and deliver brown parcels containing a half-dozen rabbits, a joint of ham or a brace of pheasants. Once he presented Mrs Saunders with a huge fresh salmon. 'All right, lads?' he'd say, greeting us cheerfully. 'Look what fell off the back of a lorry this time. Don't go telling anyone, now. There's plenty more where that came from if you play your cards right.'

Smithy was the brigadier's *fixer*. Shady deals were his forte.

One of his other tasks was to lead us in weapons training. Some thirty yards or so from Mulberry lay a large, deep depression in the forest, creating a sort of basin. This was the firing range in which weapons could be discharged with reasonable safety. Emerging from the stables, clutching an armful of guns and ammo, Smithy would lead us there and proceed to brief us in the handling of firearms ranging from Smith and Wesson and Luger pistols to the Thompson sub-machine-gun – affectionately known as the Tommy – and the Sten gun. And then there were the special devices, dreamed up by men with vivid imaginations. One was called the welrod. It was little more than a slender tube, about a foot long. It contained a single bullet and could be supplied with a silencer. An agent carried it inside the lining of a coat or suspended on string down a trouser leg. It was hard to detect unless he or she was searched thoroughly. It wasn't particularly accurate, but if you were in a tight corner it might just get you out of a nasty scrape. Smithy's favourite, however, was the Sten. It quickly became mine too. I liked its simplicity. It looked more like a few bits of a car exhaust pipe welded together than a real gun. It came in three pieces, barrel, body and butt. It was light and could fire single shots or rapid bursts from magazines that fitted at right angles to the left-hand side. It wasn't particularly accurate but you could get it wet, muddy even, and it would still function.

'That might prove useful when your backs are against a wall,' Smithy informed us. But, as with most things, the

Sten had its problems. Jolt it suddenly and it was prone to go off. Fill the magazines completely and they'd jam. Hold the gun incorrectly and you could wave goodbye to the ends of your fingers.

Weapons drill was approached in a spirit of competition. Wearing blindfolds, we repeatedly stripped and reassembled various rifles, pistols and machine guns against the clock. Usually Loki was quickest, Freya or me a close second. Jacques was rather slow and cackhanded, frequently fumbling and dropping bits. Max wasn't bad but Amélie struggled with anything heavier than a Colt pistol. Despite our frequent practice, Smithy was at pains to drum into us that actually having to use our weapons in a real Special Operation would probably be a last resort. It would almost certainly mean our cover as agents was blown and we were fighting for our lives. It was a sobering thought.

It was also down to Smithy to acquaint us with the latest methods of demolition, a task he undertook with frightening relish. Much damage was inflicted on the forest, old railway tracks and disused outbuildings, as we learned the finer points of plastic explosives, pressure switches and clever timing devices called time pencils. We were also taught how to stuff a dead rat to create the most disgusting explosive device imaginable. 'They are simply terrific!' Smithy enthused. 'Place them in a factory or woodpile and the enemy will either ignore them or bung them onto the fire to get rid of them. Either way, Mr Rat has an unpleasant surprise in store for Jerry!'

★ ★ ★

A human battering ram of a fellow nicknamed Kip 'Killer' Keenan taught us unarmed combat on the lawn behind Mulberry, a daily activity that largely involved him twisting our limbs and throwing us painfully to the ground.

When our bodies weren't getting a battering, our brains were being tested to the limit: hours were spent practising our Morse and coding techniques. Freya excelled. She had what Sergeant Walker called a 'good fist' – the ability to tap all those dots and dashes in a constant rhythm and rarely make mistakes.

Slowly we were being turned into real secret agents. Our progress, according to Walker, was 'satisfactory'. Having settled us in, Nils started disappearing for days at a time with the Special Duties squadron, flying missions out of Tangmere, an RAF station located further east along the coast.

In the few precious evenings we had to ourselves, Loki, Freya and I would play board games in the lounge, Max often joining in. It was a good opportunity to talk. Amélie usually had her nose in a book, while Jacques went for long walks in the grounds – alone. He always insisted on walking alone. 'I worry about him,' Freya said one evening, deliberately loud so that Amélie would overhear. 'Jacques shouldn't keep himself to himself. It's not healthy.'

Max snorted in a couldn't–care–less way. Amélie lowered her book and looked up.

'Don't you agree, Amélie?' Freya added.

'My brother has a lot to think about,' she replied. 'He's not always been like this, you know. Before . . .' She broke off mid sentence.

'Before what?' I asked.

'Never mind.'

'No, come on, Amélie,' said Loki. 'Tell us.'

She came and sat on a stool next to the rest of us. Speaking barely above a whisper, she began, 'Jacques used to be much happier. But after the Germans invaded France, he changed.'

'Go on,' I said encouragingly.

Amélie swallowed hard. 'I shouldn't really tell you this, so don't let on to Jacques. *Please!* Keep it to yourselves. He'd' − she looked to the heavens for inspiration −'*Faire fonder un fusible*, how you say, erm, ah, *oui* . . . *blow a fuse*, if he knew I was telling you.'

This sounded interesting! We all shifted forward on our chairs.

'Our father has been forced to work for the Nazis. It's tearing Jacques up inside. He won't talk to me about it.'

Seeing Amélie was growing upset, Freya reached out to comfort her. 'It was the same in our country,' she said softly. 'Many men were taken to work in the labour camps. They had no choice.'

'You don't understand, Freya. Our father is a brilliant engineer. The Germans insisted he went to Berlin to work on a vital project. Something *très, très important*.'

'What project?' I asked.

Amélie grew exasperated. 'I don't know, Finn. But Jacques does. That's what's making him so unhappy.'

Loki had been fiddling with a chess piece; now he placed it back down on the chequered board and said, 'What exactly does your father do? I mean, before France was invaded.'

'He was chief engineer at a . . .' She snapped her fingers hurriedly, trying to find the right words. '*Un compagnie électronique*. It's called Mouton et Mouton.' She looked exasperated. 'You understand?'

'An electronics firm,' Max said. 'I've heard of it. They make communications equipment, don't they?'

'*Oui*,' said Amélie, relieved Max had grasped what she was saying.

Between us, we encouraged Amélie to talk about her life back home, and we coaxed out of her the fact that her escape from France had been almost as hairy as ours. She and Jacques had slipped out of their home in the dead of night, stealing a small sailing dinghy. Battered by a gale, they'd ridden a violent and frightening storm but reached the Sussex coast in one piece. Once ashore they'd made themselves known to the authorities and had been whisked to London. Jacques, it seemed, had information for men in high places. Information he'd not shared with Amélie. Was that just to protect her in case they'd been caught during their escape? After all, he was very protective of his little sister. I couldn't help wondering whether we had the whole story, or whether there was much more to it.

Two days later the mystery slowly began to unravel. It began with Sergeant Walker summoning Loki, Freya and me to the brigadier's office.

'Ah! Come in,' bellowed the brigadier. 'And close the door behind you,' he added once we'd filed inside. 'Sit down.'

There was something different about the brigadier that afternoon. His manner had changed. He looked excited. Walker was there too, leaning against a filing cabinet. 'We've got a job for you three,' the sergeant announced. 'That's assuming you'd like a change of scenery.'

The brigadier rose from his chair, removed a pipe from his breast pocket, and sucked air through it before reaching for his tobacco pouch. 'It's a funny old world,' he began, tamping a wad of his favourite mild Virginia into the pipe's bowl. 'I never thought I'd see the day we'd end up working alongside the ruddy SIS. But that day has arrived.' He struck a match and lit up. 'Apparently the buggers need our help.' Pipe wedged between his teeth, he grinned wickedly.

'It's an opportunity for us to show them we're no bunch of amateurs,' Walker added. 'X is keen that we do a good job.'

Engulfed in a cloud of sweet smoke, the brigadier reached across his desk for a bulging file stamped MOST SECRET. He flipped it open, removed a photograph and handed it to me. 'Take a good look at him,' he said. 'Memorize that face.'

We took turns to study the picture of a very suave, sophisticated man in his early thirties. His dark hair was slicked back with oil and his moustache was neatly clipped. The photograph showed him emerging from a building wearing an expensive-looking long dark coat and carrying a cane. 'That, my dear friends, is the face of the enemy!' said Walker. 'We believe him to be a Nazi spy, codenamed Renard – the Fox!'

'Where and when was this taken?' Freya asked.

'Good question, Miss Haukelid,' the brigadier replied. 'Two weeks ago outside a hotel called The Melksham. It's located in the centre of a town called Bournemouth, less than an hour's drive from here.'

Walker continued, 'The rascal thinks he can steal vital information from us and get away with it. Well, we've got news for him!'

The brigadier sat back down. 'The SIS has been keeping a close eye on him.' He removed another picture from his file and handed it to us. On observing the beautiful young woman smiling into the lens of the camera, Loki wolf-whistled and promptly got a prod in the ribs from a less-than-amused Freya.

'Just kidding,' he said sheepishly.

'She is rather attractive, isn't she?' observed the brigadier, sighing fondly. 'That smile could melt hearts at twenty paces. Women are one of Renard's weaknesses, apparently. Can't say I blame him. She's what we call a *honeytrap*. Her codename's *Véronique*. She is a member of the SIS.'

'With a codename like Véronique, I suppose she's French then?' I said, handing the photograph back.

'Yes. As is Renard. He's fallen for her, hook, line and sinker, allegedly. Precisely what the SIS hoped would happen.'

'What's all this got to do with us?' asked Loki.

Walker began to explain: 'A week ago, the blueprints for a top-secret device were stolen from a place called Worth Matravers. Their disappearance has sent shivers through the corridors of Whitehall. If those documents get into enemy hands it could prove disastrous.'

'What sort of device?' I interrupted.

'That's classified,' the brigadier snapped. 'You don't need to know. What we can tell you, however, is that the SIS is certain Renard is behind the theft. And we have our own reasons for believing they might well be right, for once.' He rose from his chair again and crossed the room to a window. Gazing out, he continued, 'I've spent most of the morning on the telephone with X. He's just met Mr Churchill and some of the top chaps from MI6. Knowing the kind of things we teach here, the prime minister felt we might be able to put our skills to good use.'

Loki raised a hand.

'Yes, Mr Larson?'

'If we know Renard's an enemy agent, then why don't we just charge in and arrest him?'

'I wish it was that simple. Unfortunately there are complications. Renard has friends in very high places. And through his father's business connections he counts many in our government as valued friends, so we have to tread carefully.'

'In any event,' said Walker, 'a cautious approach is best. After all, we don't know how many people Renard may have recruited to assist him. So, it's one step at a time. Best to watch him like a hawk and be ready to pounce when the right time comes.'

'And that's what we need you three to do – watch Renard like a hawk,' said the brigadier. 'We think he's either about to try and make a run for it, or he'll pass the blueprints to an accomplice who'll courier them all the way back to Berlin.'

I glanced round to Loki and saw him grinning. Like me, he was relishing the opportunity to get away from Mulberry for a while, to join the real world and see some real action!

Walker expanded our briefing: 'As well as a large house in Belgravia, Renard has an apartment in Bournemouth.' He held up a map. 'It's right there,' he said, pressing the tip of a fingernail into the paper. 'Number twenty-three, Cranford Mansions. For the past few weeks he has been spending rather a lot of time there. That's somewhat surprising given that Bournemouth's not very popular during the winter months except for troops on leave. But it's an easy half-day's travel from Worth Matravers, where the blueprints were stolen. No coincidence, I can assure you! Tomorrow you will be driven into Bournemouth and dropped off. There is a café called the Cadenza opposite Renard's block of apartments. We want you to wait there and watch. If and when he emerges, follow him. Not too close, mind. We don't want him getting suspicious. See what he gets up to. Then report back. That's all. It couldn't be simpler. No heroics involved.'

'What if we discover one of his contacts? Do we follow them as well?' I asked.

'That's up to you, Finn,' said the brigadier. 'The key objective is not to let Renard out of your sight. So keep your eyes peeled. But play it by ear: we don't just want him, we want everyone who's aiding him. They're as much enemies to this country as he is.'

'How do we report back?' asked Loki.

'You will be relieved of your duty at midnight. A car will pick you up outside a building called the Pavilion. Naturally we'll drive you round the town centre first so you can get your bearings. And, as well as a map, we will give you a telephone number you can call should there be any trouble.'

'*Trouble?*' Freya asked.

'Renard is extremely dangerous. We have to assume he is utterly ruthless,' the brigadier replied. 'If nothing else, this should be a good opportunity to put what you've learned into practice. No slip-ups, mind, or you could jeopardize Véronique's cover.' He examined his pipe before tapping out the ash into an ashtray. 'Splendid! That's all for now. We'll reassemble at o-nine-hundred tomorrow morning for a final briefing.'

We all stood up, saluted the brigadier and left his office fizzing with excitement. We were about to embark on our first real work as secret agents. Sergeant Walker headed back through the hall behind us. Freya had a question for him. 'Renard's his codename, you said. What name does he usually use?'

'His real one,' Walker replied. 'Félix Mouton.'

Mouton! I gasped. Suddenly I saw a connection, although I didn't know what it meant. Mouton was the name of the company Jacques and Amélie's father worked for. That couldn't be a coincidence – it simply couldn't. My brain fizzed. Did Jacques know this Renard, this *Félix Mouton*? 'About our mission. Why us three?' I asked. 'Why not Jacques and Amélie as well?'

'Out of the question, Finn,' Walker replied.

'Why, do they know this Renard fellow?' I added.

Walker saw the look on my face and stiffened. I guessed I'd hit a nerve. 'No more questions, Finn. Understood?'

His tone betrayed him. I was right. Jacques and Amélie couldn't join us on our mission in case Renard spotted them. He'd recognize them instantly. And he'd know that the chances of them all accidentally bumping into each other in a small English town were a million to one – he'd realize people were on to him. As soon as we were out of Walker's earshot, Freya and Loki revealed that they'd each reached the same conclusion. We went for a walk in the grounds to discuss the mystery.

'Why all the secrecy?' Loki complained. 'If we're right, I don't see any harm in us seeing the whole picture: surely it would be best.'

We sat down on a bench beneath a leafless mulberry tree, some distance from the front door to the house.

'OK, so there's a link between this Félix Mouton, alias Renard, and our French colleagues,' I said, thinking aloud. 'Amélie told us that when they arrived, they went to London as Jacques had important information for the top brass. Maybe it was about the fact that Félix Mouton is here as a spy.'

Loki nodded vigorously. 'That would explain a great deal. Maybe all those meetings Jacques has been summoned to were about Félix. Maybe he's been providing information. You know, background stuff.'

Freya frowned. 'Perhaps. But just now Walker and the brigadier behaved as though this was all sudden and unexpected. And if you're right, Loki, if Jacques *has* been involved, then that doesn't quite add up.'

Loki sprang up and turned to face us. 'I *am* right, Freya. Otherwise, how come the brigadier had that file? And those photographs of Renard and Véronique? That file was bulging with paperwork. They've known about Renard for some time.'

'I wonder what those blueprints are for,' I said. 'And what goes on at that Worth Matravers place they mentioned. Some sort of device, they said. Got any ideas?'

'Jacques' father's an engineer, working for the Nazis on something important, and the Mouton business is all about electronics – communication stuff,' Loki interrupted. 'What if this is all connected to Renard and whatever device is contained in the blueprints?'

Something else clicked into place inside my head. 'Those doodles of Jacques', all those towers and dishes – perhaps they've got something to do with this.'

Our train of thought was interrupted by the arrival of two cars. Nils was in one, back from his latest mission with the Special Duties squadron. He looked shattered, his face grey, his eyes weary. The other car was delivering Madame Dupuis for our daily French lesson. The driver hopped out and ran round the car to open the passenger door for her.

Just as she stepped out, Freya sprang up. '*Rayon de la mort*,' she muttered, hurrying towards Madame Dupuis. Nils waved a hello. I waved back.

Freya reached Madame Dupuis. I saw her ask our teacher something. Madame Dupuis balked with surprise before replying. Freya then charged back to us with a look of alarm on her face. '*Rayon de la mort*,' she said breathlessly. 'That's what Jacques wrote, wasn't it?' We nodded. 'Well, according to Madame Dupuis it . . . it . . . it . . . means *death ray*!'

Chapter Seven
Watchful Eyes

The waiter at the Cadenza Café grew suspicious of us after our third cup of pale, brackish-tasting tea. I noticed him staring at us from behind the wooden counter as he slowly wiped a damp cloth over it. He was a middle-aged chap, of stocky build, and had faded tattoos of coiled serpents on both arms. The Cadenza proved a pretty cheerless place with cheap tables and chairs, and the menu offered little except spam sandwiches and coffee that smelled suspiciously of chicory.

Loki had shifted his chair sideways and, arms folded, was staring out of the partially misted window towards the other side of the square. In fact, it was more of a circle than a square, with roads radiating from it like the spokes of a bicycle wheel. In the middle was a clock tower and a shelter for those queuing for the next electrically powered trolley bus. The centre of Bournemouth was full of tall buildings, some seven storeys high, housing department stores and other shops. Lewis guns were stationed on their roofs in case of an air raid. There were blocks of residential apartments too, including Cranford Mansions, the one occupied by Félix Mouton – alias Renard.

As life drifted past the window of the Cadenza, we discussed whether Britain and Germany were in some sort of race to develop a death ray. If they were, then whoever succeeded first was likely to win the war.

'Christ, imagine such a weapon,' said Loki. 'Maybe it's some sort of high-energy beam of light that fries anything that stands in its way.'

'Or maybe like a bolt of lightning,' I suggested. 'Do you think it could destroy tanks or ships or aircraft?'

'Probably,' he replied.

Freya tutted. 'If it exists then it's almost too terrible to contemplate. I just hope such a thing proves impossible to make.'

We both nodded in agreement, but I thought the fact that some blueprints had been stolen surely had to mean a device existed, at least on the drawing board.

'Still no sign of him,' Loki muttered, wiping the mist from the window with the sleeve of his coat. 'I'm not sure he's even at home.'

Bournemouth was a lucky town, I decided. When Walker drove us round to give us our bearings, I noticed few obvious signs of bomb damage: he told us that the gap close to the square had been the Central Hotel until the Luftwaffe decided to close it down for good. It was a seaside town rooted in a valley where the sea cliffs temporarily gave way, allowing easy access to sandy beaches and promenades. War, however, meant that steel-reinforced concrete anti-tank defences called dragon's teeth, vicious barbed wire and heavily armed soldiers barred entry to the golden sands, which Walker had told us had been extensively mined anyway. He'd stopped our car on the cliff top within sight of the pier.

Anyone wanting a gentle stroll along it was in for a disappointment: the railings and decking had been removed and a sixty foot middle section deliberately blown up by the Royal Engineers to prevent its use as a landing stage during an invasion.

'Three hours and we've seen nothing – and the light's fading fast.' Freya complained. 'This is cruel. All those shops but I can't go shopping!'

Loki laughed. 'You haven't got enough coupons for a hanky, let alone a new dress.'

I noticed the waiter staring at us again. We'd been whispering in Norwegian, and I wondered if he'd caught an earful. Towns like Bournemouth were full of troops and people who'd fled Nazi persecution and the streets rang with foreign tongues, so I doubted that alone was the reason he was watching us so determinedly. It made me anxious. I had an awful feeling he suspected us of something – as if we were up to no good. 'We'd better find somewhere else,' I said finally. 'We can't hang around here all afternoon.'

'Good idea, Finn,' said Loki, quickly rising to his feet and grabbing his gas-mask case. 'I'm bored to tears sitting here. Let's go for a wander.'

The waiter's stare followed us outside. I could sense it burning into the back of my neck. God, he gave me the creeps. On the pavement we took stock of our surroundings. The overhead electric cables fizzed and sparked as trolley buses trundled past with their masked headlamps, painted windows and camouflaged roofs. I spotted couples strolling to and from the Pleasure

Gardens that sliced through the town centre, ending down by the pier. Seagulls and pigeons circled and swooped frantically above our heads, squawking and fighting as if re-enacting the aerial dogfights of the previous summer. It was quite a bustle – just what we needed.

'I'll go right,' said Loki, having glanced briefly at his map. 'Come with me, Freya. Finn, you go left. Walk up past those shops and then wait for a couple of minutes. Look in the windows or something but keep us in sight. At the top, we'll turn and head back. After we pass Renard's apartment, you start moving. That'll ensure someone keeps the entrance in view at all times. We'll go back and forth, like pendulums swinging in opposite directions.'

'OK,' I said. 'But what's the signal if one of us spots Renard?'

'Take out your handkerchief and blow your nose.'

For twenty minutes we played out our game. It seemed to work a treat. Nobody paid any attention to us. Sometimes I walked with a bit of a swagger, hands in pockets, coat unbuttoned. Other times I walked briskly, straight-backed, arms swinging, coat done up tightly. Yet we had a problem. It was getting dark. The shops were closing, the streets were growing quieter. We were beginning to look out of place. 'What now?' said Loki as we met up again. 'Back to the Cadenza?'

I glanced across the square and saw that the sign in the door of the café had been turned over – CLOSED –

and blinds had been pulled down. 'Not an option,' I replied. I was rather glad about that.

'Erm . . .' As Loki spun round trying to come up with a new plan, the door of the Cadenza suddenly opened and the waiter stepped out. He shut it behind him, locked it, tightened the belt of his mackintosh and adjusted the brim of his hat. He walked a little way to his right and then dipped into another doorway. In the gloom I saw the flash of a lighter as he lit a cigarette.

I had an idea. 'Give me your paper, Loki,' I said. 'There's a bench over there by the clock tower and a little light spilling out of the bus shelter. I'll position myself there. You two huddle in that recess next to the department store.'

'And do what, Finn?' said Freya.

'Improvise!' I said.

Loki grinned. 'I like the sound of that.'

So I took up my position on the bench and began to read while Loki held Freya in a lovers' embrace in the shadows.

Casually I turned the pages of my paper, peeking over the top of it; just brief glances, nothing too obvious. The best bit about my chosen vantage point was that by merely flicking my eyes from one side to the other, I could observe both Renard's building and the waiter on the other side of the square. Slouching with his shoulder pressed against a wall, he kept his head deep in the shadows. Just as I got to the back page, a woman emerged from the entrance to the apartment block. She trotted out quickly and appeared in good spirits.

She laughed, held out her arms and twirled on her high heels. Véronique! Renard tumbled out too. He seized her and they kissed. Laughing and waving they parted company, heading in opposite directions. I grabbed my handkerchief from my pocket, dropped my paper into my lap and pretended to sneeze – very loudly. Loki had spotted them too and nodded towards me over Freya's shoulder. I got up, folded my newspaper under my arm, and was all set to follow the smartly dressed Nazi spy when I paused. Renard had walked a short distance, but then he stopped and removed a cigar from his coat pocket. While holding the bold three-inch flame of his lighter to the tip of his cigar, he peered over towards the far side of the square. Flicking my eyes to the right, I saw the waiter emerge, cast down the butt of his cigarette and, thrusting his hands into the pockets of his coat, begin walking briskly in the same direction as Véronique. Was his timing pure coincidence? Or had Renard signalled to him? I wasn't sure.

Loki ran up and grabbed my shoulder. 'What are you waiting for, Finn? Come on, we mustn't lose sight of Renard.'

'Hang on.' I said. A sixth sense, something deep inside, told me something wasn't quite right. 'I'm following Véronique. You two keep Renard in your sights. I'll catch you up.'

'Don't be stupid, Finn. They're going in opposite directions. And Véronique isn't our target.'

'Get going, Loki. I've got a hunch, and I want to test

it out. Worst case we'll rendezvous outside the Pavilion at midnight.'

I didn't wait for a reply. I set off, trying to keep both Véronique and the waiter from the Cadenza in view.

'Damn you, Finn!' Loki cursed. I didn't look back.

Véronique strutted briskly along the pavement, the steel tips on her high heels clicking loudly. As I followed, I noticed the kerb stones were painted white, trees and poles had white lines painted round them too, some about a foot from the ground, others at eye level. I realized that it helped prevent people from tripping up or bumping into things in the dark. There were no streetlights allowed during the blackout: people had to carry torches. We had each been given one by Walker and told it was best to aim their feeble beams down at the ground in front of us, so we could see where we were going. Without hesitation Véronique suddenly turned and trotted down a set of steep steps that led into the Pleasure Gardens. The waiter paused at the top of the stairway, glanced briefly left and right and then descended as well.

He *was* following her. I could think of only two possible explanations. One, he worked for Renard, and Renard didn't trust Véronique so wanted her followed. Or two, he was just some creep. I couldn't decide which. But all afternoon I'd thought there was something shifty about him.

I remained about fifteen yards behind the waiter, taking the opportunity to discard my newspaper as I passed a litter bin. I didn't really relish being so close, but any further back and I ran the risk of losing them both in the gloom. For his part, he kept a constant ten yards or so behind Véronique. Couples strolled past me. One or two nodded a polite hello: I tried to acknowledge them, to smile, to look normal and carefree, not like someone from Special Ops following a big bloke with tattoos on his arms. There was a small ornamental stream running to my left and I recalled from the map that it ran the full length of the gardens. There were paths on both sides of the stream with numerous little foot-bridges linking them. I made a decision and hurriedly crossed one. I was no longer directly behind the waiter, but I could still see him. I reckoned this was good secret-agent work. If the waiter now turned and looked behind him, there was nothing to suggest he was being followed. My chosen path also ran next to some rhododendrons and other bushes that would offer me some cover in an emergency.

Véronique headed in the direction of the pier. Just as its entrance came into view, she abruptly turned left and skipped up another set of steps back towards the street, in the direction of the big building Walker had told us was our rendezvous – the Pavilion, a music hall where shows and dances were staged most nights, air raids permitting.

The waiter followed her up but stopped on the top step. I cursed under my breath. I was stuck below them both and I could no longer see Véronique. I glanced round frantically. My only option was to climb through the undergrowth towards the street above and hope she'd not disappeared from view by the time I got there. I dipped into the shrubbery and, grabbing what branches I could, hauled myself up the steep slope. At the top I crouched down, parted some leaves, and peered into the street in front of me.

Where had she gone? I noticed that the waiter's eyes were firmly fixed on a hotel across the street – The Melksham! I recalled the photograph we'd been shown of Renard, and that the brigadier had mentioned the hotel's name. Then, through the glass window I saw Véronique in the lobby, standing in front of the reception desk. I turned my head to see what the waiter would do next. Eventually, dodging the traffic, he hurried across the street.

I had a terrible thought. Maybe Renard had rumbled Véronique's cover, and knowing she was with the SIS had decided to deal with her? Was she a liability that needed to be disposed of? Had this tattooed oaf been sent to bump her off? It felt like an air-raid siren was going off in my head. I had to do something.

Emerging from my hiding place, I ran across the street, thumped into a glass panel of the revolving doors at the entrance to The Melksham and pushed. Once inside, I observed Véronique disappearing into a lift. The doors pinged and closed. The waiter hurried to a second lift, waited for the doors to open and for an elderly couple to slip out, then leaped inside. Véronique *was* in danger, I decided. The waiter had to be stopped and it was down to me to do it. But my first problem was that there were only two lifts, both now occupied. I also had no idea which room Véronique was in. Hell, I didn't even know her real name or the name she was registered under. Worst of all, I didn't have much time. I rushed to the reception desk. 'That woman who just came in. The really pretty one. I've got an urgent message for her. What room is she in?'

The smartly dressed man behind the desk peered at me over the top of his spectacles. 'We don't give out that kind of information, I'm afraid. Especially not to young riffraff,' he said, looking down his nose at me. 'Give the message to me. I'll see she gets it.'

About to scream that someone's life was in danger, and equally tempted to leap over the desk and grab the register to look at the list of guests, I managed to stop myself. There simply wasn't time. I turned and ran towards the lifts and the stairs that wound up behind them.

'Oi! You, come back here!' the man at the desk bellowed.

As I ran, I fixed my eyes on the dial above Véronique's lift. The arrow on the half-moon swung slowly clockwise. The lift climbed past the second, third and fourth floors before the arrow settled on the number five. She was on the fifth floor! I made for the staircase and raced up three steps at a time, turning right, then right again, always to my right. A couple were heading downstairs. I bumped into them and sent them flying. 'Sorry!' I yelled. More steps – three at a time. I was getting breathless, and my heart pounded. Still I ran. I turned another corner. There was a sign on the wall with a big, glorious number five on it. I grabbed a handrail and, bent double, sucked air into my burning lungs. What now? Pressing myself against the wall, I poked my head round the corner and glanced up and down the corridor. The waiter was at the far end, to my left, with his back to me. He was standing in front of a door – the door to Véronique's room? His left hand was in his pocket. He knocked with his right. *Don't answer, I prayed. Ignore it, Véronique. For God's sake!*

Chapter Eight
Véronique

Gritting my teeth, I set off down the corridor as fast as I could force my legs to go. The waiter heard me pounding towards him and turned sharply. Startled, he whipped his hand from his pocket. I saw the grey steel of a revolver. The door to Véronique's room opened and her face appeared. The man raised his gun. Between me and him stood a trolley piled high with clean linen. I grabbed it and pushed it forward with my full weight behind it. Letting out a determined cry, I ploughed ahead, slamming the trolley into him as hard as I could. Driven by my momentum, the oaf was forced back into Véronique's room. She only just managed to step aside in time. As the waiter spun backwards and fell heavily, catching the back of his head on the corner of a table, I heard a pop and something shatter. A cloud of white dust filled the room and the powerful odour of scented talc reached my nostrils. I realized he'd fired a single shot as he fell, demolishing a bottle resting on the dressing table. Terrified, Véronique let out a cry of '*Dieu tout-puissant!*' and took several unsteady steps back. Raising her hands to her face, she seemed about to scream. But she didn't. The waiter's gun bounced across the carpet and came to rest beneath a radiator amid fragments of broken glass. Holding a finger to my lips, I closed the door behind me and hurriedly picked up the gun, pointing it at the unconscious figure lying at my feet. The weapon was familiar to me: a Smith and Wesson – complete with silencer. 'He was sent to kill you,' I said, trying to catch my breath. 'Looks like I got here just in time.' Suddenly overwhelmed by a feeling of relief and exhaustion, I slumped to my knees and gasped for air.

Véronique gathered her wits, overcame her shock and divided her stare between the waiter and me. 'Who is he? And who are you?'

'Well, I don't know his name but he works at the Cadenza Café, opposite Félix's apartment.'

'You know Félix Mouton?' she asked with surprise.

'Not personally, although I understand he sometimes goes by the name Renard, *Véronique*,' I replied.

She gasped. 'How do you know his . . . and my . . . ?

'Let's just say you and I are on the same side,' I interrupted. 'Is he dead?'

She peered down at him. 'Don't think so, but he's going to have one hell of a headache when he wakes up.'

Putting his gun in my coat pocket, I seized a lamp from the dressing table and tore the flex from it. 'I'll use this to tie him up,' I said. 'Help me turn him over.'

As I bound his hands behind his back, Véronique sat down on the edge of her bed and allowed the events of the previous two minutes to sink in.

'Looks like your cover's been blown,' I said, tying a really tight double knot. 'Do you have any idea how?'

'What? No.'

I glanced up and saw she was nibbling the end of her fingernails nervously. Her clear hazel eyes were scrutinizing me closely and it was almost as if I could hear the hundred thoughts and questions bouncing round inside her head. Yes, she was in shock, but she was also highly trained, I reckoned, and her training was now kicking in, taking control. She had to assess the situation, work out what was happening and make some decisions. I did too. I pulled my handkerchief from my pocket, rolled it up and used it to gag the waiter. 'There! He's not going anywhere.'

'Who exactly do you work for?' she asked.

'Special Ops,' I said proudly.

A slight crease formed on her otherwise porcelain-smooth brow. Reaching for her handbag, she took out a slim enamelled gold case, opened it and removed a blue cocktail cigarette. Inserting it into a long, slender holder, she lit up and took a series of short, sharp puffs, all the while never taking her eyes off me.

Happy the waiter wasn't going anywhere should he regain consciousness, I dragged a chair across the room and sat down opposite Véronique. 'The way I see it,' I began, 'Renard must be close to making his move. Does he still have the blueprints?'

'How long have you been following me?' she asked cagily.

'Just from when you left Renard's apartment,' I replied. '*The blueprints . . . ?*'

'What? Oh, I don't know.'

'Have you seen them? Ever heard Renard talk about a *rayon de la mort?*'

She gave me a puzzled look, then shook her head.

'We believe he's either going to pass the blueprints on to a courier, or take them to Germany himself,' I said. 'Do you know which? Has he let on what his next move is?'

'You're not English, are you?'

'No. But where I come from is unimportant.'

She studied me, squinting slightly. 'North European, I'd say. Not German or Swedish though. Danish, maybe, or Norwegian.'

'Can we stick to the important stuff, please?'

She got up and began pacing the room. It was large with expensive furnishings, heavy drapes and frills – nothing but the best for our Véronique, I thought. It struck me that the longer she paced and mulled over her predicament, the more nervous she grew. I sensed she was thinking at breakneck speed. 'When you parted company earlier, where was Renard heading?' I asked.

'He said he had some business to attend to.' She flicked ash onto the thick carpet and then took another drag of her cigarette. 'We'd planned to meet up later at the Pavilion. There's a dance there tonight.'

'What time?'

'Eight o'clock.'

I inspected my watch. Six-fifteen. 'Only, I don't suppose he'll be expecting you to turn up this evening, will he?' I added sharply. 'He'll assume you're already dead. So, the question is, will he be there?'

'I don't know.' Her expression hardened. 'Only I *shall*,' she insisted.

'Is that wise?'

'If he turns up, I want to see the look on his face!'

'That's a bad idea, Véronique,' I said, shaking my head. 'You've had a narrow escape. Do you want to tempt fate? Although . . .' I paused, my brain racing like a runaway train. 'Maybe we can cover you. Be there in case it turns nasty. There are others, you know. Like me, that is. Right now, they're following Renard.' It suddenly dawned on me that I had no idea where Loki and Freya were. If we were to meet by eight o'clock, I had to find them quickly. 'Did Renard say where this business of his was taking place?'

'He didn't, but it will be the same as always, I expect. The Flamingo Club. That's where he normally hangs out.'

I removed the small map of the town centre from my pocket. 'Show me.'

Véronique leaned over me and I watched as she traced a perfectly painted nail over my map. I caught a whiff of her scent over the pungency of the talc that still hung in the air. She smelled nice, of strawberries. 'The club's about there,' she said.

'Thanks.' I returned the map to my pocket. 'Don't suppose you know who he's meeting?'

'No. Félix always plays his cards close to his chest.' She sat down on the edge of her bed again and gazed at me with a pained expression. 'You look so young. It's not right. It's not fair.'

I recalled X's initial briefing to us at Mulberry. 'This war is dirty, vile, downright underhand,' I said, repeating his words. 'There are no rules.'

She nodded slowly, her eyes still locked on mine. They were gorgeous eyes too, full of courage and hope; eyes I could easily lose myself in. I felt really odd inside. It was as if I wanted to reassure her; to tell her that I was no naive boy, that I knew precisely what was at stake. I wanted to tell her everything – that my father was dead, my mother and sister prisoners of the Gestapo, that I'd once been locked up in Trondheim's Kristiansten Fortress and interrogated, that I'd witnessed three men from my village face a firing squad, that I'd escaped from Norway with vital photographs and maps, that I'd stolen a plane and flown her to Scotland, that long ago I'd made up my mind to fight back in any way I could to help defeat the Nazis . . . *that looks could be deceptive*! Then it struck me. What about her? How come she was involved in all this? We were like icebergs. Both of us. What you could see of us were just the bits above the surface. Beneath, hidden from view, lay much, much more.

She stubbed out her cigarette and took a deep breath. 'What's your name?'

'Finn.'

She leaned forward and kissed me on my cheek. 'Thank you, Finn.'

I felt my cheeks redden.

She smiled. 'OK. What about him?' she said, stiffening and jerking a thumb in the direction of the waiter.

'Good question. Is there a phone in this hotel?' I asked.

'Yes. There's a kiosk in the lobby. Why?'

'I'm going to call and request some assistance. I expect my commanding officer will enjoy interrogating him.'

As I got up from my chair, she grabbed my arm. 'Be careful what you say on the telephone, Finn. The operators have a nasty habit of eavesdropping.'

At the bottom of the hotel staircase I sneaked a look into the lobby to locate the telephone kiosk and see whether the awkward man was still in reception. Luckily he was engrossed with a customer. I shot across the lobby and into the kiosk, closing the sliding door behind me. I took out the piece of paper with Brigadier Devlin's telephone number on it and picked up the handset.

'Which number please?' chirped a voice on the other end of the line.

'Beaulieu five-one-five-four, please.'

'Thank you. I'll try to connect you.'

The wait seemed endless. Come on, *come on*! I thought. Pick up the phone.

'I'm sorry for the delay,' the operator said. 'Still trying to connect you.'

'Hello?' It was Walker.

Finally!

'It's Finn,' I said.

'Is there a problem?'

'*Yes!*' I hesitated. How could I explain everything

without letting the operator – who I assumed was eavesdropping – hear it all. I had an idea. 'Is Nils there?' I asked.

'Yes. Wait.'

Nils came onto the line. 'Finn?'

I switched to Norwegian and spoke quickly. 'We've got a big problem,' I said. I told him where I was, that Véronique's cover had been blown and an attempt made on her life, that one of Renard's men was tied up in a hotel room awaiting collection by the brigadier, and that Véronique was presently getting ready to confront Renard at the Pavilion dance.

'Good Lord, Finn! And what about Loki and Freya?' he asked.

'They followed Renard. He's gone to the Flamingo Club. To do a spot of business – maybe to make arrangements or hand over the blueprints. I'm heading there as soon as we've finished talking.'

'Not so fast, Finn. Hang on a minute while I speak to the brigadier.'

I sat in the tiny, cramped, stuffy kiosk that reeked of wax polish for what felt like a lifetime.

'Finn?' Nils said, returning to the phone. 'Listen carefully,' he said, still in Norwegian. 'We're on our way. Best thing for you to do is locate Loki and Freya and then sit tight. Back off. No more heroics. The situation is far too dangerous. And Véronique must stay put. The brigadier's orders are that under no circumstances should she confront Renard before we arrive. Is that clear? Under no circumstances! Make sure she understands. It's best Renard thinks the attempt on her life was successful. OK?'

'Understood.'

'Great. We'll meet you outside the Pavilion dance hall at about eight o'clock. Well done, Finn. Sounds like quite an adventure.'

He hung up.

I raced back upstairs. Reaching the end of the fifth-floor corridor, about to knock, I realized the door to Véronique's room stood slightly ajar. I remembered that I'd closed it behind me. I definitely closed it! Through the gap I saw something that sent a chill through my bones. Where was the waiter? He wasn't where I'd left him. '*Véronique?*' I whispered. 'Is everything all right?'

Chapter Nine
The Flamingo Club

Something was very wrong. I just knew it. Reaching into my coat pocket, I removed the waiter's revolver and held it tightly. Was our weapons training about to be put to the test? This situation was real, and it felt totally different from our practice sessions taking pot shots at makeshift targets in the woods behind Mulberry House. No amount of training can prepare you for the awful sense of trepidation in your belly. I gathered my thoughts and tried to calm myself. After all, I'd been in tight corners before. And good old Smithy had prepared us for exactly this situation – close combat in confined spaces. He'd called it *instinctive firing*. Basically, you forget about taking careful aim. Simply point and shoot – two quick shots. At close range it works because it's fast – hopefully faster than the enemy. That's all that matters. I took a deep breath, moved to one side of the door, then kicked it open with my foot and glanced in. Maybe my imagination was running wild. Maybe I was being stupid. Perhaps I had forgotten to close the door, after all. 'Véronique?'

No reply. There was nothing for it. Counting to three quickly under my breath, I leaped into the room and spun around, trying to look in all directions at once. I saw a gun pointing at me. I fired twice. Two dull pops emerged from my silencer, followed by little wafts of smoke. The large mirror on the wall shattered. I'd shot my own reflection!

Regaining my composure, I realized the room was empty. The door to the bathroom, however, was open. 'Véronique? You in there?'

Still no reply. Cautiously I stepped forward, my brain full of frightful visions of what might lie inside the bathroom. Maybe the waiter was in there, his arm tightly gripped about her neck. Perhaps he'd drowned her in the bath! Holding my gun in front of me, I couldn't stop my hand from shaking. 'Véronique?' My voice quivered.

Holding my breath, I shoved the door open hard, so it swung right back on its hinges and would smack anyone hiding behind it. It crashed against the wall and slowly returned towards me. I stepped inside. There was no sign of Véronique or the waiter. Totally baffled, I moved back into the bedroom. I sat down on the edge of the bed and scratched my head. What had happened? Where were they? I'd not seen them pass me in the lobby. Had they taken the lift while I'd used the stairs? Had they gone out a back way? None of it made any sense. Then I had a horrible thought. *A really awful thought*. What if the waiter had regained consciousness while I'd been talking to Véronique? What if he'd overheard everything, managed to wriggle free and overpower her? I'd mentioned that others were following Renard – Loki and Freya! If I were the waiter, I'd be rushing to warn Renard, and that meant Loki and Freya were in great danger. I'd had to find them – fast.

Leaving the hotel, I walked briskly in the direction of the square. According to Véronique the Flamingo Club was situated on the other side of town. Keeping one hand inside my coat pocket, I was conscious that my grip on the handle of the revolver was tight, and that my palm was sweaty. I wanted to run as fast as I could, but knew that could be a big mistake. People would be suspicious of someone running. It was best to walk confidently and with purpose, to look like you knew where you're going. At the same time I wanted to keep an eye out for Véronique and the waiter. For all I knew he may have been waiting outside the hotel, intent on seeking revenge. The urge to keep looking over my shoulder was powerful. But I remembered what Jacques had said during our lessons at Mulberry – *Keep your head still and move your eyes. Don't under any circumstances peer over your shoulder – it's a real giveaway.* The last thing I wanted was to draw attention to myself. So, shining my torch onto the pavement, I headed across town, dreading a tap on my shoulder or an arm being wrapped about my neck from behind – an arm covered in coiled serpents, belonging to a man with a thumping headache and with a huge grudge against the person who gave it to him!

It began to rain, gently at first, but it soon became a deluge, giving me the perfect excuse to run the last few hundred yards. I turned a corner and entered a quiet side street. If Véronique's directions were correct, somewhere on the left-hand side was the Flamingo Club. Dodging the puddles, I walked slowly along, looking and listening carefully. Where the hell was it? Hearing voices behind me, I spun round.

Two men in army uniform staggered out of an alley. They were drunk and boisterous, their hats perched on their heads at precarious angles, their coats unbuttoned. They pushed past me, one giving me a fuzzy look, the other barely noticing my existence. 'The Flamingo Club?' I asked hopefully. One of them turned, almost falling over in the process, and waved a hand in the general direction of the alley. 'Thanks,' I said. They went on their way, singing at the tops of their voices.

Rain poured from broken gutters, splashing down on abandoned crates. The alley smelled of cat pee and I thought I heard rats scratching in the darkness. There were other noises too. They sounded like the vibrating, hollow notes of a double bass being plucked and the sharp tinny slap of cymbal against cymbal. A faint glow leaked out from beneath a shabby wooden door. As I approached the music grew louder. I turned the handle and entered.

Inside I was greeted by a dimly lit narrow hallway, staircases leading both up and down and a small counter, behind which sat a rather plump woman dressed in a hideous but revealing purple dress. Her make-up was so thick it looked as though it had been applied with a shovel, and a cigarette dangled from her lips. 'What can I do for you, young man?' she asked, her voice unnaturally deep and gravelly.

'Is this the Flamingo Club?'

'Downstairs,' she replied.

I looked and saw that an arrow painted on the grubby wall helpfully pointed towards the basement. 'Thanks!'

Placing my foot on the first step, the woman barked, 'And where the hell do you think you're going?'

'You said the club was downstairs.'

'You're too young. More than my job's worth. If we get raided I'll be in the soup again.'

'*Soup?*'

'Never mind. Now hop it.'

'Hop it?'

She frowned at me. 'Are you as stupid as you look?'

'Listen,' I said. 'I'll only be a minute. I've got a message for a friend. And he's downstairs. Asked me to meet him here.'

'Really? If that's true, then my name's Vera Lynn!'

Where had I heard that name before . . . ? Then I remembered. The wireless at Mulberry. Mrs Saunders loved to sing along to tunes, and Vera Lynn was one of her favourites. 'Nice to meet you, Vera,' I said jokingly.

She laughed. Actually, it was more of a cackle that rapidly deteriorated into a splutter, then a hacking cough that reddened her cheeks and had her reaching for a tissue. 'You a comedian?'

'No.'

'Sorry, but like I said, it's more than my job's worth.'

I took out my wallet and removed the crisp one-pound note we'd been issued with in case of emergencies. I folded it and placed it down in front of her. I could almost see her drooling. 'It really is important,' I said.

She hummed and hawed a minute and then reached out and snatched up the money, quickly making it disappear by wedging it down her ample cleavage. 'Who's this *friend*?' she asked.

'I expect you know him,' I said. 'He's a regular here. Mr Mouton. Félix.'

Her eyes lit up. 'Félix! Why didn't you say so? You could have saved yourself a lot of money. Go ahead.'

I considered asking for my money back but decided against it. I sped down the stairs and through another door, entering the heart of the candlelit Flamingo Club. In one corner a jazz quartet thumbed, strummed and bashed out crazy improvised rhythms amid a haze of cigarette and cigar smoke. Couples danced in a small area in front of them. There was a bar, tables and chairs dotted about, and snug-looking booths down one wall. The place was packed. Many people were in uniform, others in civvies, a good few in evening dress. The party-goers were a smart crowd, just like Renard, although the surroundings appeared far less salubrious. I'd never felt so out of place in my life. I cast my eyes about the room in search of Loki and Freya. There was no sign of them, but the place was so crowded they could well have been hidden from view. I couldn't see Renard either, or Véronique, or the waiter. I noticed the barman peer at me curiously. I couldn't loiter. I had an idea and headed towards him. 'I've got a message,' I called out over the hubbub. 'For Mr Mouton.'

He studied my face for a moment and then beckoned me forward to within earshot. 'You can give it to me. I'll see he gets it.'

'Sorry. I have to deliver it personally. Is he here?'

The barman responded by nodding towards a door at the rear of the club. 'Mr Mouton doesn't like being disturbed. Best if you wait out here.'

'Oh, I see. Thanks.'

He leaned forward again. 'Want a drink?'

'Sorry. No money,' I replied.

He took pity on me. 'Have it on the house. What'll it be?'

I peered at all the bottles lined up on shelves behind the bar. Most I didn't recognize. 'Whisky?' I said hopefully, fully expecting the barman to refuse.

He snatched up a tiny glass and reached for a bottle. He poured me a shot. I couldn't believe it. 'There you go.'

'Thanks!' It was the first drink I'd ever ordered in a bar. Clutching it, I wandered around the club, soaking up the rhythm, breathing the thick, smoky air, listening to the high-spirited laughter and chatter while doing my best not to bump into the revellers. I like this place, I thought. It buzzed, it breathed, it had life. Of course, it was all rather shabby and seedy, but I felt a million miles away from wartime Britain and its self-imposed austerity. Someone grabbed my arm. I jumped out of my skin, spilling half my drink.

'Finn! What are you doing here?'

It was Loki. He and Freya were huddled in one of the cosy booths. I squeezed in beside them and filled them in on all that had happened.

'Jesus!' said Loki, wide-eyed with astonishment. He glanced at his watch. 'It's after seven.' Then he pointed across the club. 'Renard disappeared out the back ages ago; through that door. We've been waiting here ever since.'

Freya leaned across. 'And we haven't seen Véronique, Finn. Or the waiter from the Cadenza.'

'Is that what I think it is, Finn?' said Loki, eyeing up my glass.

I nodded and then told Freya, 'Whatever plans Renard had for this evening, I bet everything will change as soon as he finds out what's happened. When he knows the authorities are on to him, he'll be forced to make a move.'

Loki grabbed my glass, downed the shot of whisky in one gulp, screwed up his face and coughed violently.

'Hey!' I said. Freya patted him on the back. Serves him right, I thought.

Recovering his breath, Loki grinned at me. 'Damn, I needed that! Thanks, Finn. I owe you one. So, what's the plan?'

I peered towards the door at the back of the club. Was Renard, the Nazi master spy, just a matter of feet away? Did he have the blueprints on him? Was he in the process of handing them over to an accomplice? Was he making arrangements to get the blueprints out of the country and to Berlin? It was so frustrating. Surely we couldn't just sit there and do nothing.

Freya leaned across the table again. 'I know our orders were to sit tight, but Walker and the brigadier don't know about what happened after you telephoned them. It changes everything, doesn't it?' Lowering her voice, she added, 'Have you still got the waiter's gun?'

'Yes.'

'Then we should take matters into our own hands. If Renard's out the back, this may be our one and only chance to take him on.'

Loki, suitably fortified by the whisky, sprang from his seat. 'Let's do it!'

Chapter Ten
The Dumbwaiter

Nobody noticed or cared when the three of us slipped quietly through the door at the rear of the club. Entering a corridor lit by a single naked bulb, we saw a steep set of steps ahead of us and to our right another door.

'Looks like those stairs lead to an exit into the alley,' Freya observed, peering up.

We focused our attention on the door. I took the gun from my pocket and held a finger to my lips. 'I'll cover you.'

Loki nodded and grabbed hold of the door handle. I stepped to one side. 'Go on!'

Pushing open the door, Loki reached for the light switch. 'Hell! We're too late.'

I followed him into what seemed to be a storeroom. There were shelves and racks for bottles but most were empty and just gathering dust. There was a small table and four chairs in the centre of the room. Three empty glasses and an ashtray full of dog-ends were the only signs that someone had been there.

Loki turned, pushed past me and hammered up the steps.

'At least we tried, Finn,' said Freya disconsolately.

Strawberries! I could smell strawberries. And

something in the ashtray caught my eye too. One of the cigarette butts looked different from the others. I grabbed it.

Loki returned. 'Just as you thought, Freya – the stairs lead to an exit. They've given us the slip.'

'What are you doing?' asked Freya, peering over my shoulder.

'Véronique was here,' I declared, holding up the remainder of the cigarette.

'What?' Loki inspected the evidence in my hand. 'How do you figure that out?'

'She smokes these blue cigarettes. And she wears perfume that smells of strawberries. Can't you smell it? She was here. I just know it.'

'Well, she isn't here now,' Freya huffed. 'Come on, you two, we'd better go and rendezvous with Nils and the others.'

I was confused. What was Véronique doing here? Had the waiter dragged her kicking and screaming back to Renard, who'd act as judge, jury and executioner? 'Wait,' I said. 'We can't just abandon Véronique. The way I see it, she needs our help.'

'And just how do you think we can help her?' said Loki.

'I don't know.' I racked my brain for inspiration. 'Maybe they've taken her back to Renard's apartment.'

'And maybe they haven't,' Loki replied. 'If Renard knows people are on to him, he'd not make such a stupid mistake.'

'And there's not enough time, anyway,' said Freya,

examining her watch. 'Finn, you said we've got to meet Nils and the brigadier at the Pavilion at eight. Best not be late. Come on.'

To get to our rendezvous point we had to pass the entrance to The Melksham hotel. There was quite a commotion. Two police cars were parked at the kerbside in front of the revolving doors, and a constable stood barring the way in. Fearing it might have something to do with my earlier visit, and not wishing to be recognized by the man on reception, I crossed the street and did my best to shield myself from view, hiding behind Loki.

Nils was waiting for us outside the plush carpeted entrance to the Pavilion. He saw us and waved frantically. 'He doesn't look too happy,' Freya remarked.

'Thank God you're all OK,' he said, looking relieved.

'What's going on?' Loki asked.

'This place is crawling with SIS. Walker's inside too. He brought Smithy and Killer Keenan along just in case. No sign of Renard yet, though. They intend to arrest him as soon as he sets foot through the door. But after what you told me, Finn – that Véronique's cover's been blown – I doubt he'll show up. By my reckoning he's long gone. Look out! Best behaviour now, I think the brigadier's on the warpath.'

Brigadier Devlin strode purposefully towards us from the direction of The Melksham; another man in civvies walked alongside him. Both were fuming. 'Ruddy disaster!' the brigadier bellowed. 'A body's been discovered in the hotel! Stuffed into a dumbwaiter.'

I gulped. 'It's . . . it's . . . it's . . . not Véronique, is it?' I asked, bracing myself.

'No,' snapped the man accompanying the brigadier.

I breathed a sigh of relief.

'What's a dumbwaiter?' Freya asked.

'It's a small lift used for carrying food or rubbish between floors, miss,' the brigadier informed her. 'This here is Colonel Shelby,' he added, gesturing to the man beside him. 'He's with the SIS. He's just identified the body as being that of the waiter from the Cadenza.'

'*The waiter!* I don't understand,' I said.

'Neither do I,' hissed the brigadier.

I explained what had happened after I'd telephoned Nils. 'I assumed the waiter had managed to free himself and then overpower Véronique. I figured he'd dragged her off to the Flamingo Club. Guess I was wrong.'

The brigadier glared at me.

'And, so,' I continued, figuring it out as I spoke, 'presumably Véronique got the better of him, after all. Killed him and then disposed of the body in that dumb-waiter thing. So there's one less of Renard's men to worry about.'

The brigadier's face grew plum-coloured with rage.

'. . . That's good, isn't it?'

From the brigadier's expression I knew that I was mistaken.

Colonel Shelby spoke up. 'The waiter was one of *our* men!'

Chapter Eleven
Jacques' Story

Back at Mulberry all hell broke loose. Everyone was ordered to assemble in the lounge. Colonel Shelby had returned with the brigadier, and from the look on Walker's face, I reckoned the very existence of Special Operations hung in the balance. It had been a calamitous day and I think Shelby wanted to shout from the rooftops that Special Ops was to blame for the loss of one of his men. As we took our seats you could cut the atmosphere with one of Mrs Saunders' extremely sharp kitchen knives.

'Unfortunately,' the brigadier began, scowling indignantly at Colonel Shelby, 'it seems that our left hand doesn't know what our right hand is doing these days. For Christ's sake, we're all supposed to be on the same side! Why wasn't your undercover agent informed of our activities?'

'Why weren't yours informed of ours?' Shelby hissed back with equal venom.

Had Shelby and the brigadier been twenty years younger, I imagined this particular conversation would have ended up with punches being thrown. As it was, they composed themselves. Nils asked the perfect question: 'Can someone explain what the hell's going on?'

Shelby sighed. 'Very well. The waiter at the Cadenza had the job of covering Véronique's back. We inserted him into the field just a week ago. You see, in Véronique's last report she hinted that Renard was growing suspicious of her. Anyway, we can only assume our chap saw you lot watching Renard's apartment. Maybe he thought you were part of his unsavoury crowd. If he reckoned there was trouble brewing, his orders were to tail Véronique to make sure she was OK.'

I held up a hand.

'Yes, Mr Gunnersen?'

'Did Véronique know the waiter was with the SIS? She told me she didn't recognize him.'

Shelby shook his head. 'No, they'd not met. Of course, like you lot, in an emergency our agents can identify themselves to each other with coded phrases or signals. However, from your version of events, Mr Gunnersen, it sounds like our man didn't get the chance to introduce himself!'

That put me in my place. I tried to explain that I'd suspected Renard had signalled to the waiter in the town square. It was that, and the fact that the waiter immediately set off after Véronique, that had raised my suspicions. My little speech was met with blank faces. I was wrong, apparently. The waiter was not working for Renard. But what about Véronique? She'd gone running to Renard. Surely that made her a double agent. I was about to point out her treachery when I saw the fury in Shelby's eyes. This wasn't the right moment,

I decided. I suspected that Shelby had already come to the same conclusion as me – that one way or another he'd lost *two* agents in a single night.

'The upshot of this *mess*,' Shelby continued, 'is that we have to assume Renard will attempt to make his escape soon. Of course, we'll try to stop him. We will double security at all ports and airfields, place extra men at railway stations across southern England and order every policeman and member of the Home Guard to look out for him. Unfortunately it's well nigh impossible to cover every river and rocky cove, every nook and cranny of Britain's coastline. We have to face the fact that in all likelihood the blueprints will find their way to Berlin.'

Sitting at the back of the room, Amélie took a sharp intake of breath and muttered, '*Désastreux!*'

'Quite, miss!' the brigadier replied.

'What exactly are the blueprints for?' asked Max.

I reckoned Loki, Freya and I already knew the answer – an abominable weapon, a hideous death ray. Eager to hear all about it, I leaned forward in my chair. The brigadier's reply, however, took me by surprise.

'Our chaps over at Worth Matravers design radar systems. They've been working on a device that's small enough to be fitted into our aircraft.'

'You mean so our pilots can see the enemy in the dark?' interrupted Loki. I too recalled what Nils had explained to us during our journey down from Glasgow.

'Exactly, Mr Larson. And we're pretty close to an

operational version. There is a vital component in it called a magnetron. *That's* what the blueprints contain.'

The confused and puzzled look on Loki's face exactly matched how I felt. 'So it's not some sort of death ray then?' I said hesitantly.

Walker and the brigadier exchanged sharp glances. Both appeared to be at a loss as to what to say next. I sensed their awkwardness had something to do with Shelby's presence in the room. Why was that? I wondered. Then I remembered the animosity and competitiveness between Special Ops and the SIS. Was that it? Was the matter too sensitive for Shelby's ears? '*Death ray?*' Walker said finally, trying to sound light-hearted. 'What on earth are you on about, Mr Gunnersen?'

Shelby, for his part, had heard enough. Muttering that he had spies to catch, blueprints to retrieve and a war to win, he headed for the door and the chauffeur-driven car parked on the gravel outside.

The moment he'd left, Jacques stood up and slapped the palm of his left hand against his forehead. '*Bien entendu!* It is my fault, sir,' he said, turning to the brigadier. 'Finn saw me writing *rayon de la mort* during lessons.'

'Yes, that's right, I did. *Rayon de la mort* – death ray. We also know your father works for the Moutons' electronics company, Jacques – or at least he did until the Nazis invaded France and shipped him off to Berlin to work on something important. And we were told that those blueprints were vital. We assumed they were linked, all part of the same thing – plans for a devastating weapon.'

Jacques shook his head at me. '*Imbécile!*' he snorted. 'What is it the English say? Ah, yes, *A little knowledge is a very dangerous thing.*'

The brigadier puffed out his cheeks and nodded. 'Explanations are in order, I think. Perhaps you'd like to begin, Mr Lefebvre. Tell your colleagues about your role in all this.'

Max was scratching his head. Interrupting proceedings, he asked, 'What about this talk of a death ray?'

Walker held up a hand. 'All in good time, Max. We'll get to that.'

Jacques fired up a cigarette and took centre stage. 'You are right, Finn, about Amélie and I knowing Félix Mouton, and about our father working for the Moutons. Their electronics company makes many things, including radios and . . . *radar systems*! After France was invaded the Nazis seized everything. Being rich, the Moutons had a lot to lose. Félix's father faced a difficult choice. He could either give up his electronics company and fortune, or co-operate with the Nazis in the hope they'd let him keep them. He decided to co-operate. Our father continued working for him. That way he hoped to avoid being shipped to Germany as forced labour. It was the lesser of two evils.'

'But they took him to Berlin anyway!' Amélie interrupted.

Jacques exhaled forcefully. 'Yes, as soon as they realized he was a brilliant engineer.'

Max snorted with derision. 'So they're all *collaborators*!'

'No!' Jacques shouted. 'Not Father. He is a true Frenchman. In Berlin, the authorities allowed him to write home once a week. We agreed a sort of code before he left. Hidden in his letters he sent us information about what he was working on. Little bits at first. Then more detail. Eventually I could see what the Nazis were developing with his reluctant help. Through his letters he began pleading with me to give the information to the Resistance, or better still deliver it to the British authorities personally.'

'So that's when you decided to leave France?' said Freya.

'Yes. Both Amélie and I were already heavily involved with the local partisans but there was a problem. The Resistance is fragmented. It is hard to know who to trust. There are at least half a dozen groups working in and around Rochefort alone. Some are communists, others just local peasants. All have their own reasons for fighting. I decided it was safest to deliver the information myself.'

Max asked, 'What exactly was your father working on?'

'*Radar à impulsions* – erm, I think it translates as *pulse radar*. The Nazis have developed a new long-range system, one that can detect aircraft or ships hundreds of miles away. It is proving devastating. British bombers are being shot down before they even get across the Channel.'

The room fell silent for a while as all this information sank in. I realized both sides in this awful war were doing their best to steal the secrets of the other. Fritz wanted to learn about our new-fangled airborne system, while we desperately needed to know about their deadly long-range equipment. Eventually Max piped up with a question, 'I understand about your father, Jacques, but do we know why Félix Mouton agreed to spy for the Nazis?'

Jacques yanked the smouldering cigarette from his lips. 'I think so. I've known Félix most of my life. He has always been in his father's shadow and he resented it. I believe he saw an opportunity. I have little doubt the Nazis promised him many things in return for his assistance – money, power, and eventually control of his father's business. I expect his greed took over. He likes being *rich*!'

The brigadier took up Jacques' story. 'After Amélie and Jacques arrived in England and passed the information to Intelligence, X recruited them to Special Operations. He was already aware that Félix was in England, and had a pretty good idea that he was a rotten egg. He came up with a plan to try and infiltrate his world. He arranged it so that Jacques accidentally bumped into him in London.'

Amélie gasped in astonishment. '*Mon Dieu!*' Clearly she knew nothing of her brother's clandestine work. Walker apologized to her for all the secrecy, saying that X thought it safer to keep her out of that part of the operation.

Something pinged in my head. 'So that's where you keep disappearing to,' I said. 'You've been meeting Renard!'

'*Bravo!* Congratulations, Finn.' The smirk on Jacques' face broadened and he clapped his hands slowly. 'Of course, I couldn't let on that I knew he was working for the Nazis, so our little meetings were just old friends getting together to chat about the war and life back home. My cover story was that I got caught up helping French soldiers evacuate the beaches at Dunkirk, and with the Germans advancing rapidly I had to escape too.

'X instructed me to find out as much as possible about what Félix was up to over here. Félix is a very careful man, although he did let several – how do you say . . . *cats out of the bag.* As you know, we all come from a town called Rochefort, near the Channel coast. The Moutons own a large château there, close to the cliffs. About ten years ago Félix's father built laboratories in the grounds. That's where my father worked. One night a couple of months ago Félix told me how angry his father was now that the Germans had taken over. He's no longer permitted inside his own laboratories. *Eintritt verboten!* signs are everywhere. Also, a large part of the estate has been sealed off. Nobody is allowed within two hundred yards of the cliffs. I think he'd drunk too much and didn't realize what he was saying. I knew instantly that this information was recent, *new* – Félix was still actively communicating with home, despite being in England. He also told me that the Nazis had built something close to the edge of the cliffs. What, he wouldn't say. I don't think any amount of drink would have loosened his tongue sufficiently to reveal that.'

'What Jacques discovered all ties in with recent reports from the French Resistance,' the brigadier added. 'And our latest aerial reconnaissance photographs of the area. As well as the usual coastal defences, there are several strange rectangular grids of aerials and some small dish-like objects sited round a partially buried concrete building. Although the setup looks completely different to our radar sites, we're convinced it's Jerry's new long-range system.'

'Hah! So that's what your doodles were all about, Jacques. You were trying to draw Fritz's new aerials,' I said. Jacques pushed up his spectacles and nodded at me.

'How can you be certain it is the enemy's new radar system?' Max asked.

The brigadier smiled. 'One of our experts at Worth Matravers, a splendid chap with bags of initiative, set out to prove it. In a flash of inspiration he realized that if Jerry really did have a system that could detect aircraft a hundred miles away, then surely we ought to be able to hear it. So, one night he packed the boot of his car with a radio receiver, drove along the coast and parked up somewhere nice and quiet. Then he began listening. Sure enough, he picked up the tell-tale rhythmic beeps of a transmitter, and by fiddling about a bit with his aerial, he pinpointed the source – Rochefort! Bob's your uncle, case proven, I think.'

Amélie frowned. 'Bob? Who is this Bob?'

'Never mind, miss,' Walker replied. 'It's just an old saying.'

'You English and your crazy sayings. Why can't you talk properly?'

'Sorry, miss,' said the brigadier sheepishly. 'You're quite right.'

The room filled with chatter as everyone spoke at once, bombarding Jacques with questions about Renard. Max almost looked impressed. Amélie repeatedly tugged at her brother's sleeve while haranguing him for keeping so many secrets from her. Jacques glowed amid all the attention.

'Sergeant Walker, what about that death ray? You said you'd tell us,' Freya called out over the hubbub.

The brigadier bellowed for everyone to listen. 'Miss Haukelid is quite correct. Please all sit back down.' He signalled to Walker, who took up a commanding position in front of the fireplace. 'What Sergeant Walker is about to tell you is highly classified. You were to be briefed about it the day after tomorrow, but I think now is as good a time as any. Sergeant, if you please . . .'

'I think everyone here has a basic idea what radar is, don't they?' Walker began.

A murmur of agreement echoed about the room.

'Excellent. Well, when you think about it, all radar really does is send invisible radio waves into the air. Of course, the waves are perfectly harmless, invisible, and yet they are deadly! They allow the enemy to be located and destroyed. They are, in effect, a death ray.' He paused and saw me staring at him intensely. 'The point is,' he continued, 'we thought Death Ray was the perfect codename for your first mission into enemy territory.' Pushing back his shoulders and clearing his throat, he was evidently preparing himself for a big announcement. 'Mr Churchill has demanded that we do something to protect our pilots and reduce our heavy losses. We're losing aircraft faster than we can build replacements and train new pilots. It has to stop. And we intend to do just that. One week from now four of you will be heading for France. Your mission will be to help our chaps steal Jerry's new radar system – the whole kit and caboodle, every last damn nut and bolt.'

I was astonished.

The brigadier caught my eye. 'Close call earlier when you mentioned the codename in front of Shelby, Mr Gunnersen. His lot don't know about it. X wants it kept that way. He doesn't want the SIS interfering with our show. I know it sounds incredible, impossible even, but we have planned every detail. Operation Death Ray *must* succeed – otherwise we will lose this war!'

Loki beat me to the question hovering on my lips. 'You said *four* of us?'

'Correct,' said Walker. 'Jacques and Amélie will be accompanied by Max and Freya on their return to Rochefort.'

'What about Finn and me?' demanded Loki.

'We don't think your French is fluent enough yet, Mr Larson. We simply can't take the risk. There is too much at stake,' said the brigadier.

'*What?*' Loki's face darkened. 'If Freya's going, then so am I.'

'Calm down, Mr Larson. It wasn't an easy decision. But we believe it's the right one. In any event, you and Finn do have a role to play.'

'And what's that?' Loki snapped angrily.

'Captain Jacobsen needs a crew to help fly them in. We're going to be using the Heinkel seaplane you stole.'

The absence of surprise on Nils' face made me realize that he knew about at least that part of the operation. 'Are you up for it, Finn?' he asked.

I nodded vigorously – the chance to fly again made me fizz with excitement. Loki, however, reacted rather differently. 'No way,' he said, shaking his head. 'The three of us promised to stick together through thick and thin. Isn't that right?'

Freya nodded slowly. I think she was in shock. She looked kind of dazed, far away.

'And, anyway, our French is just as good as hers,' Loki complained. 'So, like I said, if she's going, then so am I. Otherwise you can forget it. Isn't that right?' He divided his stare between Freya and me. 'Well? Back me up, you two.' Anxiously awaiting our support, he was dismayed when we remained silent. '*Well?*'

'It's not our decision,' I said finally. I realized it wasn't much of a reply, and certainly not the one my best friend wanted to hear. He gave me a look that spoke of my betrayal.

'Mr Larson,' said the brigadier sternly, 'Freya's French is by no means perfect, but Jacques needs to have a dedicated wireless operator in the field. Freya's proven herself to be gifted. It's essential that she goes. It's a calculated risk.'

'Why can't Amélie operate the radio? Or someone in the French Resistance?'

'That's enough! X has made his decision,' the brigadier replied. 'It is not for you or me to question it.'

'Like hell it isn't.'

'Get a grip of yourself, Mr Larson,' said Walker. 'Or else we'll have to reconsider whether there is any kind of active role you can play in this mission.'

Seething, Loki stormed out of the room, slamming the door behind him.

Disgusted by the outburst, Jacques shook his head. 'His temper is too short. One day it will get him killed!'

'I'll go and talk to him,' I said. Freya got up too. 'No, maybe it's best if I speak to him alone.'

I found Loki sitting on a bench outside, busy sulking, his head in his hands. 'I just can't believe it. They know the three of us are a team, Finn. We told X that we rely on each other. It's not fair. It's not right!'

'I know.'

'I want to go home. Right this minute. That's where our war is. That's where our families are. *They*'re the ones we should be fighting for. When we agreed to join Special Ops I assumed X would eventually send us back home, to help the Norwegian Resistance, to help free our country. Not France, for God's sake!'

Of course, what lay at the heart of his rage was that

he and Freya were going to be separated. Worse, she was heading into great danger. We all knew that the work of wireless operators was probably the most hazardous of all Resistance work. Fritz had an uncanny knack of capturing them. Their life expectancy could be measured in terms of weeks. And good though Freya's French was, I doubted it would withstand close scrutiny. It would be down to Jacques and Amélie to protect her.

'And why's Max going?' Loki added bitterly.

'They want someone in the team who can read and speak fluent German.'

I looked round and saw Nils approaching. 'You knew all about this, didn't you?' I said accusingly.

'Some of it. Mind if I sit down?' He didn't wait for a reply and plonked himself next to Loki. 'I understand your feelings, and I share your concerns. But this operation really is important.'

'You sound just like the brigadier,' said Loki coldly. 'Why don't they just fly in and bomb the place to hell? Then there'd be no need for Freya to go; for any of us to go.'

'Think about it, Loki. If we blow it up, the Nazis will simply build another one, and another, and another. Maybe they'll find ways of camouflaging the system so we don't even know it's there. But if we got hold of one, one that worked, we could figure out how to beat it, to jam it or confuse it. There is a great deal at stake. The brigadier was right when he said the outcome of the war may depend on it.'

'It sounds a crackpot plan, anyway,' said Loki. 'How

on earth are they going to steal a radar system from right under Fritz's nose?'

'Not far from here a group of commandos and sappers from the Royal Engineers have been practising day and night, climbing cliffs and dismantling life-size models of the setup. It'll be their job to sail in and grab the equipment. Special Operations has been given the job of creating diversions in order to draw the local German garrison away from Mouton's château.'

Loki was unconvinced. 'Huh! I can't see Jacques and Amélie pulling that off, not even with Max's help.'

'I agree,' Nils replied. 'Jacques will have to co-ordinate the various disparate groups of partisans and try to get them all to pull in the same direction for once. At least they know him. I just hope they're willing to take their orders from him. The one thing on his side is that he'll return with the authority of Britain's top brass. And if that's not enough, a little blackmail can always be used.'

'Blackmail?'

'Yes – all the partisan groups rely heavily on RAF parachute drops for fresh supplies. As Jacques has control over the drops, the locals will realize that co-operating with him will ultimately be in their best interests too. Listen – about who's going in and who's not . . . A word of advice from a friend. I am your friend, aren't I?'

Although Loki's mouth remained shut, I replied for us both, 'Of course you are, Nils.'

'Good. The way I see it is like this,' he began, 'I know you three rely heavily on each other, but ultimately you each have to make your own decisions. Freya has to decide by herself whether she's willing to take on the responsibility. She knows the risks as well as you do. From what you told me of her father, Heimar, it strikes me that she takes after him. She seems pretty level-headed and courageous.'

'There are few braver,' I said. 'Remember that awful day, Loki, when we rowed across the fjord, only to discover that her father had been shot and captured by the Germans? When we caught up with Freya and I told her what had happened, she didn't even flinch. She just looked me in the eye and said we had a job to do and we'd better get on and do it. I was gobsmacked. I mean, I expected her to burst out crying or collapse or something. But no, she just gritted her teeth and got on with it. She said it was exactly what her father would have wanted her to do. Remember?'

Loki lifted his head out of his hands and stared at me. 'Of course I remember.'

'War has done strange things to us,' said Nils, 'brought out strengths none of us knew we possessed. I mean, take Amélie, for example: who'd have thought . . .'

'Thought what?' said Loki.

'You've heard their story, I take it.'

'Yes. That they stole a boat and escaped to England,' I replied. 'That's all Amélie told us. Jacques won't talk about it.'

'Ah! Well, there's a little more to it. The night they left France, they'd just reached their boat when two German guards stumbled across them. The soldiers quickly realized something was going on and proceeded to arrest Jacques. If it wasn't for Amélie they'd never have made their escape.'

'Why? What did she do?'

'Bashed hell out of one soldier with an oar, seized his pistol and shot the other one before he knew what was happening. The noise raised the alarm and pretty quickly other soldiers were rushing to the scene. She was all ready to stay ashore – to hold the soldiers off, to sacrifice herself to give her brother time to escape. It took all Jacques' efforts to get her into the boat in time.'

'*Little Amélie!*' The shock on Loki's face equalled my own.

'Yes. Innocent, harmless little Amélie. Tiny, but with the heart of a polar bear. Don't underestimate your fellow students. They are all extremely capable. Just like the two of you.'

Chapter Twelve
From Freya to Odette

During the following few days Mulberry House buzzed with frenetic activity. There were endless briefings, although often Loki, Nils and I were excluded. Our job was simply to fly the others in. What happened once they were on the ground didn't concern us. The brigadier was keen to keep the spread of information strictly on a need-to-know basis. When Loki wasn't sulking, he helped Nils and me draw up our flight plans. We spent hours poring over maps and examining aerial photographs, reading the latest reports from the French Resistance about the coastal defences and making lists of landmarks for us to look out for when flying in. On the face of it, the plan seemed reasonably straight-forward. The cliffs were high along that part of the French coast, some stretches measuring almost four hundred feet, but five miles west of Rochefort they gave way to form a river estuary. We decided to be bold and fly straight up the river valley for about ten miles, land and offload our passengers, then fly straight back. We'd fly in and out low, hoping that we could maybe squeeze beneath the enemy's radar. Our choice of landing site was based on two main criteria – a straight stretch of river and an area that seemed pretty rural and remote. Anything too close to towns or villages had to be avoided – towns and villages meant soldiers and patrols.

Having chosen the landing site, we radioed the co-ordinates to the nearest local Resistance group in a town about eight miles from Rochefort, to forewarn them in case they knew of any difficulties we weren't aware of. The exact date and time of our arrival, however, would only be communicated to them just before we set off.

Within twenty-four hours the Resistance replied that the location was OK and they informed us that they would signal as we approached, waving lamps with green filters if it was safe to land, red ones if not. A rowing boat would be used to take everyone ashore. They also asked whether we might be able to bring along some additional supplies. The brigadier promptly instructed Smithy to see what he could lay his hands on at such short notice. As always, Smithy didn't disappoint.

'All right, lads,' he said, grinning at us as he unloaded his stash from the back of his truck. 'All pukka gear, this. These Stens are brand new.' He opened a couple of crates to reveal fifty Sten guns, plus enough ammunition to retake Paris. 'Only the best for our chaps working for the underground. Just wish I was delivering them personally,' he said wistfully, revealing the contents of several tightly packed canvas holdalls. I observed grenades, plastic explosive, detonators and various timers, including pressure switches and time pencils.

'There's enough there to start a small war,' Loki observed.

'No, Mr Larson, sir,' Smithy replied. 'There's enough

there to *end* a bloody big war!' He scratched his jaw thoughtfully. 'Now, have I forgotten anything? Oh, yes, those dead rats. Where did I put them . . . ?'

For Max and Freya, life at Mulberry turned into a living nightmare. They had to learn their false French identities, absorbing countless facts – from their new names, where they were born, schools they'd attended, their imaginary families and friends, to their reasons for being in Rochefort. The list was endless. And they had to learn it in enough detail that they could convince an inquisitor that they really had lived where they claimed. This struck me as a hard enough task, but two compli-cations made it utterly mind-boggling. They had to understand the questions and reply to them in French. Harder still, their responses needed to be fluent, natural, without hesitation, just as they would be if they were true. Anything less could cost them their lives.

Locked away in a dimly lit back room at the house, Freya and Max faced interrogation by men dressed in the uniforms of the dreaded SS. Late into the night, they emerged from their sessions looking shell-shocked, as white as sheets and so shattered they just wanted to sleep.

One morning over breakfast Freya remarked, 'It is all so hard.' Peering at the tea leaves in the bottom of her cup, she went on, 'But I think Madame Dupuis was right when she told us that, to be convincing, we should become our new identities in every way. We can't simply pretend. We should make ourselves believe it. And to do that we must think of our real selves as being dead!'

Mrs Saunders was busy scrubbing pans in the sink at the time but she froze when she heard Freya say this. A stony-faced Loki screeched back his chair and stormed out of the house. '*Freya!*' I said in dismay. 'Don't say that. That's awful.'

The strain was beginning to show. She looked exhausted, her face pale and her shoulders hunched.

'Listen, are you certain you want to go ahead with this?' I asked. 'There's still time to back out. Remember what X said to us when we arrived. It's better to back out before an operation gets underway. There'd be no shame in it.'

She reached across the table and took my hand. 'I don't know, Finn. I just don't know. I'm afraid. But that's only natural, isn't it? And I'm worried about Loki.'

'It's tearing him apart,' I said.

'I know.'

Our eyes locked together and I felt as if I could see right into her. I think it was at that moment I realized Loki's feelings for Freya were matched by the way she felt about him. 'You have to talk to him,' I said. 'You must.'

She nodded faintly. 'Yes, Finn, I must.'

Later I noticed that Loki and Freya had wandered off together. When Walker came looking for them, furious that they'd skipped important lessons, I told him to back off, to give them a little space. He would have none of it. 'This isn't the time for those two to be off canoodling,' he snapped. 'I'll ruddy well go and fetch them myself.'

I was surprised at my reaction. Even though Walker

was much bigger and stronger than me, I grabbed the collar of his tunic, yanked him forward so that our faces were inches apart, and hissed through clenched teeth, '*Leave them alone!* Please . . . ! Sir!'

Taken aback, Walker got the message. Composing himself, he replied, 'Just make sure they're back by lunch time, Finn.'

I think Freya's willingness to play her part in Operation Death Ray lay in the balance that morning. It would not have taken much to sway her either way. And had it simply been left to Loki, I think she would have decided that whatever work we agreed to do, the three of us would either do it together or not at all. But later that morning things changed for ever for Freya. For all of us, in fact.

It began when Nils arrived back from RAF Tangmere with bad news. I saw him step gingerly out of his car and I was immediately filled with a sense of dread. It was the look on his face.

'Finn, where are the others?' he called out.

I ran across to him and explained.

'Oh!'

'What's the matter? You look like you've seen a ghost.'

He grabbed my shoulder tightly. 'I've got some terrible news,' he said softly.

'*What?*' Instantly my head filled with pictures of our families back home; of Mother and Anna being marched out to face a firing squad. Hell, I could even hear the shots ringing in my ears! '*What?*'

'It's Freya's father,' he said. 'My brother finally managed to get a message out of Norway via a courier. He said he tried his best for him. But Heimar never recovered from the gunshot wounds he received when he was taken prisoner.'

'Poor Freya,' I said. 'I guess we'd better go and find her.'

Nils hesitated.

'Is there something else?' I asked. 'About our families?'

'No. It's nothing like that. It's just . . . Listen, Finn, if I tell you something that I'm not supposed to, will you keep it to yourself. Do you promise? Only I'll be in big trouble if anyone finds out I've repeated it. But I feel I need to share it with someone. Someone I can trust.'

'Of course.'

'Well, at a place called Bletchley we have people who intercept and decode all sorts of different radio transmissions and other intelligence reports. My brother's message was decoded there before being forwarded on to me at Tangmere. When I went to collect it from my squadron leader's office, I took the opportunity to glance through all the other latest intelligence reports.'

'And . . . ?'

'There was a really strange one. It was the record of a conversation between a Luftwaffe pilot flying off the French coast and his HQ. One of our people at Bletchley had scribbled a footnote saying that the source of transmission on the ground had been narrowed by triangulation to within a few miles of Rochefort. The puzzling bit is that in the conversation there was a reference to *Freya Meldung*.'

'Freya what?'

'*Meldung* is German for *detection* or *announcement*, Finn.'

'Freya detection? Freya announcement? Does that mean what I think it does?'

'No, I don't think so. It wouldn't make any sense, Finn. No one over there could possibly know anything about Freya or the rest of you. In truth, nobody in intelligence has a clue what it means. It's a real puzzle. Intelligence is stumped. They assume it's a codename for something. But what?'

He saw the worried look on my face. 'I'm sure it's just a coincidence, Finn. There are hundreds of code-words being used by both sides in this war.'

'God, I hope you're right!' Then I was struck by a thought. Why was he telling me this if it wasn't relevant? If it was simply a coincidence, then why trouble me with it? 'Are you sure there's nothing more to it, Nils? Remember, we're friends and you can trust me.'

He put his hand on my shoulder again. 'I know I can trust you, Finn. I'm telling you all I know. Honestly! It's just . . . well . . . I'm not always sure we get to hear about everything. Know what I mean? If it was important, maybe X or people in the SIS would want to keep it from us. Save us worrying about it. Anyway, all I'm really saying to you is make a mental note of it. Just in case something relevant crops up. OK?'

'Yes. Of course.'

★ ★ ★

A dark shadow was cast over Mulberry House that spring afternoon. Understandably Freya wanted a while to herself, although at tea time Amélie went off in search of her. When they returned, Freya had made her decision and called Loki and me to one side.

'I've thought long and hard,' she said. 'It would be easy to back out now. The brigadier said he'd understand, that it was terrible timing, and that now might not be an ideal moment for me to go into the field. But . . .' She paused and took our hands in hers. 'Please understand. I asked myself a question. What would Father want me to do?'

'Heimar would have wanted you to be safe,' Loki interrupted.

'Of course – under normal circumstances. But he also believed that some things were truly worth fighting for. Your father was the same, Finn. That's why he flew to England at the outbreak of war to join the RAF. And yours too, Loki; that's why he joined the local Resistance. And we're just like them. All three of us. That's how we got *here*, to Mulberry House, training as agents in the middle of nowhere. All over Europe there are men and women facing impossible choices, having to put their own feelings to one side. There are battles to be fought. Like X said on our first night here, this war is good versus evil, and it requires all sorts of different sacrifices, big and small. It's simply my turn now. I've decided. I *will* go to France.'

Loki bit his lip and nodded. I reached out and gave her a hug.

Forty-eight hours later it was our last evening together at Mulberry. The brigadier wanted to give the team a good send-off and instructed Mrs Saunders to provide us all with a slap-up dinner. X would be attending. She had to pull out all the stops. Just the thought that our housekeeper might be tempted to *experiment* put the fear of God into us. Luckily, knowing how we'd grown sick of eating anything that came out of a tin, Smithy came up trumps. That morning he wandered into the kitchen carrying an entire deer carcass across his shoulders, head and all. 'All right, lads,' he said to Max and me as we ate our toast. 'Look what leaped out in front of my truck last night. Never saw it. Still, waste not want not. That's what my mum always used to say.'

We didn't question his story, although it failed to explain the bullet hole located plum between the poor beast's eyes.

That evening we assembled in the dining room at eight o'clock. The room had been cleared of our small desks and chairs, and a single large trestle table erected, neatly covered with white linen and sparkling silver cutlery. X duly arrived. Then, having called us to attention, the brigadier spoke: 'Dear friends, we all know what faces you in the following days and weeks and, having got to know you a little, I have no doubt you will all serve Special Operations well. Before we eat, however, you will notice that two of you are absent. Sadly, Freya and Max couldn't make it tonight.'

There was a murmur of consternation around the room, but the brigadier raised a hand and added, 'However, I would like to introduce you to two new colleagues, Luc and Odette Ravoir.'

The door opened and in walked Max and Freya. Or rather, it wasn't them. Freya's lovely blonde hair had been cut short and they both wore clothes we'd not seen before; in fact everything about them seemed different. Freya wore a simple pale-blue blouse and stylishly pleated tailored skirt beneath a smart coat. Max wore a fairly worn jacket with leather patches on his sleeves and a cap on his head that somehow *completely* altered the way he looked.

'*Bonsoir, mes amis,*' Madame Dupuis chirped. There followed a lengthy conversation between the three of them in French. I struggled to keep up and realized that maybe the brigadier and Walker had made a wise decision when evaluating my proficiency. Loki just stood next to me open-mouthed. The sight was astonishing. If they really had been strangers, I would have been convinced they were French. When Loki finally managed to speak, all he could say was, '*Utrolig!*'

It was indeed an *incredible* spectacle. When the conversation with Madame Dupuis ended, X said, 'Splendid! Simply splendid.' Jacques rose from his chair, and with his cigarette dangling from his lips he applauded energetically. '*Bravo!*'

We sat down and ate a truly sumptuous meal of venison pie served with lashings of rich gravy. It was the second revelation of the night – Mrs Saunders could cook after all! X gave a rambling speech, and we were glad when he finished; then we raised our glasses to toast the success of Operation Death Ray. Although there was much light-hearted chatter about the room, Loki said very little, and I noticed that while his eyes seemed glued to Freya – or should I say Odette – she managed to avoid his stare. It was as if he wasn't even in the same room. I felt for him. She was playing her game well.

I'd assumed that when the two of them disappeared together that morning a couple of days earlier, they'd told each other how they truly felt. But Freya had lied: she'd told Loki she was fond of him but nothing more. Loki had told me she'd effectively given him the brush-off, saying that now wasn't the time to get involved, that her feelings weren't strong enough for him, that she'd hate to lead him on. But I knew she was lying. I'd seen that look in her eyes. I guessed she was being cruel to be kind in case she didn't make it back from France, but Loki remained inconsolable. When we'd finished eating, we moved to the comfort of the lounge. Loki went for a walk. I was about to go and join him when Amélie, who'd been admiring Freya's clothes, let out a hideous shriek. '*Bougre d'idiot! Merde! Merde! Merde!*' Her outburst was directed at a rather startled Madame Dupuis.

Amélie held up her hand, in which she clutched one of Freya's gloves. 'How could you be so stupid?' she shouted. 'Do you want her killed?'

Walker snatched the glove from Amélie's hand and inspected it. His face grew scarlet with rage and he flashed Madame Dupuis a piercing, accusatory look. 'You know you must check everything *meticulously*,' he snarled. 'Double check and then triple check. Examine every damn seam and stitch.'

I realized Amélie had turned the glove inside out and, deep inside, in a fold in the material, she'd found a label which innocently stated – MADE IN ENGLAND.

The blood drained from Madame Dupuis' cheeks. '*Je regrette infiniment!* I checked everything. Jacques, you helped me. Neither of us spotted it, did we?'

Jacques shrugged apologetically.

'Well, sorry simply isn't good enough,' Walker chastised. 'Freya and Max, go and change. Then Madame Dupuis will help you go through every item of your clothing with a fine-tooth comb. Make sure there's *nothing* that could give you away.'

Oddly, although it took place in the safe confines of Mulberry House, the episode felt like a really close shave. It unsettled everyone, and the evening drew to a premature close. X shook each of our hands, said he'd eagerly await everyone's safe return, and then departed after a short private conversation with the brigadier; a conversation I suspected had something to do with the fact that there'd been no sign of Renard and the stolen blueprints. Max reckoned he'd been picked up by a U-boat. Smithy had a different theory – he bet that Renard had disguised himself as a merchant seaman and hitched a lift on a boat heading for Lisbon – a popular escape route, apparently. According to Walker, Véronique hadn't been seen or heard of either since the night she and I met in Bournemouth. But it was all speculation. It was really a case of no news being bad news, and it meant the pressure for us to succeed was growing by the day.

Grabbing a torch, I went in search of Loki in the garden; he didn't answer my calls, but I homed in on the strange banging and splintering sounds that appeared to be coming from one of the sheds. I found Loki demolishing it with an axe. 'Jesus! What the hell do you think you're doing?'

Axe poised above his head, Loki paused. 'Had to get it out of my system, Finn. It felt like I was going to explode. Smithy told me this old wreck of a shed was due to be replaced, anyway, so I figured I'd lend a hand.'

'Has it made you feel better?'

He lowered the axe. 'Not really.'

I explained what had just happened. Loki shook his head in dismay. 'Damn it, Finn, I've got this really bad feeling. I can't explain it. Am I being stupid?' In the torch light his eyes glowed at me.

'I don't know. I guess we're all on edge.'

He cast the axe down. 'You can say that again.'

'Listen,' I said. 'About Freya . . .'

'I don't want to talk about her, Finn. *All right?*'

'She feels the same way about you as you do about her,' I continued. 'I just know it.'

'Yeah, right, Finn. Of course she does.'

'No, really.'

Loki puffed out his cheeks and sat down heavily on a mound of debris.

'It'll all turn out fine,' I said hopefully.

'Huh!'

'There you two are,' Max called out, approaching through the gloom. He saw what had happened to the shed and laughed. 'Captain Jacobsen was asking for you, Finn. I said I'd help him look.'

'What about checking your clothes?' I said.

'That can wait. Poor old Madame Dupuis. It wasn't her fault, you know. Jacques checked Freya's gloves earlier, not her. I saw him doing it. It's entirely his fault. I told the brigadier as much.'

There was a hint of glee in Max's voice. He'd never really hit it off with Jacques and seemed to enjoy pointing the finger at him. He slapped Loki on the shoulder. 'Don't worry. I'll look after her for you. I'll see she makes it home safely.'

Loki peered up at him but said nothing.

'Are you scared about the mission, Max?' I asked.

'A little, but I suppose this is what it's all about, isn't it? It's time to get our hands dirty. I just pray there aren't any more slip-ups. We're going to be relying heavily on Jacques, and I can't say that fills me with confidence. In truth, I wish you two were coming along too. I'd feel a whole lot happier.' He looked up at the night sky. 'Tomorrow's a full moon. Walker's sent confirmation that we're going in. Let's hope Fritz wasn't listening and managed to decode his message.'

I was reminded of what Nils had told me about

the intercepted conversation between the Luftwaffe pilot and his base somewhere near Rochefort. It had been troubling me ever since. Despite my promise to him, I found myself blurting it out – and instantly regretting it. Loki tore at his hair. 'God, Finn, they know about Freya. I reckon they know all about us. Bloody hell!'

Repeating what Nils had said, I tried telling him not to be so hasty, not to jump to conclusions, that it was probably just some code for something. After all, why would a Luftwaffe pilot mention Freya while out on patrol? That didn't make any sense unless he was referring to something else. 'Maybe the message was garbled,' I said. 'Maybe the people at that Bletchley place misheard or got the decoding wrong.' I think my words fell on deaf ears. In the end I decided it was best to go and find out what Nils wanted before I landed myself in any more trouble.

I found him standing in the hall outside the brigadier's office. He was clutching a canvas bag. 'There you are, Finn.' He beckoned me into the office and closed the door. 'I've got something for you. I figured you'd need it for tomorrow night.' He handed me the bag.

Opening it, my heart stopped and I gasped. My father's leather flying jacket! The one he gave to me on the morning he left for England; the jacket I'd worn with pride the night we stole the Heinkel and flew her to Britain; the jacket that had given me the courage to face great danger. 'Thanks.'

He smiled. 'Well, that's us all set, I think. Try and get a good night's sleep, if that's possible. Tomorrow's going to be a long day.'

Clutching the jacket, I turned to go.

'About Loki,' Nils added. 'He'll be all right, won't he? I mean, it's going to prove a difficult night for him.'

'He'll be OK,' I lied. In truth, just the thought of Freya clambering out into enemy territory made me feel sick to the stomach. I could only imagine what Loki was going through. 'That intercepted message you told me about. The one about "Freya detection". You haven't found out any more, I suppose?'

'No, except that it's not the first time they've over-heard pilots mention it.'

'Really?'

'Apparently so. It's quite a mystery, isn't it? Still, like I said the other day, don't go mentioning it to the others. I think they've got enough to worry about.'

Biting my lip, I said nothing.

Chapter Thirteen
Friend or Foe

At precisely nine o'clock the following evening we all climbed nervously into the back of Smithy's truck for the short journey to Calshot, a small RAF station located on a spit of land jutting into the sea, where our Heinkel plane was being readied. There was an uneasy, contemplative hush among the seven of us. Freya and Max – or should I say Odette and Luc – were fully kitted out in their French clothing, their pockets filled with money and false papers, and each carried maps of northern France printed on silk and stitched into the seams of their coats. Their heads were filled with code-words and phrases known only to a select few. Freya clutched a small suitcase close to her chest. She had to guard it with her life. It contained her transmitter.

The brigadier's parting gesture had been to offer each of them a small gift: a tiny blister containing a single tablet. They were called L-pills, the L standing for *lethal*. They contained potassium cyanide and acted quickly, causing death in just a few seconds apparently, saving them from suffering the worst horrors of the Gestapo should they be captured. Max hesitated and then reluctantly took his. Freya simply refused. 'That isn't how I want to go,' she said softly but determinedly.

Smithy was unusually tight-lipped as he helped the

girls aboard his truck, which was most unlike him, as was the fact that he'd turned out in a pristine, freshly pressed uniform, with polished boots and buttons, and snapped to attention and saluted us with such precision it was as if he was standing before the King of England. I also noticed something else. There was a single medal pinned to his chest. It caught my eye because it looked vaguely similar to the ones my father had earned. They too were made of bronze. Smithy's, however, dangled from a crimson ribbon whereas my father's bore the colours of the Norwegian flag. Once we were underway, winding through the narrow country lanes in the dark, I asked Nils about it.

'That, Finn, is the Victoria Cross. It's the highest decoration and is awarded for conspicuous bravery.'

'Really! How did Smithy get it?' asked Loki.

'I don't know the details,' Nils replied. 'Smithy doesn't like talking about it. For something he did during the evacuation of Dunkirk, I think Walker said. Whatever it was, it was undoubtedly pretty special. They don't award them for anything less.'

'Old Smithy – who'd have thought it?' I said. 'Why was he wearing it tonight?'

Nils shrugged. 'Probably out of respect for you lot. You've got to hand it to the brigadier. It couldn't have been easy getting hold of some of the finest men in the British army to train you all.'

Driving at great speed, Smithy hammered along the twisting lanes, the truck's tyres screeching every time he took a sharp bend a little too fast. As we neared our destination my belly felt oddly empty. Turning suddenly hard left Smithy came to a standstill, then called out from the cab, 'We're here.'

I heard voices and footsteps. Then the truck's canvas awning was drawn back and a powerful torch beam was shone into our faces. Nils shielded his eyes with one hand and handed over some papers with the other. 'I'm Captain Jacobsen. We're expected. There are seven of us.'

As my eyes began to adjust, I noticed a tall fence smothered with coils of barbed wire. We clambered out of the truck and unloaded the supplies for the Resistance group near Rochefort. The guns, ammo and sabotage equipment had been packed into waterproof holdalls. We each carried two, except Freya, who lugged her small suitcase. It was heavy, weighing in at thirty-two pounds. Once in France she'd need to carry it through the streets as though it was as light as a feather – certainly not hefty enough to conceal a transmitter – otherwise German soldiers might grow suspicious. If they stopped and searched her, that would be it – there'd be no way she could talk her way out of the situation. She'd be arrested, interrogated and ultimately shot. Maybe, I thought, she'd been a bit hasty to decline her L-pill. As she walked, with her raincoat buttoned up and beret perched on her head, I suppose I expected her to look full of trepidation. Instead, she stood tall and proud, striding forward with purpose, her eyes bright as if filled with fire. I understood. She was thinking of her father, Heimar. She wasn't thinking of Operation Death Ray, so much as her own personal mission – one of revenge.

We were escorted along the shingle spit by a young soldier with three pips on his shoulders. He made straight for a large hangar. The cold night was crisp and I could taste the saltiness of the sea. Waves rolled in and crashed against the stony shore barely a dozen yards away. The soldier talked incessantly, probably under orders to try and take our minds off matters. 'We service seaplanes and marine craft here,' he said, almost as if we were on a school outing to the local museum. 'This place is pretty famous. Back in 'twenty-nine the Schneider Cup was held here.'

'The what?' Freya snapped irritably.

'High-speed air races, miss. It was reckoned a million people came to watch, lining the shores of the Solent. Britain won with a seaplane called the S-six. It averaged over three hundred miles per hour during the race. It was designed by a man called Reggie Mitchell. He also designed the Supermarine Spitfire.'

On any other day, at any other time, I would have been all ears. At that moment, however, I just wished the fellow would button it!

A man in blue overalls ran out to greet us from a nearby hut. 'Jolly good. Right on time. I'm Chief Engineer Roberts. She's ready and waiting for you.' He stuck two fingers into his mouth and whistled loudly. '*Open sesame!*' he bellowed before turning to me and adding, 'Just my little joke.'

Slowly the huge hangar door slid open and I gasped. There she was – our Heinkel 115 float plane! Roberts ushered everyone inside. 'We keep her under lock and key,' he remarked. 'After all, she must remain top secret. We can't let any old Tom, Dick or Harry see we've got her. We took her out of the water as soon as she arrived. She's been under armed guard ever since.'

The hangar was vast. There were various seaplanes and motorboats undergoing repair and servicing under the bright glare of arc lights, some half dismantled, their engine parts neatly laid out beside gantries and ladders. There was a heavy smell of oil and kerosene, and sounds of hammering and of metal striking metal. It was an amazing sight. The Heinkel had been removed from the water using large wheeled dollies inserted beneath each of her floats. She looked bigger than I remembered. Her wingspan was over seventy feet and she was close to sixty feet long. I recalled that her official maximum speed was over one hundred and eighty miles per hour at about three thousand feet, although I reckoned she could do more. On seeing her dullish grey-green camouflage paint, the black and white crosses on her fuselage and the swastika on her tail fin, Max whistled loudly. '*Ach du meine Fresse!* You two can fly this thing? *Mein Gott!* I'm impressed.'

I walked around the plane. The metal of her twin nine-cylinder, nine hundred and sixty horse power radial engines clicked and pinged. She was cooling down. 'We ran her engines for twenty minutes to make sure everything was OK,' Roberts called out.

'And?' Nils asked.

'Purrs like a kitten.' Roberts beamed. 'And we carried out the modifications you requested, Captain Jacobsen.'

'What modifications?' I asked while surveying her sleek lines.

'We've fitted her with IFF.'

'What's that?'

'It's a very clever system,' Nils replied. 'It stands for *Identification Friend or Foe*. As soon as we take off, our radar stations will pick us up. Without IFF they wouldn't know whose side we're on. The system is ingenious. There's a device on board that detects our radar and then transmits its own signal back – a kind of reply, if you like. It tells the radar operators that the blip on their screens is friend, not foe. It should stop Fighter Command from scrambling some Spits to intercept us.'

'What else have you done with her?' Loki asked.

'Well, as we discussed, we're going to fly in low, to try and squeeze underneath Fritz's radar. What I didn't tell you is just how low we'll be flying.'

'How low?' I enquired.

'About fifty feet.'

'That's impossible,' I said.

Roberts nodded to me. 'Indeed, under normal circumstances flying that low over the sea is well nigh impossible. Your altimeter isn't that accurate and it's easy to get disorientated at night, especially over featureless terrain. One mistake and you'd splash into the briny. But we've come up with something.'

I was still trying to get my head round the magnitude of our task, when Roberts headed for the plane's starboard wing tip. 'We've fixed a lamp in each wing and adjusted their beams so that they meet at exactly fifty feet below the plane some hundred yards ahead of her. All you have to do is watch where the beams strike the ground or water and make sure they remain together. That'll tell you you're at exactly fifty feet. Think of it simply like a triangle.' Roberts looked mighty pleased with himself.

'But won't the enemy see the lights?' asked Freya.

The smile faded from Roberts's lips. 'I can't work flipping miracles!'

'It sounds splendid, Mr Roberts,' said Nils. 'Thank you. Loki, as you'll be in the forward-gun position I want you to keep one eye on the lights. OK?'

Jacques, Amélie, 'Luc' and 'Odette' were taken to Roberts's hut while Nils, Loki and I checked over the plane and then watched a dozen brawny men put their shoulders and backs into pushing the dollies out of the hangar, guiding the Heinkel towards a wide slipway. There, all the equipment was loaded before the plane was pushed into the water and tied up. There was just time for checking the latest weather reports, grabbing a cup of piping-hot tea, and worrying about everything that might go wrong, before Nils tapped me on my shoulder and said to everyone, 'It's time.'

Chapter Fourteen
To France

Scaling a ladder fixed between the fuselage and one of the floats, the team boarded. Loki headed for the forward-gun position in the nose of the plane and I made for the cockpit, while Nils ensured the others strapped themselves in properly within the cramped confines of what's called the 'crawl way'. I took a deep breath, the strong kerosene fumes and peculiar but distinctive burnt-like odour of electrical stuff filling my lungs, and sat down behind the controls. For a split second I had a flashback. My sister's one-time boyfriend, Dieter Braun, a Luftwaffe pilot, was sitting next to me just like he had on that day when he took Loki and me for a short flight in this very plane over the fjords back home. He knew I was crazy about flying and had thought it a perfect sixteenth birthday present for me. I'd watched him run through the pre-flight checks and then start her up. Oddly, I had him to thank for making me believe I could fly this plane, although as it turned out Dieter was dangerously two-faced. While he charmed my sister and me, he was simultaneously seeking the maps and photographs that had fallen into my hands. He stopped at nothing to retrieve them. In the end it cost him his life.

Nils arrived and sat in the co-pilot's seat next to me. 'OK, Finn?'

I swallowed hard and nodded.

He strapped himself in and we hooked up the radio sets in our flying helmets to the control panel so we could still communicate once the engines were running. He checked Loki had done the same, then turned to me. 'I've grabbed a few hours on her, Finn. All-night flying, too, so we should be fine. We'll run through the pre-flight checks together. Shout if you think I've forgotten anything.'

Nils was asking me! But I knew the drill. Dozens of times in the past I'd helped my father check over his plane before setting off. 'Flaps and rudder, first,' I replied hesitantly.

'Yes, Finn. Flaps and rudder controls first.'

While he checked them, I cast my eyes over the instrument panel: the altimeter, airspeed indicator, oil pressure and temperature gauges. 'I'll set the controls for takeoff,' I said. Reaching forward, I got to work, talking through my actions. 'Opening throttles and adjusting the carburettor air-intakes to their start positions. Main ignition and magneto switches on . . . As Roberts has already run the engines the oil temperature is OK. No need to let her warm up.'

'Good.' Nils sat back and cracked his knuckles. 'Port engine first please, Finn.'

I hit the starter switch for the port engine and we both peered out of the cockpit, watching the propeller blades begin to turn amid a loud whine. The engine spluttered into life, spewing puffs of black smoke. The blades spun faster and quickly became a blur. Nils adjusted the throttle slightly. A minute later the starboard engine hummed loudly too. Nils slid open the cockpit, stuck an arm out and signalled for the plane to be untied. Then he flipped a switch that looked new to me. 'That's the IFF we were talking about, Finn. For God's sake always make sure it's on otherwise you'll have Spits on your tail before you know it. Well, this is it. Next stop France!'

He reached for the throttles and shoved them to their maximum positions. The hum of the engines rose to a whining din and then a frenetic howl. Everything shook and rattled. Slowly we moved forward, away from the slipway, out into the open water. According to the weather reports, the wind was north-westerly, gusting about fifteen knots. We headed away from land and, easing the throttles slightly, Nils used the rudder to turn her into the wind. Then full throttle again. She shook and rocked violently as she smacked and cut through the slight swell. We gathered speed rapidly. The din of her howling engines was ear-splitting. Our ground speed reached forty miles per hour. Then fifty, sixty, seventy. At eighty miles per hour we pulled back our columns. 'Gently does it,' I muttered under my breath. The rocking, wallowing and wave-smacking gradually subsided as the plane lifted slightly. Then, like some great bird almost too heavy to fly, she rose clear of the water. The pounding ceased. Everything was suddenly smooth. We were airborne.

Climbing fast, Nils reached forward and made some adjustments. Then he set us on a tight left turn towards the southeast. Checking the compass, I made a note of the time and our airspeed on my copy of our maps.

'I'm going to take her to five hundred feet, Finn. Let her settle and make sure everything's OK, and then we'll drop to fifty feet.'

'I remember Dieter telling me that at cruising speed we need eighty-five per cent power,' I said.

'As we'll be going in so low we'll take it nice and steady. We won't push the engines so hard.'

Levelling off at five hundred feet I gazed out of the cockpit. It was a full moon and there was just a little broken cloud. I could see countless stars, and the sea stretched out before us like a shimmering silk carpet.

'Everything all right, Loki?' I said into my mouthpiece.

'Yeah. When are you going to switch on those lights?'

Nils reached out and flipped a switch. 'They're on now. Can you see them?'

I leaned forward and peered at the sea in front and beneath us. There were two barely discernible oval shapes of pale light on the surface, far ahead of us and some distance apart. 'Here goes,' said Nils. He throttled back and pushed his control column forward. The plane's nose dipped and we descended. Keeping one eye on the altimeter and the other on the patches of light beneath us, I saw the ovals gradually move closer together, growing smaller and brighter. It felt like the sea was rising up to swallow us. Instinctively I braced myself.

'Almost there.' Loki's voice crackled through my earphones. 'That's it! Fifty feet. Hold her nice and steady.'

Nils levelled the plane. Again I noted the time and our airspeed – ten minutes past eleven and one hundred and fifteen miles per hour. The prevailing wind was at our tail now. I calculated the time to our next change of course, which wouldn't be until we approached the French coast, and got Nils to check my sums. He nodded approvingly. I set about plotting our position and route on my map.

'Do you think they've picked us up on their radar?' I asked.

He shrugged. 'Guess we'll soon find out, Finn. We'll either find a Messerschmitt on our tail or have Fritz challenging us on our radio. Fingers crossed though.'

I recalled the hours we'd spent studying the aerial photographs of Rochefort while compiling our flight plan. From what we could see of the structures that were supposedly Fritz's new-fangled radar system, they looked totally different to the huge tall aerial towers Nils said lay at the heart of our system. All we could make out were some small dish-like objects and rectangular grids arranged in a triangle, although it was hard to tell exactly what shape they were from the angle the photographs had been taken. 'Are they absolutely sure there's a radar installation at Rochefort and not something entirely different?'

Nils nodded. 'Everything seems to point to it. I had a bit of a chat with one of the experts from

Worth Matravers last time he visited the brigadier at Mulberry House. There's a theory to explain why our boys are getting intercepted so early once they approach the coast. They think Fritz's system has three parts: two accurate but short-range devices – one to track our planes and the other their own fighter aircraft; and a single long-range device that they use as an early-warning system. As soon as they see us coming, they get their fighters into the air and wait until we show up on their short-range system. At that point they can track us accurately enough to talk their fighters into intercepting us.'

'The bastards!' I shouted into my mouthpiece.

Nils laughed. 'Don't underestimate them, Finn. Their *Nachtjagd* is pretty formidable.'

My German was good enough to know he was referring to their night fighting. Unfastening my harness, I turned to look back at the others – lit by the glow of a feeble red lamp, they were sitting quietly with their backs to the fuselage, staring blankly ahead, lost in their own thoughts. 'Luc' briefly looked in my direction but, solemn faced, quickly looked away. It wasn't long now, I realized, and there was no going back. I refastened my harness and pulled the straps tight.

Nils began fiddling with the dials of our radio. Since we were under orders to maintain radio silence I was puzzled. 'What are you doing?'

'Adjusting the frequency to see if we can pick up Fritz's transmissions. If anyone's up here with us we stand a good chance of hearing them.'

Having flown with the Special Duties squadron, I knew this wasn't the first time Nils had made forays into France. 'Had problems before?'

He nodded.

I gulped. 'What can we expect? Will the coast be lit up by searchlights?'

He shook his head. 'Fritz doesn't care about anything other than his industrial heartland. Close to cities like Hamburg and Bremen they drench the night sky with beams of light, creating a so-called *Lichtdom* or cathedral of light. It's about twenty miles wide. Our chaps just fly round it. On the coast, Finn, I don't anticipate seeing more than the occasional searchlight, and that'll only appear if they hear us and get twitchy.'

Breathing a sigh of relief, I took my turn on the controls. Keeping to fifty feet proved even harder than I'd expected. I repeatedly had to make small adjustments every time Loki yelled into my ears that we were too high or too low. Sweat formed on the nape of my neck and trickled down inside the collar of my leather jacket. I found myself gripping the column so tightly my knuckles looked like they were about to explode.

Then it happened. Without warning a distorted, faint voice crackled over the radio. A German voice . . . And he was talking to us!

Chapter Fifteen
Nachtjagd

The hairs on the back of my neck prickled. 'Bandits, Loki! Can you see them?'

'No, Finn. They must be on our tail. Being this low, we're sitting ducks.'

'Keep your eyes peeled.'

Nils reached down and switched off the lights in the wing-tips. 'Hold her steady, Finn, while I try to get him off our backs.'

Nils explained over the radio to the German pilot that we were on a special mission – at least that bit was true! We had prepared for this situation and our response was based on several things in our favour. First, we were in a German Heinkel in Luftwaffe colours and markings, albeit the wrong ones for this area; our plane actually belonged to a Luftwaffe squadron based in Norway, not northern France. Second, we were flying low and slowly because we had engine trouble and so were limping home. Third, we spoke reasonable German, Nils more or less fluently, so we reckoned that would help convince the enemy. While I frantically scanned the night sky, Nils spoke to the pilot, trying to sound natural and reassuring, telling him that everything was otherwise fine, or, as the Germans say, *Alles in Ordnung*. Unfortunately the rather suspicious enemy didn't buy it for some reason and kept mentioning something about our *Zwilling*, which had me baffled. I knew was that *Zwilling* was German for 'twin' but as far as I could tell, he was saying our *Zwilling* wasn't on, whatever that meant.

Remembering something, Loki came to our rescue. 'Finn, when we flew that first time with Dieter Braun, his navigator mentioned to me that a special system was fitted to the plane. I think he called it something weird like *Zwilling* and, although I didn't understand everything he said about it, I reckon it sounds a bit like that IFF system you mentioned earlier, Nils.'

'Thanks, Loki.' Nils began frantically scanning the instruments.

It hadn't occurred to me that the Germans probably had a similar system. If there was one, then there had to be some controls for it. Nils located a small group of switches to his left and, reaching out, said that he might as well try them.

'Wait!' I said, grabbing his arm. 'It would look rather odd if we suddenly turned it back on. Can't we say it's broken?'

'Good point. Let's give that a try.' He flipped the transmission switch on the radio and proceeded to inform the enemy that our *Zwilling* was totally *kaputt*, that we'd been hit by flak over the English coast and that it had screwed up some of our systems.

A few heart-stopping moments of silence were eventually followed by the pilot's reply. It began with a groan of sympathy, followed by, '*Kein Wunder! So ein Pech!*'

'Above us at two o'clock!' Loki yelled into our ears. I looked up to my right and saw the silhouette of a small plane. My mouth went so dry I had trouble swallowing. At first I assumed she was a Messerschmitt 109 but then I saw that she was too small and her wings were tapered like those of the Hurricane. 'What is she?' I asked.

Nils gazed at her a moment. 'Looks like one of their new Heinkel 113s, Finn. They're even faster than the Messerschmitt 109. No way can we outrun or out-manoeuvre her.'

'Want me to blast her to hell?' Loki called out.

'No, Loki,' Nils snapped. 'Wait. I think we're OK.'

The enemy kindly offered to escort us. Nils set about dissuading the pilot, saying we hadn't far to go and that we were fine as we were. He was getting nowhere, however. Just as I was thinking that we'd dug a mighty big hole for ourselves and that Loki might be forced to have a go with his machine gun, the enemy pilot suddenly said, '*Es tut mir Leid, aber wir haben noch eine Freya Detektionsmeldung empfangen . . . Gute Reise . . . Wiedersehen.*'

Without further explanation his plane turned sharply left, cut across our path and disappeared into the night. I felt even more choked. *Freya Detektionsmeldung empfangen* – he'd made another Freya discovery. What on earth did that mean? I turned and saw Nils staring at me, his eyes narrow and questioning.

'Bloody hell!' Loki exclaimed through our head-phones. 'Told you, Finn. I said they knew we were coming. They were looking for Freya.'

Nils angrily unfastened his mask. 'You told him?' he snapped at me.

I removed my mask too. 'Yes. It just slipped out. Sorry.'

'Do the others know?'

'No . . . Well, only Max – I mean Luc.'

He shook his head at me in disappointment.

'But I still don't get it,' I said. 'What does it mean?'

Nils looked up at the night sky in exasperation.

'Do we turn back?' I asked.

'Too late,' he replied. 'There's the French coast, Finn. And if we were to turn round now they'd know something was up for sure.'

Straight ahead I could see the horizontal grey smudge of a line: the tall cliffs of France. We were almost there. And Nils was right, we had to press on. To turn round now, with the enemy so close, would look suspicious, and undoubtedly they'd be swarming all over us like flies around a rotting apple within minutes. I squeezed my eyes shut and said a quick prayer. Then I opened them again, took a deep breath and said, 'Right, Nils. Let's do it.' I checked the time and our airspeed, then calculated our position. 'Turn parallel to the coast heading east. We should see the river estuary in about five minutes.'

Chapter Sixteen
A Rough Reception

We flew in the shadow of the cliffs. They lay to our left, towering above us almost within touching distance. In the moonlight they looked like a solid black wall. The wind was stronger than forecast too, and seemed to be drawing us towards the cliff face as if we were caught in the strong pull of a magnetic field. Having to continually adjust our position, we knew that one slip and in the blink of an eye we would become little more than a mangled wreck encased in a ball of flames. I didn't like the way we kept lurching from side to side either, everything not securely bolted down rattling as if jittery with nerves. For once I wished I was one of the others, huddled against the fuselage in the crawl way, oblivious to the risks we were taking.

'There's the river, Finn.' Nils pointed.

I saw the estuary ahead, a broad sweeping gap in the cliffs where the sea seemed to be eating into the land. Nils turned away from the coast and then set us on a gentle turn so that we ended up approaching the river head on. The waterway curved and snaked inland, slowly narrowing to little more than a twisting sliver of silver. It reminded me of a snail's slimy trail. Nils leaned forward and turned our wing lights back on. 'I figure we need all the help we can get going in so low. Better tell the others, Finn. Less than ten minutes to landing.' He flashed two handfuls of fingers at me to make sure I'd understood.

I climbed out of my seat and headed back, stretching out my arms and pressing my hands against the plane's fuselage to steady myself. Four pairs of eyes looked round at me expectantly. I crouched down. 'Ten minutes, give or take,' I shouted. In the dim glow of the small red lamp I was startled by just how scared Freya looked. She had never looked this fearful. Never! Her knees drawn up, she hugged her suitcase against her chest. Amélie, full of nervous energy, was fiddling with a crucifix on a slender gold chain about her neck, while Jacques stared as if held in a hypnotist's trance. Only Max, or should I say Luc, responded to my message. He nodded, smiled at me, and held out a hand. I leaned forward, grasped it tightly and shook it. He said something to me but I didn't catch it over the din of the engines. So I just smiled back. As I turned to head for the cockpit, Freya stopped me, calling out, 'Finn!'

I crouched back down in front of her, so that our noses were almost touching. 'Finn, I just wanted to say . . .' She hesitated. 'Take care of yourself. I love you two, both of you. You and Loki.' She kissed me on my cheek.

Overwhelmed, I reached out and hugged her tightly. 'I've got the easy bit,' I said. 'Your father would be so proud of you. And you're going to be just fine. I know it. Max here has promised to look after you. Isn't that right, Max?' He didn't hear, so I shouted at him,

'Isn't that right, Max? You'll see Freya's still in one piece when we come to pick her up.'

Max gave a thumbs-up.

'See! Told you.'

Freya managed to force an unconvincing smile onto her lips.

'Loki and I love you too,' I said, squeezing her.

When I was back in my seat, we prepared for our tricky landing. 'About four miles to the rendezvous,' said Nils. 'Keep your eyes peeled for their signal. Green light and we're OK, a red one and we're out of here before you can say *Gute Nacht, Fritz*. Once we land, I want you and Loki to go and help the others. Arm yourselves with a couple of Stens and stay out on the floats until everyone's safely in the boats and heading for the river bank. Then get back into the plane double quick. I don't want to be here a second longer than is necessary. I'll keep her engines running just fast enough to hold our position against the flow of the river.'

Looking at our instruments, I realized we were hurtling up the middle of the estuary at eighty-five miles per hour, at an altitude of about fifty feet. Our airspeed was gradually falling. 'Won't she stall if we go too slowly?'

Nils' reply hardly filled me with confidence. 'We'll soon find out, Finn.'

The landscape was hard to make out, but struck me as flat. I saw only occasional lights and the outlines of buildings whizzing past. I guessed that anyone at home would get the fright of their lives as we roared past their bedrooms or rooftops, but by the time they ran to their windows or doors we'd be long gone. The river looked scarily narrow in places too, and it seemed as if our wing tips were trimming the branches of trees lining both banks. Strange dark shapes in the water caught my eye: boats were moored mid-river and I dreaded unwittingly crashing into their masts. My other worry was German patrols out there in the darkness. They could be anywhere, even on the river itself, and we could do nothing about it. That was a job for our reception committee, the local Resistance. It was down to them to keep a lookout.

'Green light. To our left. Three to four hundred yards,' Loki announced.

Spotting it as well, Nils wasted no time. He throttled right back and set the flaps to their maximum angles, creating as much drag as possible. His treatment of the controls was so fierce, the plane seemed to jolt as if it had struck something. Our airspeed plummeted and we descended rapidly, everything rattling like bones in a metal coffin. Flying in so low, it took only seconds for our floats to strike the surface. We bounced off the water, the nose of the plane lifting about thirty degrees before pitching forwards again. Like a pebble skimming across the surface of a pond, we struck the water four times before the plane's massive floats settled, the sudden drag slowing us down sharply. 'Get going, you two. There isn't a moment to lose,' Nils shouted. 'I'll turn and position us as close to the bank as possible.'

I unbuckled and headed back, pressing past the others

and making for the hatchway. Flinging the door open, Loki joined me and handed over a Sten, plus several magazines of ammunition. Moments later we were outside, crouching on the floats, machine guns poised, scanning the gloom. Jacques clambered down the ladder next and then set about catching each of the waterproof holdalls as Max threw them out. Although the engines were barely ticking over, the noise seemed frighteningly loud – I reckoned we could be heard for miles.

Thankfully the river was broad where we'd chosen to land, which made it slow flowing. When the moon briefly hid behind a cloud, the night grew as black as coal. It was chilly too, and a thin veil of patchy mist seemed to hang in the air, partially shrouding the banks.

All the supplies had been unloaded by the time I spotted the strange insect-like shapes of two rowing boats heading towards us, the rhythmic lifting and dipping of their oars making them look like bugs crawling over the surface of the water. Max helped Amélie and Freya clamber out of the Heinkel and then he slid down the ladder too.

The first rowing boat arrived, clonking hard against the metal of the float. The man in it hurriedly drew in his oars, flung Max a rope and said, '*Bonsoir. Faites vite! Vite!*'

Our contact was a hulk of a fellow with a huge moustache. Clad in dark jacket and hat, he struck me as extremely nervous, flashing glances up and down the river and at the opposite bank.

Jacques startled us all by drawing a revolver and

pointing it at the oarsman. 'Where is Monsieur Truffaut?' he asked sternly in his native French. His hand was shaking. 'We were expecting him.'

'Albert was rounded up by the SS three days ago,' the man snapped back. 'Along with several others. Now get a move on. We haven't much time.'

Jacques looked uncertain about what to do next. Was this a trap? I wondered. We'd been taught to be on our guard at all times, to be suspicious of everyone we met, and not to take unnecessary chances – and that was when everything seemed to be going according to plan! Any change, anything remotely unexpected happening, required urgent reassessment. Loki helpfully pointed his Sten at the boat and released the safety catch. Amélie grabbed Jacques' arm. 'It's Monsieur Blanc,' she said. 'The butcher from Rochefort, remember? It's OK.'

A boy arrived in the second boat and cursed aloud as he struggled to get into position. He saw what was happening and shouted, 'Jacques, it's me, Pierre. My father's been arrested. We had to get some others to help us at short notice. Henri Blanc can be trusted. I give you my word.'

Pierre Truffaut was a tough-looking boy. Amélie seemed especially heartened to see him.

'Hurry up, for God's sake,' he added. 'The noise those engines are making will wake up half of Normandy.'

When Jacques lowered his gun I allowed myself to breathe again. Hurriedly we set to work, throwing all the bags and cases into the boats. Pierre held out a supporting hand and Amélie hopped across into his arms. Freya turned to Loki. They both stood there, neither knowing quite how to say goodbye. Instead, Loki lowered his machine gun and wrapped his free arm about her. They would have remained entwined for ever if Pierre hadn't been hissing '*Vite!*' at them with ever-increasing urgency.

Freya let go and unwrapped herself from Loki's grip. Without a word she turned and seized Pierre's outstretched hand. Max and Jacques were already in the other boat and had pushed off. Loki and I stood and watched them disappear into the night.

'Come on, let's get out of here,' I said. But Loki just stood and gazed after Freya's boat. I grabbed his sleeve. 'We must go!' I pushed, shoved and cajoled him back up the ladder and into the Heinkel.

As I was about to haul myself up the last rung, some-thing caught my eye. Up river two flares arced their way high into the night sky, then seemed to hang there like newborn stars. Their shimmering glow was so intense, so bright, it hurt your eyes to look at them. I blinked, looked down . . . and saw her — a boat heading in our direction. She was quite some distance away, although precisely how far, and how fast she was travelling, was hard to tell. She had a searchlight on deck and it was pointing straight at the Heinkel, although the beam barely lit us. Then I noticed tiny flashes. It dawned on me. *Jesus!* She'd opened fire. I flung myself into the plane. 'There's a German patrol boat heading our way! She'll be on top of us in seconds, Loki!' I shouted.

'Hell! We've walked right into a trap, Finn. I told you

I had a bad feeling. All those intercepted messages about Freya, then that Resistance man was arrested and now this! I can't abandon her. I can't do *nothing*.' He grabbed a bag containing some emergency gear Smithy had prepared in case we crash-landed over enemy territory, swung it over his shoulder and pushed past me.

'What on earth are you doing?'

Loki was already on the third rung of the ladder. 'Going to rescue Freya, Finn. Coming?'

What a nightmare. I knew there was no way I was going to stop him, or change his mind, or explain the rashness of his impulsive decision. And, of course, the truth was simple: I couldn't abandon Freya either. 'Give me a second!' I yelled before scrambling up the crawl way to the cockpit. There I grabbed hold of Nils just as he was about to push the throttles to full power. 'There's a boat on your tail. We'll try and deal with it. Give us about thirty seconds and then get the hell out of here. It looks like the Germans are on to the others as well. We've got to do something to help them. You'll have to fly back alone. OK?'

I expected Nils to remonstrate but he didn't. I think he realized that we had few options. As I tore off my leather flying jacket, he simply nodded to me. I threw it down into the empty seat beside him. Knowing I was about to get wet, the last thing I needed was the extra weight. 'Look after it for me. I'll be back to collect it.'

'For God's sake be careful, Finn. And good luck. Go! Go! Go!'

Ten seconds later I was out of the plane, sliding down

the ladder. Kneeling on the float, Loki was already well through his second magazine of ammunition, returning fire at the rapidly approaching patrol boat. Nils must've counted to thirty mighty fast and pushed the throttles to maximum because the Heinkel's engines suddenly roared like some fearsome beast. It was deafening, and the propellers whipped up a gale and a shower of water that hammered and buffeted us, almost knocking me off my feet. I grabbed one of the struts between the float and the fuselage and held on for dear life. Emptying another magazine, Loki somehow managed to maintain his balance and hit the searchlight on the approaching boat – it was pure fluke, a damn lucky shot.

The plane surged forward and gathered speed. Loki stood up precariously and grabbed hold of me. 'Time to jump, Finn. Before she gets airborne,' he yelled. Throwing the strap of his Sten gun over his shoulder and grasping the bag of emergency equipment against his chest, he let go of me and threw himself off the float, splashing into the turbulent, churning water of the plane's wake. He'd done it. He'd actually jumped! He quickly disappeared from view. My grip on the strut remained vice-like. It was as if I just couldn't let go. I'd frozen. Something deep inside was holding me back. We were going so frighteningly fast. Then I felt the Heinkel lifting beneath me. I'd run out of choices. In seconds we'd be airborne. I took a deep breath, shut my eyes, let go and jumped.

Chapter Seventeen
Lost in France

I struck the water at an awkward angle and with such force it felt as if I'd fallen onto solid concrete. Winded, I had to resist trying to gasp for air as I sank beneath the surface. Instantly the cold embraced me and my ears filled with the strange hollowness of an underwater world. I wanted to panic, to thrash my arms about, but our training in the Scottish lochs now paid off. Reaching the bottom, I turned and kicked with my legs. I shot upwards and seconds later broke the surface. At last I could breathe! I coughed and spluttered and frantically tried to tread water. My dark woollen sweater and trousers were heavy and threatened to drag me back under. The strap of my Sten gun was thankfully still wrapped about my neck but the gun had twisted round several times, the strap tightening like a tourniquet – I was slowly being throttled.

As I tried to unwind it I looked northwards, in the direction of the coast. Nils was airborne and the Heinkel was climbing steeply, now little more than a black speck in a dark sky, its engines already sounding distant. I realized that in the other direction the German patrol boat had given up the chase and slowed. She was nearly two hundred yards from me and had drawn close to the river bank. The last of the flares fizzled out as it returned to earth. I saw what looked like flashes of torch light aimed at the shore too, but they were feeble in comparison to the searchlight Loki had managed to put out of commission. His lucky shot might just prove to be a life-saver, I thought. Having freed the gun strap from around my neck, I headed for dry land, trying to make as little noise as possible. As I swam, it struck me just how far I was from where we'd off-loaded the others. The plane had taken us a good distance along the river before we'd jumped. Even in the few seconds between Loki leaping and me following, the plane had travelled another hundred yards or so. My first task was to find him.

Reaching a tall reed bed in the shallows, I waded breathlessly through thick mud and then crawled out onto firm soil. Remaining on my belly, I reached back, scooped up a handful of mud and smothered it over my face. I slapped a second handful of the slimy, gritty, stinking silt over my ears and neck. I needed camouflage as even a feeble torch beam would be able to pick out the white of my face. During training we'd used burned cork to blacken exposed skin and I'd always hated the stuff. But now I realized it was tons better than the smelly grime I had to improvise with.

Next to the reeds and mud lay a narrow strip of grass and a well-trodden path on a raised-earth embankment. I was too exposed. I had to reach the trees and bushes beyond. Keeping low, I checked the coast was clear, then darted across the path and into the undergrowth. I was just in time! Distant voices gradually grew louder, as did the burbling chatter of a diesel engine running at barely more than idling speed. Removing the magazine from my Sten, I drained out the water and reattached it, praying Smithy was right when he'd said you could get it wet and muddy and it would still function. Just don't go jamming on me, I thought as I rose to my knees and pressed my right shoulder up against a tree trunk. I caught glimpses of torch light. The boat was drawing near. Shrinking back so the tree obscured me, I listened as she slowly motored past. The voices of those aboard were German and they sounded irate. Rays of light flashed and danced through the branches and leaves, creating an eerie world of moving shadows. I tightened my grip on the Sten, held my breath and flicked the safety catch off.

The boat continued north for about another thirty yards and then thankfully the captain suddenly gunned the throttle, turned her through one hundred and eighty degrees and opened her up. She sped back past me at quite a lick, her bow creating waves that quickly washed up and over the bank. Keeping to the trees, I headed after her, back towards where Loki must've scrambled out of the water, crossing my fingers that he was either patiently waiting for me or was heading my way, and that we wouldn't slip past each other in the darkness.

Moving stealthily from bush to bush, from tree to tree, I was shaking, and it wasn't because of the chilly, clinging damp of my waterlogged clothes. Was Fritz waiting in hiding? Had our team been rounded up? Was it game over before it had even begun? Or had Pierre Truffaut and Henri Blanc led the others to safety?

I heard a faint groan. It came from the tall reeds. *Loki?* I risked crossing the path again to find out and, on reaching the edge of the water, I saw him lying amongst the forest of tall, stiff, slender stems. He looked barely conscious. 'Loki! You OK?' I whispered.

No reply. Scrambling down to reach him, I knelt and gave him a good shake to bring him round. Extremely groggy, he let out a groan as I tried to move him. Hunting for the bag of emergency supplies, I spotted it caught in the reeds about six feet further out. I waded in to collect it. Unzipping it, I began rummaging inside. As well as some high-energy biscuit rations, bottled water and a box of matches, there was a revolver and a box of bullets, three grenades and a handful of plastic explosive plus timers and detonators. Digging deep, I found what I was looking for: a small pen torch. I shone it onto Loki's bedraggled face and saw a trickle of blood from his scalp. Closer inspection revealed a nasty gash. Placing the torch between my teeth, I shone it into the bag and dug right to the bottom to locate the small first-aid tin. Carefully popping it open, I saw it contained some syringes, small glass ampoules of morphine, some bandages, antiseptic, tweezers and scissors, mostly stuff for someone who was seriously hurt. What I wanted was the tiny brown bottle which I seized and opened, exposing the rim, then stuck it beneath Loki's nose. The bottle contained smelling salts, and the sharp, stinging odour brought my friend back into the here and now with a jolt. 'Finn? Ow, my bloody head hurts.'

'You must've fallen on a stone or something. You've got a nasty gash. Wait a minute.' I soaked a piece of gauze in some antiseptic. 'This is going to sting, so don't cry out.' I placed the gauze on his head and got him to hold it there. 'We can't stay here. We must get to the trees. Can you make it?'

He was unsteady on his feet, but with him leaning heavily on me we made it back across the path. I got us deep into the bushes, where even the brightest torch light wouldn't reach us. We'd been lucky. The reeds had provided just enough cover for Loki as the boat crawled past him. Had he been lying a few feet either way, Fritz would have seen him for certain.

As if suddenly waking from a dream, Loki snatched up his Sten, looking extremely alarmed. 'Where are they, Finn? Have they been captured?'

'Calm down. I've no idea. I've not seen or heard anyone other than that German patrol boat.'

He seemed even more confused. I was too. Had Fritz been lying in wait I would have expected to hear some gunfire, maybe even one hell of a firefight. Even if he had pounced before a single shot was fired, surely we would have heard shouts, maybe the barking of guard dogs, or the roar of engines as our friends were taken away in cars and trucks. But I'd heard none of those things. 'You know, we may just have been unlucky,' I said.

'Unlucky?'

'Yes. Perhaps that patrol boat simply happened upon us . . . Or came to investigate the noise of our engines . . . Or maybe some local patrol or coastal observer saw us fly in and put everyone on alert.'

'Are you trying to tell me that they weren't waiting for us after all, Finn?'

'I don't know. It just all seems so quiet now that boat's gone. *Too* quiet.'

He slumped back onto the soft earth and swore. 'This was a bad idea, wasn't it, Finn?'

'I think so. Probably in your top five worst ideas ever.'

He didn't laugh. 'Sorry.'

'Too late for that.'

'Thanks, Finn – for staying, that is.'

The thought of leaving Freya behind and in great danger was never an option. We could hardly have left her and the others to face the Germans alone. I felt a wave of guilt and I reached out and grabbed Loki's shoulder. 'You know, it's me who should be sorry. You were right when you said the three of us should stick together through thick and thin; that we rely on each other. That evening they announced Operation Death Ray, I should have backed you up when you said as much to the brigadier and Walker.'

'I suppose we were all taken by surprise.'

'True. And I think I was sidetracked by the chance to fly again. It clouded my judgement.'

'We're in a mess, aren't we?'

'You could say that.'

The true horror of our predicament was beginning to sink in. We were in occupied France and it was crawling with Nazis. We didn't have any French documents such as identity cards, travel permits or ration cards, nor were our clothes convincingly French. Our grasp of the language was untested, but it hadn't even been good enough to convince our instructors to send us on this mission, and unlike Freya and Max we didn't possess false identities and well-rehearsed cover stories to fall back on. Worst of all, we were Special Ops, not RAF or soldiers, and that meant we weren't in uniform. If we had been and we were captured, we'd be treated as prisoners of war. Without uniforms, we didn't have that protection. The authorities would rightly treat us as spies and question us before having us shot.

Wincing, Loki tore the gauze from his scalp. 'We've wasted enough time. We need a plan of action. I think the first thing we should do is check out further up-river – the spot we used for the drop. We'll soon see if there are any signs of a struggle.'

This was a better idea, although I thought it was about as flawed as a boat with a hole in its bottom. 'It may be dangerous staying too close to the river. If I was right – that the patrol boat just stumbled across us – then it changes everything.'

'How?'

'They saw us land. They'll be highly suspicious, despite us being a German plane in Luftwaffe colours. I reckon they'll figure out that a drop has been made for the Resistance and alert their HQ. And if I were them, I'd flood this area with troops to search high and low.'

Loki summoned his strength and rose to his knees. 'We'd better get a move on then. Come on, Finn. *Chop chop*, as Walker's always telling us.'

Hugging the trees and bushes, we headed alongside the river, back towards the drop-off point. Where was everyone? It was as if they'd landed and then vanished into thin air. Loki tapped me on my shoulder and pointed. He'd spotted the rowing boats used by Henri Blanc and Pierre Truffaut. They'd been tied to the trunk of a sturdy silver birch leaning out over the water. I shone the pen torch onto them and observed that they were empty and undamaged. So I presumed that at least the others had all made it safely ashore. A mass of fresh, deep boot prints in the mud was the only sign of recent activity.

'Let's carry on, Finn. They didn't head our way so they must've gone south.'

Continuing along the path, listening and looking out, Loki faced forwards and I walked backwards so we kept both directions covered. A slight breeze whispered through the trees, shaking the leaves, creating a rustling sound that kept my heart firmly in my mouth. I knew from the maps we'd studied when planning the drop that this stretch of river was nearly a mile from the nearest dwelling, and two from the closest village. Beyond the trees lay open fields. I also remembered that there was a road, a minor one, that split the fields and followed the path of the river, albeit some distance away. Had they escaped that way? Had they cut across the fields to a waiting car or van or truck? Suddenly I felt a hand seize me and drag me over to the cover of the bushes. 'Lie still, Finn! Someone's coming!'

Chapter Eighteen
Keeping One Step Ahead

Why couldn't it have been some old Frenchman out walking his dog, keen to help two boys in it up to their necks? No such luck. It was a German patrol, at least half a dozen men, methodically searching the bushes, moving slowly towards us, leaving no stone unturned. There was nothing for it. We rolled over and crawled into the undergrowth, scrambled on all fours through prickly brambles that clung and clawed at our clothes, and only rose to our feet when we could see the pale glow of moonlight beyond the trees. 'Christ, Finn, I can't see any cover for miles. It's all open fields. We'll be sitting ducks if they hear us. There's nowhere to hide.'

It wasn't all bad news, I thought. When studying the maps I hadn't really taken in just what exactly all those tiny contour lines meant. The full moon's glow enabled me to see that we were in the middle of a broad, flat-bottomed river valley. I had little doubt that the fields were dangerous to cross, but guessed that beyond them, where the land rose up to form gentle hills, there'd be some sort of cover. 'We'll be OK as long as we wait until the moon goes behind that cloud,' I whispered.

'Are you sure?'

'Yes. Remember our training in the Scottish mountains? Major Baxter's men kept reminding us to stay on lower ground, and certainly never to use the ridges or hilltops: otherwise our silhouettes would give us away. Once the moon's hidden, nobody will be able to make us out in the darkness against the backdrop of those hills over there.'

We waited, peering up at the broken clouds drifting slowly across the heavens while listening out for the approaching German patrol. It was going to be touch and go. And the particular cloud I had my eye on was moving annoyingly slowly. Loki began fidgeting, repeatedly turning and peering back towards the path. 'I can hear them. They'll be on top of us any time now. We could try and take them on. There's only a handful. We have two machine guns and surprise on our side. What do you think?'

I didn't reply. I was too busy willing the damn cloud to get a move on. In my head I was trying to give it a shove, to haul it along just a little faster. The first wisps trailed across the moon and the light faded slightly. But we needed more. It was still too bright. 'Shit, shit, shit,' Loki muttered nervously.

Just a little further. Go on, cloud, you can do it! My heart was racing. God, those German voices sounded loud, I thought. Almost as if they were standing right behind me. Then, at last, the glow faded just like the light in a room when a candle finally burns itself out. In a flash we broke cover and were gone.

We raced at full stretch across open farmland, only to

discover that the field had been newly ploughed, and recent rainfall had turned it into a claggy quagmire. We slipped and slithered, stumbled and fell, but somehow managed to keep getting to our feet and carrying on. We ran and ran, repeatedly overtaking each other, our breathing heavy, our boots squelching. Reaching a shallow ditch, we flung ourselves down just as the moon emerged. I was buzzing inside, my senses heightened. I guess I'd just found out what it was like to be a fox trying to outwit the hounds. Rising to my knees, I looked back towards the river. There was no sign of the soldiers. So far so good. Loki slid up beside me on his belly.

'All clear the other way, Finn.'

The moonlight dimmed again and we set off for a second time. The next field proved even lumpier, with deep ridges and furrows of heavy clay-laden earth. And something was growing there – cabbages? It was hard to tell, but it felt like I was treading over endless soft footballs glued to the ground. With every stride and skid, I felt we were getting further and further away from danger; or was it a horribly false sense of security?

At the boundary of the second field we hit upon the narrow lane I'd recalled seeing on the map. While I racked my brain trying to remember exactly where the road led to, Loki pointed left and said between rasping gasps, 'Well, Rochefort must be that way, back towards the coast.'

No sooner had he said it than lights appeared in the

distance from the direction of Rochefort and moved slowly towards us, like a clowder of cats on the prowl. The unmistakable clattering of diesel engines drifted in the night air. Frozen and uncertain, we stayed down. They were army trucks. Having trundled noisily to within a couple of hundred yards of us, they began peeling off, three to the left and three to the right. Then they stopped and dozens of soldiers piled out, forming neat, practised rows and columns. My heart sank. Our problems had been doubled and redoubled all in one go.

The soldiers began dispersing and I guessed at the orders they'd been given – file out and form a long line across the fields. We didn't wait to see them begin their search. Cloud or no cloud, this time we couldn't wait for nature's helping hand. And despite needing to go left to reach Rochefort, or straight on to the distant hills, we went right. It was our only option.

We ran for miles. We just kept on going. Field after field passed beneath our boots; we leaped over small streams without altering our stride, and waded through larger ones with barely a moment's thought for how deep they might be. Hedges were leapfrogged or scrambled through despite our clothes being ripped to shreds by thorns so sharp I reckoned they'd make a fantastic alternative to barbed wire. Finally, utterly exhausted, our chests heaving, we were forced to stop. Lying as flat as I could, I desperately tried to figure out what we should do next. Loki glanced at his watch – one-fifteen. I did some quick mental calculations. The soldiers would have advanced at nothing quicker than a brisk march, so surely we must've put plenty of distance between us and them. And yet, I also knew that despite our efforts it was highly likely that Fritz had off-loaded more soldiers at the other end of the valley, in the direction we were heading, leaving us trapped in a pincer movement. Our situation seemed hopeless.

'Where's the nearest village, Finn?'

'I'm not sure. Why?'

'I reckon it's our best chance. Out here they'll close in on us eventually. I'd rather find some barn or shed or outhouse to hide in.'

'First place they'll look.' I didn't want to sound negative but I reckoned we were surrounded and it was only a question of time before we got caught. The Germans were no fools. They knew how to close an area down, how to search it systematically, how to find any needles in a haystack.

'OK, maybe a church crypt or bell tower or something.'

'Second place they'll look.'

'Damn it, Finn, have you got any better ideas?'

'No . . . Actually, yes!' I'd been struck by a flash of inspiration. It came from nowhere. I'd remembered something X had said to us the very first evening we arrived at Mulberry House; something the prime minister of Great Britain, Mr Churchill, had told him. 'You're a genius, Loki! You're right, we should head for the nearest village.' I rolled over and scanned the valley.

Spotting a shape, I pointed. 'Over there. See it? I reckon that's a church tower. It can't be more than a mile or so.'

'And what shall we do when we get there, Finn?'

'We'll set about waking the whole place up!'

Chapter Nineteen
Setting Europe Ablaze

Making for the village, I realized that what had struck me as an absolutely splendid idea was in truth a pretty potty, harebrained scheme, but I didn't let on. I kept telling myself that we could make it work. We had to make it work. While running, I began filling Loki in.

'Let me get this straight, Finn. You want to wake everyone up by setting fire to something.'

'Uh-huh. A house maybe. Perhaps even two houses. But they'd have to be next door to each other, of course. Otherwise it would look suspicious. But the bigger the fire the better.'

'You're talking utter nonsense.'

'No I'm not. Remember what X told us Mr Churchill had said to him? "Go forth and set Europe ablaze."'

'Yes, but I don't get it.'

'You will.'

He stopped in his tracks and grabbed hold of my arm. 'If I'm about to commit suicide, I'd like to understand why. This is crazy, Finn! Surely the last thing we should be doing is drawing attention to where we are.'

'Exactly! It's the last thing Fritz would expect.'

He frowned at me incredulously. 'I was the one who

got a bang on the head, Finn. Not you. Have you gone mad?'

'Listen,' I said. 'Think about it. It's the middle of the night. Most people are going to be tucked up in bed fast asleep. We know the Germans have initiated one of their *razzias* as we saw them begin the search. At some point they'll pile into the village, start banging on doors and order everyone to produce their papers while they set about searching everywhere. Agreed?'

'Yes, but?'

'Right. Fritz has surprise on his side and total control over the situation. Everyone will be bleary-eyed and confused. They won't know what the hell is happening or why. But – and here's the beauty of my plan – what if when Fritz arrives, everyone is already up and rushing about trying to put out the fire? It'll be chaos, and a hundred times harder for Fritz to conduct the search properly. Chances are he'll be distracted. If we make it look accidental, then I bet you the soldiers will simply check a few papers, maybe search half a dozen houses or so and then move on. They'll know that otherwise the search could take hours. And, if the fire's big enough they're hardly going to encounter a compliant local population, are they? Villagers won't appreciate their untimely arrival.'

Loki stared at me blankly while my plan sank in. 'So . . . we'll be able to find somewhere safe to hide because Fritz won't bother searching every nook and cranny.'

'Precisely! Look, we'll find somewhere to hide and

make the necessary preparations. If Fritz doesn't turn up, then terrific. We just regain our strength and figure out our next move. But if we hear them coming, we'll set off our diversion. OK?'

'It's the barmiest scheme you've come up with since you had that idea to steal the Heinkel seaplane from under the Luftwaffe's nose, Finn. But, you know what, it might just work!'

We entered the village cautiously, keeping to the darkest paths and frequently dipping into doorways and passages where only the local rats had eyes sharp enough to see us. It turned out to be larger that I'd anticipated, at least a hundred houses, I reckoned, with two separate huddles of shabby buildings on either side of a tributary of the main river linked by an ancient stone bridge. Recent rain meant the water ran swiftly, burbling and gushing over a stony bed. It created quite a noise, useful for obscuring the sound of our footsteps. Beneath the bridge, I took the opportunity to wash the mud from my face. Our clothes, however, looked like they'd been dragged to hell and back. It was a problem that I knew we'd have to solve eventually, but it was a case of one thing at a time.

I spotted a sign pointing down a side street and made a mental note – the place had a small station. There was a tiny market square too, at the centre of which stood a tall stone memorial with seating around it, and a large stone trough into which spring water was pouring from a piece of lead pipe. The village also possessed several small shops in a neat row, a *boulangerie*, a *boucherie*, and a third shop I couldn't quite fathom, although I suspected it was some sort of general store or ironmonger's. Drawn blinds meant we couldn't see inside but above the door there was a metal sign – Paraffin oil. Perfect!

A dog barked somewhere far away but soon settled again. 'We need to get inside that shop,' I whispered. 'Best if we try round the back.'

'And then what?'

'We borrow some paraffin.'

Edging our way down a narrow passage between the *boucherie* and our target, we scrambled quietly over a brick wall and dropped down into a large yard paved with cobblestones. There were several outbuildings and the walled area was accessed from the road running behind it via tall wooden gates firmly secured by a heavy chain and padlock. Unzipping our bag of emergency supplies, I hunted out the pair of tweezers from the first-aid kit. I knew that just a little modification by bending the arms would form the perfect implement for undoing simple locks. I had Sergeant Walker to thank for that. He'd taught me well. As I worked, Loki explored the yard before returning and tapping me on the shoulder. He led me to a space between two of the outbuildings. On a raised concrete plinth next to the wall stood two pumps – one for petrol, the other for paraffin. 'There's a container over there, Finn,' he whispered under his breath. 'A milk churn. It's perfect. It'll hold at least a couple of gallons. That'll be enough, won't it?'

Figuring petrol would be an even better option, we set about unpicking the small padlock to release the chain that was supposed to prevent theft of the precious juice. The handle operating the pump squeaked like mad so we reverted to my original plan and turned our attention to the paraffin. To my relief this pump's handle didn't make such a noise. Slowly we filled the stainless-steel churn to about a third full. Taking my bent tweezers, Loki then picked the padlock on the gates and we slipped out into the narrow lane beyond, lugging the churn between us. Now all we needed was a suitable target, preferably somewhere central that was either unlived in or unused. The last thing I wanted to do was set fire to a building with people inside.

Loki spotted the perfect place. Just off the square and in sight of the bridge and the road leading out of the village lay what looked like a hall or meeting place. It was two storeys tall, timber-framed and in a poor state of repair. It was also detached, which was a bonus. Hopefully, if we were forced to set it alight, the flames wouldn't jump to neighbouring dwellings.

Inside, the ground floor was divided into a main hall with wooden trestle tables and chairs neatly stacked up against one side, a small kitchen and a lavatory that appeared to be little more than a hole in the ground. We positioned ourselves by the main window and kept a lookout.

'Suppose they don't come?' Loki whispered. 'What do we do when it gets light?'

'We'll have to leave well before dawn. Our strange faces will stick out here like sore thumbs. Even if we looked French we'd not be able to hang around long before people started asking awkward questions. In these wet, stinking clothes, we've got no chance. Hopefully by sunrise the Germans will be winding down their search. I think this is our best chance. The other alternative is that we sit tight here for twenty-four hours and let things cool down a bit.'

'We could go to the church and put ourselves at the mercy of the priest there. He'd help us, wouldn't he? Not hand us over?'

'Maybe.' I reached for our bag and hunted out the box of matches. 'Grabbing these emergency supplies at the last minute was one of your better ideas. Without them we'd be stuffed.'

Loki quietly opened one of the windows a fraction and listened for Fritz. We didn't have long to wait. 'I think I can hear something, Finn.'

I placed my ear to the gap and strained to hear – the sound of distant vehicles, lots of them! Hurriedly Loki got to work, splashing and sloshing the paraffin over the floor while I grabbed our bag and moved it to the door.

'As the French say, we've *préparé le feu*!' Loki announced. 'Do you want to do the honours, or shall I?'

'I'll do it.' Striking a match, I waited for its flame to glow strong and bright and then flung it down into a puddle of paraffin. The flame fizzed and died. I tried again. Once more the match fizzled out.

'Try holding it just above the floor. Let it ignite the fumes.'

Third time lucky. A sheet of orange-blue flame unfolded and crept across the floor, then climbed the walls. It crackled and spat nicely. I could feel the heat against my face.

Hurriedly tumbling out of the door, Loki whispered, 'Now let's wake everyone up!'

Running through the streets, we hammered on doors and shouted, '*Au feu! Au feu!*' Making for the churchyard, we leaped a wall and hid ourselves in dense bushes. At first, nothing. Then I saw lights come on. Then a voice. More voices. Then shouts of panic. Frantic footsteps hurried to and fro. I heard someone shout to fetch buckets, lots of buckets.

The hall was ablaze! Even from our place of hiding we could see the glow. Several motorbikes roared into the village, followed by trucks. Within minutes, the yells from men with thick rural French accents were joined by others speaking German. Eventually Loki couldn't resist. He had to take a peek. Rising up, he parted the branches of the bush, looked out over the wall, and gasped. Tapping me on my shoulder, he encouraged me to look too.

The fire had taken hold and was tearing through the building. There were two lines of villagers, one strung out to the trough of water in the square, the other towards the river, each frantically passing buckets, pots and pans to one another. The men nearest the building were flinging the contents at the blaze – theirs was a hopeless task. But what amazed me most was that amid their lines stood Germans. *Loads of them*. They were helping!

Feeling jubilant, I realized my plan was working better than I could ever have hoped for. Fritz wasn't just distracted, he'd been roped in. They weren't questioning people, or inspecting papers, or searching anywhere.

Just as Loki began congratulating me, we heard a terrifying scream, the sort of scream that leaves you cold, as if death is tapping you on your shoulder. It was a young girl's scream, and it was twice as loud as anybody else's voice. Loki pointed to a small window in the eaves of the building. 'Oh my God, Finn. Look! At the upstairs window! There was somebody in there. We didn't check upstairs. What have we done?!'

Chapter Twenty
Sofie's Choice

'*Saute, Sofie! Saute!*' a woman cried. But the little girl was hysterical and refused to jump. I could see the flames flickering and licking the walls behind her. She just kept screaming, even when briefly disappearing in clouds of black smoke.

'What on earth was she doing in there?' I whispered angrily. 'The place looked empty to me.'

'We should have checked, Finn.'

'There wasn't time.'

The hurriedly moving chain of men and buckets, pots and pans looked like some sort of giant centipede, and reminded me of the party game, Pass the Parcel. Only this was no game. The horror of seeing the little girl at the window caused the conveyor belt to stop abruptly as everyone looked up. More villagers began calling out, encouraging the little girl with shoulder-length flaxen-coloured hair to swallow her fear, close her eyes and jump, before it was too late. Three men braved the searing heat to stand beneath the window, their arms held wide, coaxing her, telling her they'd catch her and break her fall, that it was safe to leap, that she *must* jump.

The frightened girl sobbed. Women turned away and covered their faces in anguish. Just as all seemed lost, the unexpected happened. A young German soldier rushed forward, grabbed a large pail of water from the hand of an onlooker, lifted it and tipped the contents over his head and over his heavy grey trenchcoat. Throwing the bucket down, he ran into the roaring, spitting inferno and was gone. A second later, part of the roof to the rear of the building gave way with an almighty crash, and sparks and cinders rose high into the night sky. People were forced back. Without explanation the girl suddenly vanished from view. Everyone stood so still, so silently, it was as if they were made of stone.

Staggering, blackened and smouldering, the young soldier emerged carrying the girl in his arms. The crowd rushed forward and surrounded him. I heard cries of '*Dieu merci!*' and '*Grâce au ciel!*'

She was alive! My heart leaped. The young soldier tore off his helmet as men jostled for their turn to pat him on his back and shake his hand. Although the corporal's hair was matted and singed and his face blackened by soot, I could tell he was probably only a couple of years older than Loki and me.

Someone – an elderly man with a stoop, I think – began to clap. The crowd joined in. The applause and accompanying cheers grew louder and louder, especially when the other soldiers added their whistles, hoots of delight and appreciative boot-stomping for good measure. For one precious moment I don't think any of them were thinking about the reason why they'd come to this village. It was hardly what I'd envisaged, but with everyone safe I hoped it would last. 'Over there, Finn.' Loki pointed.

A senior Wehrmacht officer was standing beside his staff car, hands on hips, surveying the scene. I could sense what he was thinking. Was the fire an accident or deliberate? If deliberate, was the Resistance to blame? Was it simply a diversion? I hoped he'd arrived at the conclusion I was praying for – that either way no partisan would be stupid enough to hang around. Squinting slightly, he looked in all directions and then said something to his driver, who merely shrugged and pulled a face. The officer then barked his orders, waved a glove dismissively and climbed back into his car. In minutes the motorbikes and trucks were revving their engines and pulling out, winding in convoy through the small square, into the narrow streets, heading for the open country beyond. I sank down to my knees and blew a huge sigh of relief. 'That took guts,' I whispered, the image of the young soldier emerging from the hall still firmly stuck in my mind.

'Yes, and now they're all pals with the locals. If anyone finds out it was us who set fire to the place, I reckon they'll either string us up from the nearest tree, or gladly turn us in.'

'I doubt it, Loki.'

'Huh! I don't want to take the chance.'

The villagers set about dousing the worst of the flames. When there was little left of the hall and it seemed unlikely the fire would spread, they gradually abandoned the task and drifted off back to their homes. One elderly man stayed behind to keep an eye on the smouldering remains. Carefully working our way through the churchyard, we found an old shed hidden in thick overgrown brambles and bushes. We quietly forced open the door and took shelter inside. The shed was full of rusty tools and dusty cobwebs. It had a heartening *forgotten* feel about it, as if no one had paid it a visit in months. It felt safe. We removed our wet sweaters and hung them on hooks to dry alongside the hoes, forks and spades, and found some smelly old cloth sacks to wrap round our shoulders for warmth.

Exhausted, all Loki wanted to do was sleep.

'How's your head?' I asked.

'Better,' he replied. 'A bit sore, but at least the bleeding's stopped.'

We shared some of the water and biscuit rations from the bag and pondered what we were going to do once dawn approached.

'The thing is,' said Loki, smacking his lips after a swig of water, 'I suppose we have to head for Rochefort even though we've no idea where Jacques and Amélie live. Maybe we can ask around once we get there.' He wiped the rim of the bottle with his hand and passed it to me.

'Sounds a bit risky. It will expose our poor French and just mentioning the Lefebvre family will draw attention to them. It could prove a death sentence if we're caught.'

'True.' We sat in silence for a while before Loki was struck by an idea. 'Hey, I've got it! That man in the boat. The one Jacques was uncertain about. Didn't Amélie know him? What did she say his name was?'

It came to me instantly. 'Of course, Henri Blanc!' I replied. 'She said he was a butcher in Rochefort.'

Loki was euphoric. 'Then we have a contact, Finn! Someone we can trust. He's our first port of call. He'll hide us and get in touch with the others. Brilliant!'

As my best friend settled contentedly onto his back, folded his arms and tried to grab forty winks, I think he believed all our problems were solved. Yes, Monsieur Blanc's butcher's shop was probably safe. The problem was – how the hell were we going to get there? Our clothes were a mess, we were a mess. We'd not last long out in the open. Spotting us crossing muddy fields, people might just look at us and think two lads were larking about in the mud. But once we were in a town we'd have no chance.

In truth we had few options to deliberate over. Loki's idea of putting ourselves at the mercy of the local church's priest was possibly the simplest. We would become someone else's problem. They'd have to make the arrangements, take the risks. But could we trust our fate to others, to total strangers? Another possibility was to make for the coast, steal a boat and head back to England. It wasn't too far away. Getting out of enemy territory as quickly as possible certainly had its appeal. But we'd abandoned the Heinkel for a reason – to help Freya and the others, and although I had the feeling they'd probably got away safely, we couldn't be sure. No, we had to stay, we had to find out. Loki began snoring. I gave him a sharp prod in the ribs. '*Shush!*'

I didn't know how he could sleep. My brain was buzzing. I tried to use the time productively. Our biggest problem remained our clothes. They were filthy and torn. We *had* to get some clean ones. But how? I could think of only two ways. We could look for stuff hung out on washing lines to dry and steal what we needed. But that would be risky, even if we could find a house occupied by two people of our age and size. Or we could do a spot of burglary. That struck me as being even riskier – although, of course, we knew how to do it. That was what some of our training at Arisaig and Mulberry had been about – surviving on the run. I laughed to myself. X had told us we were embarking on a career not far removed from that of the common criminal. How right he was.

As the hours passed I found my eyes wanting to shut, my chin desperate to rest itself against my chest. The desire to sleep was so powerful it felt as if I'd been drugged. I forced myself to remain awake. My mind wandered over many things, including Véronique and Renard. I shivered when I thought of how the smartly dressed Renard had brazenly walked the streets of Britain as if he hadn't a care in the world. I pictured him standing before the German High Command in Berlin, gleefully handing over the blueprints while saying how *easy* it had been. And here I was, hiding out in an old shed somewhere in rural France, clad in sodden, filthy clothes, barely able to speak the lingo. We were both secret agents but there the comparison ended – *abruptly*. I suddenly felt way out of my depth, a rank amateur.

I drew up my knees tightly and wrapped my arms about them.

At five o'clock in the morning I woke Loki. 'Best if we move on. There's about two hours before daylight and I reckon we can put some healthy distance between us and the village in that time.'

The air was breathlessly still and damp, and filled with the horribly sharp, acrid smell of a wood fire extinguished with water. Reaching the wall of the churchyard and peering over the top, we soon realized that we weren't going anywhere for a while.

The elderly man who'd stayed to keep watch on the remains of the hall was talking to another man sitting astride a bicycle. Their rural accents made it doubly difficult for us to work out what they were saying, but the cyclist pointed in various directions and grew quite animated. However one word I did recognize, peppered his sentences like the lead pellets from a shotgun cartridge – *barrages.*

Roadblocks!

Fritz wasn't giving up quite so easily. For now, it was simply too dangerous to move. Quietly we crept back into the shed and closed the door. We decided to spend the day cleaning our weapons. It was also a good opportunity to rest up and regain our strength. But we remained on edge, continually listening out for approaching footsteps. With the arrival of spring I dreaded that someone might think it was time to tidy up the churchyard, to cut the grass, to trim the bushes. Or maybe some old dear had died and a fresh grave needed to be dug. I prayed our luck would hold, that we'd remain undiscovered.

I lost count of the number of times I peered at my watch. It felt as if it would never get dark; as if the hour and minute hands were deliberately going slowly just to torture us. Apart from a few vehicles and occasional distant voices and the whistles of approaching and departing trains we heard virtually nothing all day. The trains came and went regularly, arriving at exactly ten minutes past and twenty minutes to the hour. As far as I could work out, those arriving just after the hour were heading in the direction of Rochefort. It was cruel music to our ears. Based on how far we'd run from the drop-off point, we couldn't be more than fifteen miles from Rochefort. Less than half an hour's train ride away. Half an hour and we could be in Rochefort! Only we couldn't. We'd never make it. As soon as a soldier spotted us, the game would be up. And all the stations and trains were bound to be guarded.

As the light began to fade, I risked taking a peek out of the shed and was heartened to see that a heavy veil of mist was forming. At last something was in our favour. We began gathering up our gear.

'So, our plan is to cut across country, Finn, avoiding the roads. With luck we'll reach Rochefort well before dawn. I don't want to spend another night hiding like this,' Loki said.

'Agreed.'

When the village lay in darkness, the mist thickening

nicely into what the English call a *pea souper*, we slipped
out of the shed, reached the wall to the churchyard and,
checking the coast was clear, climbed over. Lights
glowed from windows and there was noise coming from
several café-bars in and around the square. A few people
went about their business in the streets, although thankfully none loitered in conversation on corners or
doorsteps. Darting from one dark passageway to the
next, we desperately tried not to make too much noise.
My heart quickly began racing, fearing that at any
second we might stumble across someone. How would
they react? How would *we* react? What could we say?
What could we do? But for now Lady Luck remained
on our side.

Having left the village square and bridge well behind,
we pressed on and were soon tantalizingly close to open
countryside. With only fifty yards to go, just one more
corner to negotiate, Loki froze, grabbed me and threw
me against a wall. Soldiers!

We dived for cover behind some bushes. 'Bloody hell,
Finn!' he whispered into my ear. 'They've still got the
roadblocks in place. We'll have to go round.'

I surveyed the scene through the thick, leafy
branches. The sight of heavy grey trenchcoats, tin
helmets and weapons made me swallow hard. There
were three of them huddled beside a wooden bus
shelter. Behind the shelter stood a tall lamppost, its light
casting a ghostly glow through the billowing mist. The
soldiers smoked and chatted, their machine guns draped
from shoulder straps, their breaths adding to the mist.

They looked cold, damp, bored and miserable. They were far from home and had been given the dullest of jobs. They didn't strike me as being eagle-eyed or intent on looking out for trouble. I guessed if anyone came past they'd probably stop them and merely glance at their papers. Possibly subject them to a quick, half-hearted search. Probably the last thing they expected was to encounter agents from Special Ops! It would be a case of whiling away the hours until someone came to relieve them of their duties and they could go back to barracks or to a bar for a nice cool beer. One looked quite old – in his fifties at a guess. He spoke and laughed in a gratingly loud and gruff tone. The other two were younger – eighteen or nineteen, I reckoned.

Loki tapped me on my shoulder, leaned forward until his lips were an inch from my ear and whispered, 'Best if we go that way. We'll double back around those houses and come out further along.'

'Wait,' I replied. 'I've got an idea. Remember what Briggs said to us during our lessons at Mulberry?'

'No.'

'Yes you do. When he was teaching us about improvising and disguising ourselves, he said that we should take risks, be daring, use whatever is to hand.'

'I don't like the sound of this, Finn. What did you have in mind?'

I slipped back a little further into the bushes and turned to face him. 'Listen: as long as we're dressed like this the odds are stacked against us. It's hell of a long walk to Rochefort. And our French isn't brilliant.'

He grew impatient. 'Get to the point, Finn.'

'Although our French isn't completely convincing, our German's pretty good. I reckon it's certainly good enough to get us to Rochefort.'

'I don't understand. What are you suggesting?'

'This might sound crazy but don't dismiss it. Hear me out, OK? What if we take them on, use surprise to get the better of them? We steal their uniforms and catch the next train to Rochefort.'

He didn't reply.

'Well?'

'That's the craziest plan I've ever heard, Finn. I mean, just how exactly do you think we're going to get the better of them?'

'I've thought about that. Like this . . .' I cupped my hands round Loki's right ear and whispered my plan. As I did so, a wickedly broad grin formed on his lips.

Chapter Twenty-one
Hände Hoch!

'Let go, it's mine,' I said in French, praying my best attempt at an authentic accent would do the trick.

'No it isn't, it's mine. Mine, I tell you. Give it here!'

Behaving as if we couldn't give a fig about stumbling across the enemy, Loki and I jostled each other along the road towards the soldiers, pushing and shoving, both with one hand on the strap of our bag. It was a pretend tug-of-war, two lads fighting over possession of it. Although startled at hearing us approach, on seeing we were just two boys arguing about something, the soldiers didn't even bother lifting their weapons. Instead, they watched us with more a sense of amusement than suspicion. Loki had loaded our revolver and wedged it behind his back in the belt of his trousers. The Sten machine guns were safely tucked in the bag, placed on top of everything else in readiness to be whipped out when the right moment came. And that moment was fast approaching.

'It's my bag. *I* found it!' I shouted, continuing our little charade.

'*Halt! Kommen sie hir,*' the oldest of the three soldiers barked. '*Was ist das?*' he snarled, pointing to the bag. '*Was ist in der Tasche?*'

Stopping, we peered at them as if they were rudely

interrupting our game. Looking at each other, we shrugged, pretending we hadn't a clue what the soldier was saying.

One took a step towards us and beckoned with a hand. In a no-nonsense manner, he spat, '*Gib mir. Sofort!*'

The soldier took delight in throwing his weight around and I think he'd grown used to people doing as they were told. Obligingly, Loki let go of his end of the strap. So far so good, I thought. The situation was unfolding exactly to plan. Clutching the bag close to my chest, I yanked at the zip as if gladly willing to share its secrets. With Fritz's attention suitably distracted, Loki snatched the revolver from his belt. '*Hände hoch!*' he ordered, flashing the gun about so it spent equal time pointing at each of them.

For a split second the soldiers were struck by astonishment and bemusement in equal measure. The eldest looked as though he might burst out laughing at our caper; as if it was a joke, or a dare of some sort. But the others failed to see anything amusing and moved to lift their machine guns. I whipped my Sten from the bag and beat them to it. '*Hände hoch!*' I ordered and took delight in the look of horror that swept across their faces in the time it takes to blink.

It dawned on them that we were deadly serious. Flashing each other uncertain looks, slowly, apprehensively, they raised their hands. Pressing his revolver hard into each of their backs in turn, Loki set about disarming them. I covered him. Gesturing with the barrel of my Sten, we then frogmarched all three behind the bus shelter and forced them to stand facing a wall. We now had to work quickly if we wanted to catch the ten past seven train to Rochefort. We ordered them to take off their uniforms, which they only did after a few encouraging prods from the barrel of my Sten. The bandages from the first-aid tin and the straps from our machine guns proved perfect for tying them up and gagging them. Job done, we hurriedly changed into their uniforms and shoved our old clothes and the spare uniform into the bag. About to do the same with our weapons, Loki said, 'Shouldn't we kill them? That way they can't talk.'

It was tempting, but to do so struck me as cowardly – and, of course, would also raise the alarm. I grabbed the barrel of the machine gun Loki was pointing at the huddled, debagged trio sitting on the ground in their underpants, shivering in the cold, and pushed it to one side. 'No. By the time they're discovered we'll be . . .' I was careful not to reveal our destination out loud. 'Anyway, they're not going anywhere in a hurry.'

With the soldiers taken care of and hidden from view, we emerged from behind the bus shelter and briefly inspected each other in the lamplight. Neither uniform fitted perfectly but they'd do. They'd have to. My grey trenchcoat felt heavy and was a size too big. It smelled funny as well, of somebody else's stale body odour. It wasn't nice. And the helmet's strap bit into my chin.

'That's the hard part done, Finn. We've got to hurry or we'll miss the train,' Loki said.

We slung the straps of our newly acquired German machine guns over our shoulders and walked briskly through the murk back towards the station, this time out in the open, our strides confident, fearless even. After all, we were Nazis! We'd conquered this damn country. We had to look and behave as if we believed it. Along the way we startled a few locals. It must have been frightening for them to see us emerge through the mist like a pair of unwelcome ghouls. Most gave us a wide berth, stepping off the pavement or hopping into doorways. I thought I detected hatred in one or two eyes as we passed, but mostly it was fear, I think. Some simply ignored us. One old lady even nodded to us kindly. I supposed she was grateful for 'our' help the previous night in saving that little girl and 'our' assistance in fighting the flames.

'Do we need to buy a ticket?' Loki whispered as we approached the tiny station through the gloom.

'Of course not, you idiot,' I replied under my breath. 'The spoils of victory – free travel!'

Loki managed a nervous laugh.

Trying to look purposeful and serious, we passed through the small ticket office and strode out onto the platform. There was a large clock suspended from the roof and the moment my eyes fell on its face the minute hand clicked forward a notch – it was five past seven. There was a woman with two small children waiting on a bench at the far end of the platform, a really scruffy old fellow ferreting through a rubbish bin in search of food and a few others dotted about, with several on the opposite side of the tracks. A single German guard clutching a rifle stood on the far platform. He saw us and nodded a hello. We nodded back.

Loki looked round anxiously and whispered, 'We're on the right side, aren't we? And the next train is going to Rochefort, isn't it?'

A distant blast of a train's whistle told us we'd soon find out.

The locomotive panted and squealed as it drew to a stop. I counted six carriages, the front two occupying the full length of the short platform. A handful of people got off and the woman and her two children got on. 'Come on, Loki. Once on board we'll head for the rear of the train. Look as if you're searching for someone. Glance at each person in turn. It'll put the fear of God into the passengers and with any luck they'll look the other way. And remember, if we come across a German officer, for God's sake remember to salute him.'

It worked a treat. As the train pulled out, we slowly made our way along the corridor of each carriage in turn, our machine guns poised for trouble and our expressions deliberately grim. The train was quite full and those passengers unable to find seats in the compartments loitered in the corridors. Most stiffened at seeing us approach and I swear half of them held their breaths as we belligerently shoved our way past. I could almost taste their fear.

A strange and growing sense of power gripped me. It felt weird. These people were all at our mercy. One wrong look, one rude gesture, one word out of line, and they believed we'd arrest them, make their lives a misery, maybe even make them disappear! They wouldn't dare question who we were, or think maybe I looked a trifle too young to be a soldier in the Wehrmacht. My confidence and swagger grew with every step. Although I'd never admit it, I was almost enjoying the experience, the total control over the situation, and I was even tempted to pick someone out at random and bark at them to produce their papers, to watch them fumble nervously, guessing that even the totally innocent would pray there wasn't some discrepancy – a missing official stamp, an expired permit – that would dump a shed load of trouble on their head.

Loki was a couple of steps in front of me when, without warning, a door to one of the compartments slid open and a tall, immaculately dressed SS officer emerged. Startled, we both snapped to attention and saluted, announcing, '*Heil Hitler!*' with what we hoped was sufficient enthusiasm and conviction. He didn't even acknowledge us. Instead, he hissed at us to get out of his way, which we duly did. With my heart thumping like a nervous rabbit, we pressed on.

'*Ein Moment!*'

I froze. The SS officer was talking to us. Slowly we turned.

'What's the latest news? Have they arrested anyone?' he called out, heading back towards us.

Oh, Lord, time to put my German to the test. '*Nein,*' I began. 'We've been searching all day, sir. Seen nothing. Our orders are to return to Rochefort and to check the passengers on the train.'

The SS officer nodded thoughtfully. From his tunic pocket he removed a silver cigarette case embossed with a skull and crossbones matching the badge on his cap. Producing a gold lighter bearing the same hideous emblem, he lit up and took a long drag. 'Do you think they've slipped through our net?' he asked.

I shrugged and pulled a *don't-know* face. Loki chipped in, 'We've covered just about every square inch for miles. If there was anyone out there I think we would have caught them, sir.'

The officer nodded. 'Perhaps. Tell me, where do you two come from?'

'Cologne,' I replied without hesitation.

Loki said, 'Hamburg,' simultaneously.

'Ah! Cologne. Wonderful city. Let's hope the RAF doesn't bomb our splendid cathedral there.'

'Yes, sir, let's hope so.' Sweat dripped down the back of my neck. And the way the officer looked at me, casting his eyes over first my uniform then the supplies bag, I couldn't help but sense that he was suspicious about something. Was he testing me? Had the RAF *already* bombed Cologne's cathedral? If they had, then any soldier from the city would surely have heard or read about it. Maybe Cologne didn't even have a cathedral! *Oh God!* I desperately tried to hide my growing trepidation.

Dismissing us with a wave of his hand, the officer said, 'All right. Carry on.'

We didn't need to be told twice. Glad that particular close shave was behind us, and not wanting a repeat, we hurried towards the rear of the train. At the end of the last carriage we found ourselves in a small space next to a smelly lavatory, nicely hidden from the main corridor. We could go no further. Loki slid down the window in the carriage door, stuck his head out and took deep breaths. The train began to slow. 'There's a station up ahead,' he said. 'I can see lights.'

'Do you think it's Rochefort?' I asked hopefully.

'No. It looks too small.'

The train clunked and clattered into the tiny station. I heard voices and the slamming of carriage doors, then a loud whistle, and we set off again. As we trundled past the platform I peered out and saw several guards. They were stopping and checking every passenger as they headed for the exit. 'See them?' I said. 'Good job we've got these uniforms on. If they're doing similar checks at Rochefort we'd stand no chance without them.'

Loki leaned up against the wall of the carriage, pressed his eyes tightly shut and let out a long, drawn out sigh. The stress and strain were beginning to take their toll. I felt it too. 'Not far now,' I said, trying to sound reassuring. 'We'll find Monsieur Blanc and before you know it we'll reunited with Freya and the others.'

He opened his eyes and stared down at the floor. I knew what he was thinking. Our journey was far from over.

The train accelerated and we were rocked by a series of jolts as each pair of wheels passed over a set of points. I figured our next stop had to be Rochefort. It couldn't be more than just two or three miles away. In my head I was preparing myself for Act Two of our little play. We'd have to step off the train full of that arrogant confidence of the victorious and head straight for the station's exit. I decided I'd try to avoid looking other soldiers in the eye. There were bound to be a lot of them about and I didn't want us to enter into tricky conversations unless forced. I still had nagging doubts about that SS officer. If he was suspicious he might single us out and test us further. We'd stand no chance out in the open, surrounded by soldiers. An awful picture flashed into my head – we'd been rumbled and were escaping by running back along the tracks, bursts of machine-gun fire chasing us, catching us up and mowing us down, leaving us strewn over the rails, bleeding from a dozen bullet wounds. I shuddered and tried to shake the nightmare away.

Hearing something, Loki frowned. Edging to the corner, he glanced back up the corridor. Panicking, he turned to me. 'Hell! That SS officer's heading this way. We're in really deep shit this time.'

'Do we stand and fight? Maybe we can get onto the roof?'

Loki shook his head vehemently. 'No. Too risky, Finn.

We've got to get off. It's the only way.' Hurriedly he began unbuttoning his trenchcoat. 'Take off your coat and put it back on inside out. *Get a move on*, we haven't much time.'

The train was gathering pace. I estimated she was doing at least thirty miles an hour. All fingers and thumbs, I yanked at the belt and buttons of my coat, let it slip from my shoulders and set about turning it inside out. Loki had been quick thinking. To get off a train at speed would take its toll on our clothes when we struck the ground. Our coats would get ruined and our disguises compromised. At least by turning them inside out there was a chance we'd preserve the outer cloth. Loki risked another peek up the corridor and was consumed with alarm. 'No time to put them back on, Finn. We've only got about twenty seconds.' He shoved past me and flung open the carriage door. I felt a gush of air rush in and the noise of the train suddenly seemed ten times louder. 'You go first.'

Every agent with Special Operations had been trained in how to do this, and every agent hoped they'd never have to do it for real. It was incredibly dangerous. Up in Scotland we'd been taken on a short trip by train from Arisaig, only we never reached our destination. About midway Major Baxter had our little steam train stopped, at which point the full horror of the exercise facing us unfolded. We learned that to jump blindly from a fast-moving train was tantamount to suicide. The *safest* way was to clamber out and lie down on the narrow step beneath the door called the footplate, with your feet facing forward. Then you count quickly to three, say a quick prayer, let go and roll off. Apparently it minimized injury, as you had less distance to fall. Trying it out at five miles per hour, we'd all believed it. It felt exhilarating, as if we were invincible. At ten we began to have our doubts. At twenty miles per hour all the bruises, grazes and twisted limbs suffered among the various students, not to mention lost teeth, suggested that *safe* was a very relative word. Right now we were going faster than in training – much faster!

Crouching down and holding onto the frame of the door for dear life, I slid my feet out onto the footplate and tentatively lowered myself down. I had to force myself to do it. My brain, my common sense, was telling me *No, don't, you'll die.* Loki rolled up my coat. 'I'll throw it out after you along with the bag, Finn. Go! For God's sake, let go!'

Trees, bushes and telegraph poles flashed by. The huge wheels ground noisily against the rails and the carriage jolted and rocked on the uneven track. I felt sick. This was going to hurt. *A lot!* I counted to three but couldn't bring myself to let go. I counted to three again. Still I couldn't let go.

Loki cursed, placed his boot against my shoulder and gave me a shove.

As I tumbled, I braced myself. In training we'd been advised to pick a stretch of track with a nice sloping, grassy embankment, down which we could roll or slide. There'd been no time to wait for such a perfect spot. I struck the ground hard and it felt like I bounced.

Spinning wildly, I rolled a full four times before I banged into something punishingly hard, my Nazi helmet clanging like a church bell as it hit something solid. My left ankle hurt with sudden shooting pains. And there was a ringing in my ears that took ages to fade. I tried to sit up but couldn't. Disorientated, I struggled frantically. Something tore. Then I realized I was wedged in a low hedge that had a barbed-wire fence running through it. Carefully I felt around and unhooked myself from the barbs before scrambling to my feet. Upright, I felt slightly giddy, as if I was still being rocked by the trundling motion of the train. As I tried to flex my ankle, the shooting pains returned, striking me like daggers. Despite the hurt, a wave of elation swept through me. I'd made it! I was alive. Trying to put weight on my left foot, I cried out. I gritted my teeth and desperately tried to ignore the agony. Hobbling and cursing, I headed up the railway line in search of Loki. In front of me the train snaked into the distance, disappearing into the mist. The sky beyond glowed faintly – the lights of Rochefort!

I'd struggled barely ten yards before I spotted something: my coat. I found Loki's draped over the hedge a little further on. Then I came across our emergency bag. Like me, it had survived intact, although it was badly scuffed and there was a small tear in the canvas. Gathering everything up, I grew increasingly anxious with every step. Where was he? I whispered, 'Loki?' then repeated it a little louder. Then louder still. I had visions of him still on the train, apprehended by that SS officer, his hands held high, a Luger pistol pressed hard into his ribs. Then, seeing a shape, a figure lying awkwardly beside the track, I froze. The body was still, lifeless. '*Loki!*' Horrified, I staggered towards it as fast as I could. Was he dead? Was I alone?

Chapter Twenty-two
Next Stop Rochefort

I could hardly bring myself to look. Throwing down our coats and bag, I dropped to my knees. I reached out, held my breath, grabbed his shoulder and turned him over. I gasped. It was the SS officer. And the front of his tunic was all wet and sticky – blood!

A scuffling noise from nearby bushes had me reaching for the bag and our Stens. A tall lumbering figure emerged from the gloom. 'It was him or me, Finn. Something must have made him suspicious. Maybe it was that bag of ours, or that our uniforms don't fit properly. Anyway, the bastard drew his pistol and tried to grab my tunic. We struggled but I got the better of him. You all right?'

'Yes, I think so. Twisted my ankle. Hurts a bit. Hopefully I can walk it off. How about you?'

'Fine.' He stood over me and the body. 'Best if we get him out of sight.'

Loki hauled the body into the undergrowth and then helped me put on my trenchcoat. I was struggling. My ankle was a far bigger problem than I'd initially realized. How on earth could we walk the rest of the way, let alone avoid drawing attention to ourselves? Our precarious situation suddenly overwhelmed me. 'You know, we should have stayed on the train,' I snapped angrily. 'Dealt with that SS officer and thrown him out of the carriage. We'd be in Rochefort by now and I'd still be able to walk properly.'

Loki sat down heavily and buried his head in his hands. 'Sorry.'

I looked to the heavens and asked God to give me strength. 'Right, well I can't walk into Rochefort, can I?' I complained. 'So we'd better set about finding some transport. Any ideas? Come on, think, Loki, think.'

He looked up at me and said, 'I killed him, Finn.' His voice sounded odd.

'Well, like you said, it was you or him. Anyway, it's not the first time we've shot at the enemy. Remember our escape from the mountains back home? God knows how many rounds we fired at that German patrol.'

'I know, but that was different. They were a long way away. We could barely make them out on their skis. He was *this* close, Finn,' he added, 'Really close. Just inches. I could smell his breath. And the look in his eyes as I pulled the trigger, Finn – I'll never forget it.'

'Try not to think about it.'

'I can't help it.'

'Then think of it like this – ask yourself how many good men he has killed. And remember you're not alone. This war will be just like the last one, like any other, and when it's all over there will be thousands of men like you and me on both sides left with nightmares about what they've seen and done. It's all part of the terrible price we pay. That's war. X was right when he said that it was vile, dirty, and has no rules.'

'You're right, of course – not that it helps much.'

I helped Loki to his feet and he gazed southwards towards the glow in the sky. 'Is that Rochefort over there?'

'Guess so.'

Leaning on his shoulder, I hopped, jigged and hobbled along the railway track. Neither of us spoke for ages. The lights of Rochefort gradually grew brighter. Eventually I saw shapes and shadows, the angles of rooftops and walls, the railway carving a canal-like path between them. The single track branched and then branched again, forming long sidings. A string of freight wagons sat waiting for a locomotive to come and drag them away. The hedges and fields to either side of us gave way to fencing and long back gardens. Loki suddenly stopped and pointed. 'There's a level crossing up ahead,' he whispered. 'We'd better get off the track. We need some cover.'

The crossing didn't have gates or barriers. Only warning signs. As far as I could tell the road wasn't a major one. In all the time it took to creep up on it, not a single vehicle drove past. I heard music drifting on the air and saw light spilling out of the windows and door of a small whitewashed guard house nestled close to where the road and rail tracks met. Having mislaid the German machine guns in our escape from the train, we removed the Stens from our bag and attached full magazines. 'Over there, Finn. See it? Parked next to the house. A motorbike complete with sidecar. Your chariot awaits! What do you reckon?'

'Looks good to me,' I said. 'Do you think you can drive it? Only I'm not sure my ankle will . . .'

'Yes, Finn, I'll drive,' he interrupted. 'But first we've got to deal with its present owners. How many do you reckon there are?'

'God knows,' I snapped irritably, rubbing my sore ankle.

'Wait here and don't move a muscle. I'm going to take a closer look.' Keeping bent low, he scurried forward, darting from side to side, finally stopping in undergrowth opposite the guard house. I watched him get as close as he dared. Even from my vantage point I could see soldiers moving back and forth inside, their shapes passing the windows and door every few seconds. I counted four of them. No doubt they were considered sufficient to guard such a small, minor crossing.

Loki hurried back. 'Four or five, I reckon. We need a plan.'

I quickly came up with two. Plan A involved using a little of our plastic explosive to create a diversion, to blast to smithereens one of the freight wagons we'd passed a hundred yards or so back. It would draw them away and give us time to steal the motorcycle. Loki thought it too risky. Plan B was simply to grab a couple of grenades from our bag, pull the pins, count to four, chuck them through the windows, then cover our ears. Loki preferred its simplicity. Plan B was decided on. But first there was the *really* tricky bit. Not wanting to hang around after the blast and being pretty immobile, I needed to get myself into the motorcycle's sidecar before the grenades went off.

Making barely a sound, Loki shouldered me to the side of the house and then to the waiting motorcycle. He helped me climb into the sidecar. It proved quite a squeeze. As I tried to get comfortable, he spent a moment examining the controls of the bike, turning on the fuel tap and yanking out the kick-start pedal in readiness. A pair of goggles was draped across the handlebars. He snatched them up and put them on. Meanwhile I removed two grenades from our bag and held them out to him. He hesitated. 'Do you want me to do it?' I whispered.

Shaking his head, he seized them from my grasp and gave me a thumbs up. He was all set. With a grenade in each hand, he ran and pressed hard up against the side wall of the guard house. I took a really, really deep breath and held it in the second he pulled the pins from the grenades using his teeth. I began counting in my head. *One . . . two . . . three . . . four . . .* Loki scrambled round to the front of the house, chucked both grenades through the door, then fled back towards me. *Five . . . six . . . seven . . . eight—*

Running as fast as he could, he leaped onto the motorcycle and kicked the starter pedal. As the engine fired up, two blinding flashes were accompanied by deafening blasts. The windows blew out. Glass fragments and splinters of wood showered down over the road. Clouds of dust billowed from the open doorway. Selecting first gear, Loki released the brake and gunned the throttle. The bike's rear wheel spun viciously on some loose stones as we sped off. Snaking up the road, he fought for control. I suddenly remembered something. Loki's father had once owned a motorbike and I'd seen Loki have a go on it a few times. He'd always ended up falling off. Time to say a prayer!

At full throttle we raced along the road. The feeble headlamp had a cover on it with just a narrow slit, making it all but useless in slicing through the mist. Without goggles, the air buffeting my face made my eyes water. Spotting a junction ahead Loki braked hard – too hard. The bike weaved horribly as the tyres screeched and struggled for grip.

'Christ, slow down a bit!' I yelled. 'Keep this up and you'll get us both killed. Turn left here. That must take us into the centre of town.'

'Right, Finn. Listen, if we come across any trouble, like another roadblock, I want you to play at being seriously hurt. Pretend to groan and act like you're semiconscious. I'll stop and tell them that the crossing and goods yard have been attacked by the Resistance, and that I'm rushing you to the hospital. OK?'

'Yes. But what if they don't buy it?'

'Pull out the Sten and let them have it!'

Twisting the throttle, he revved the engine, snapped back into first gear and we set off again. Bouncing in my seat, I focused really hard on the road ahead. What little I could see of buildings and parked vehicles flashed by in one big blur as we tore through waves of mist hanging in the air like sheets billowing on a washing line. We travelled a further half mile or so before a roadblock emerged out of the gloom, complete with barbed-wire barriers and a truckload of soldiers. A long queue of vehicles patiently waited their turn in line for inspection. Without hesitating, Loki drove on, speeding past the line of parked cars, vans and trucks. At the last second he slammed on the brakes and skidded to a halt.

'*Achtung! Schnell!*' he yelled.

An alarmed sentry hurried towards us. Loki lifted his goggles and tried to look frantic and breathless. 'The Resistance!' he shouted, still gunning the throttle of the bike so he was hard to hear. 'They raided the goods yard. Attacked the guards' house at the crossing. Everyone else is dead.' He jerked a finger in my direction. 'He's badly hurt. I'm taking him to the hospital.'

Meanwhile, clutching my chest, I'd thrown my head back and was groaning as if both my legs had been chopped off. In fact, hidden inside the sidecar I'd pressed my left foot hard against the front of the cramped space deliberately, so that my sore ankle sent waves of pain through me. I wanted my hurt to seem real. It was!

The sentry bought our story. Stepping back, he waved for the barrier to be dragged open. Loki nodded in gratitude, lowered his goggles and we tore off. We didn't dare look back.

Chapter Twenty-three
Blood and Guts

Rochefort was a larger town than I hoped it would be. Locating Monsieur Blanc's butcher's shop was proving mighty difficult. Slowly, methodically, we worked our way through the streets. Although thankfully the mist had thinned in places, the lighting was still poor and I had to lean precariously out of the sidecar in order to read the shop signs. It was now late evening and most shops were shuttered or had their blinds drawn. I looked to my right, while Loki peered left. Pausing at a junction, he leaned over in my direction and said, 'Can't we ask for directions, Finn? This is impossible.'

'No. We'll keep looking,' I replied, worried that talking to anyone might create a mighty deep hole for us, not to mention Monsieur Blanc. In any event, the suburbs were pretty deserted, with little traffic and few people wandering the streets. That all changed as we drove deeper into town. The roads narrowed and the buildings took on a medieval feel. I realized Rochefort had been here for centuries. The ancient stone buildings of the old town were crammed together. Many looked shabby and neglected. There was barely a straight roof, wall or doorway to be seen. Turning a corner, we suddenly found ourselves in a huge square that was buzzing with life. The scene took me by surprise and sent a tingle of trepidation down my back. There were bars, hotels and a large church. The town hall, or *hôtel de ville*, was situated opposite, across the square from us, a swastika was draped from a flagpole above the large entrance. I guessed the French *tricolore* had been torn down the day Fritz arrived, just like our Norwegian flags had been back home in Trondheim. There were Germans milling about everywhere, mingling with the few locals brave enough to venture out. I felt increasingly sick as Loki slowly did a circuit round the cobble-stoned square, partly because of the scary spectacle and partly because the sidecar's suspension was unable to cope with the uneven surface. My insides were getting horribly shaken up.

Military vehicles were parked up by the kerbside around the edge of the square. Loki suddenly spotted a gap and, without warning, turned and parked between two other motorcycles. Switching off the engine, he turned to me and announced, 'I've got an idea, Finn. Don't go running off. I'll only be a minute.'

Before I could remonstrate, he leaped off the bike and hurried into a busy café-bar that appeared popular with the Germans. What the hell was he doing? The lunatic! He was taking unnecessary risks. But I could do nothing except sit there and try not to draw attention to myself. I knew I'd struggle to get out of the sidecar without a helping hand, and even then, I'd only be able to hobble. Running was out of the question. Out of view, I held the Sten gun tightly in my lap. I waited one minute, then two, then five . . . What was keeping Loki?

I felt ridiculously exposed and helpless. It struck me for the first time just how alien France was to me. Everything looked different from what I was used to; even the smell of the place was unfamiliar. Ten minutes passed. I was nearing the end of my tether. A boisterous group of soldiers passed by and shouted hello to me. I nodded and smiled. *Bloody hell, Loki!*

I took to looking anywhere there weren't soldiers. I spent a few minutes studying the *hôtel de ville* and then switched my attention to a smart hotel, La Grand Maison, a few doors further along. It had huge tall windows from which light spilled onto the street. I was dazzled by what I could see of the sparkling crystal chandeliers inside. A Mercedes staff car entered the square and drew up outside the hotel. A solider leaped from behind the steering wheel, ran round the front and opened both doors the other side. A chubby, very senior-looking German officer stepped out. A colonel, I reckoned, maybe even a general, but he was too far away for me to be sure. Instinctively I sank down in my seat as far as I could and tipped down the front of my helmet to obscure my face and hide the fact I was watching him. Then another man clambered out. I squinted. Was it . . . ? Could it be . . . ? Oh, my God, I thought, *it is*! A fizz ran through me; that slicked-back hair, clipped moustache and immaculate clothes were unmistakable. *Félix Mouton*, alias Renard! I sat bolt upright and lifted the front of my helmet. Then out stepped a woman dressed to kill in a long, figure-hugging red velvet dress – *Véronique!* They climbed the steps and entered the swanky hotel, guards snapping to attention, the doorman giving them his full attention. I sat in a state of shock, barely reacting when Loki reappeared, jumped onto the saddle and fired up the engine. He pointed to a side street. 'It's somewhere down there!' he shouted cheerfully in German. As he manoeuvred the bike, I watched Véronique go inside La Grand Maison – *You traitor*, I thought.

We did not have far to go. Loki slowed as we passed the sign above the shop. Monsieur Blanc's name was written in tiny red letters beside the larger and more elaborately scrawled *Boucherie*. A little further on, Loki turned into a narrow cobbled street and cut the engine. 'We'll leave the bike here, out of sight, and try round the back of the shop. We don't want people thinking he's being raided.'

'What the hell kept you back there?' I hissed angrily, tearing off my helmet. 'What were you thinking?'

'Oh, that bar was packed with soldiers. It took me a while to get to speak with the barman. I told him I'd heard that Henri Blanc's sausages were legendary and wanted to know where his shop was. On my way out I bumped into a couple of corporals from Dresden and they insisted I had a beer with them. Well, I could hardly refuse, could I?'

'You left me out in the open! If there'd been any trouble . . .'

'Well there wasn't, was there, Finn? And we saved ourselves a lot of time.' He grabbed my arm. 'Come on.'

My ankle had swollen and I still couldn't put much

weight on it. I slung my arm over Loki's shoulder for support. 'Guess who I saw just now.'

'Who, Finn?'

'Guess.'

'Hell, I don't know . . . Adolf Hitler?'

'Don't be stupid. I saw Renard and Véronique. They arrived in an officer's car and headed into that posh hotel in the square.'

'*Really?* Now that is a surprise. Renard must be a fast worker, escaping Britain, reaching Berlin, passing on the stolen blueprints to his superiors and heading home to Rochefort, all in little more than a week. That's what I call impressive! We must inform London as soon as we can get hold of a wireless transmitter. I bet it'll raise a few eyebrows back at Mulberry House.'

He was right. And eyebrows within the SIS, I reckoned. Renard was good. So good he was being wined and dined by the enemy as a reward. And Véronique was sharing in his success. Damn her! Recalling the one and only time we'd met, that evening in Bournemouth, she'd not struck me as likely material for a double agent. I'd spotted nothing in her manner or in what she'd said. She had to be a master at concealing the truth. In the end it was her actions that betrayed her, first running to warn Renard at the Flamingo Club, and now popping up alongside him in the company of the wretched Wehrmacht. I had little doubt that members of the Gestapo and SS would also be seated at their table.

Treading carefully, one awkward shuffling step at a

time, we made our way through a stinking passageway
leading to the rear of Monsieur Blanc's shop. Although
it was dark at the front, I could see lights at the back of
the property. Loki removed his helmet, and we both
took off our heavy coats and unbuttoned our tunics so
as not to scare the living daylights out of Monsieur
Blanc. Resting me up against a wall next to the door,
Loki took the Sten from me and said, 'Well, here goes,
Finn. Let's hope for a warm welcome.' Grabbing the
handle, he threw open the door, stepped inside and
called out, '*Bonsoir!*'

I hobbled in after him. My stomach turned at the
spectacle confronting us. There was blood everywhere.
Hanging from a hook in the ceiling was a pig, its belly
slit open. I reckoned it had been slaughtered just
minutes before we'd arrived. A man wearing a heavily
stained apron and holding a frighteningly long knife was
pulling the foul red, grey and greenish-white organs and
guts from the beast. The animal's entrails slipped and
slopped to the floor, forming a pile that slithered and
wriggled, steam rising from it. Feeling myself retch, I
placed a hand over my nose and tried not to breathe.
The butcher was a big chap, with black, greasy hair, a
huge moustache and massive arms. Startled, he turned
and dropped his knife but quickly reached out and
snatched up an even scarier meat cleaver.

'Monsieur Blanc?' Loki enquired.

The butcher raised the cleaver threateningly and then
tentatively nodded. He looked ready and willing to
make a fight of it. In poor French I announced, 'We

need your help. We're Special Operations. We flew in with the others, with Jacques and Amélie Lefebvre, and Luc and Odette. Do you speak English?'

Suitably confused, Monsieur Blanc's eyes narrowed.

'Give him your gun, Loki,' I said.

Hesitantly Loki held it out. Henri Blanc stiffened and shuffled backwards. Seeing that he wasn't going to take it, Loki gently placed the gun down on a wooden table and stepped back as well.

His gaze firmly fixed on us, Henri Blanc cocked his head towards an open door behind him and called out, 'Hélené! Come quickly!'

A young woman appeared at the door, lifted her hands to her face in dismay and let out a shriek. I guessed she was Henri's daughter because she had the same dark hair and heavy bones. He spoke quickly to her while her eyes dashed back and forth between us. She gasped. 'You're English?' she asked disbelievingly.

'Well, we're *from* England,' I replied. In a kind of *Franglais*, we slowly explained what had happened to us while Hélené and Henri listened attentively. It was hard finding the right words in French, much harder than it had been in Madame Dupuis' lessons. When we'd finished, Hélené took us upstairs and gave us some water, a wedge of crusty bread and a little soup from a large pot resting on a stove. Henri came too, and sat in the corner of the room just staring at us. He was still clutching the meat cleaver. I decided Henri was a careful man. He wasn't taking any chances.

The soup, full of hearty chunks of meat, tasted

wonderful. No sooner had we begun tucking in, than Hélené and Henri exchanged words. Hélené then set about throwing on her coat and scarf. In broken English she informed us, 'I go fetch Pierre Truffaut. He will know what to do and how to contact the others. I'll be gone an hour. I'll get him to bring you some new clothes. You can't stay dressed like that.'

She disappeared and we waited in silence. Henri Blanc didn't move from his chair, and never took his eyes off us.

Chapter Twenty-four
Friends Reunited

When Hélené reappeared with Pierre on her heels, I sensed all was not well. Pierre studied us suspiciously and asked question after question about the drop that only those involved could have answered correctly. Even so, he didn't relax. I suppose he didn't recognize us from the rendezvous despite the fact we'd been standing on the Heinkel's float, just feet from him. When I first set eyes on him in his rowing boat, he'd struck me as a tough young man. Now, in the lamplight, I saw a sharpness in his face too, the look of someone used to living with danger, used to relying on their wits. I could see he was extremely bright and quick thinking. Like Henri, he was being careful. We tried asking a lot of questions such as whether the others were safe, where they were hiding out, when could we get to meet up with them? All were ignored. He wasn't going to tell us anything. He threw over a bag containing some hastily gathered old clothes. As we sorted through them and began changing, I remembered that it was Pierre's father who Jacques had expected to meet at the drop. Henri Blanc had come instead only because Monsieur Truffaut had been arrested by the SS. 'Any news about your father?' I asked.

Pierre moved to the window overlooking the street

below and cautiously peered through a narrow gap between the curtains. 'He's dead,' he declared coldly, in a startlingly matter-of-fact way.

I felt awful for asking. 'I'm sorry. How . . . ?'

Pierre turned and looked at me. 'The Gestapo tortured him and when they'd finished they took him into the woods to the east of Rochefort and put a bullet in his head.'

Hélené added, 'We only found out this morning.'

'Do you think he talked?' Loki asked, somewhat hesitantly.

Pierre glared at him. 'Probably. Wouldn't you if they tore your fingernails out one by one?'

I gulped. The room fell silent. Then Hélené sighed and said, 'Well *someone's* been talking. Over the last month so many partisans have been rounded up. We have to be twice as careful as before.'

'We trust no one,' Pierre snapped. He peered across at my left leg. 'How is your ankle? Is it broken?'

'I don't think so. Probably just twisted.'

'Good. I will need to get papers made for you. They will take a few days. Without them you cannot go anywhere. You must stay here. Rest that ankle. I will talk to Jacques. He is in charge now. When it is safe for you to be moved, I'll return.' He turned to go. 'Oh, and Hélené, tell your father not to worry. I'll have someone move that motorcycle and sidecar. We'll hide it. It may come in useful.'

For four days we hid out in the dusty attic above

Monsieur Blanc's shop. In the event of a raid, we were instructed to make our escape onto the roof via a tiny skylight. Once outside we'd be on our own. Neither of us fancied our chances. My swollen ankle slowly improved and after two days I found I could put my weight on it. After four, it didn't hurt much at all.

Hélené brought us food and water three times a day but never any news. Idling away the time, we had a growing sense we were an unwanted burden on people who already had enough problems of their own. But despite the fact that our discovery by the Germans would be a death sentence for Henri Blanc and Hélené, they did not complain, at least not openly. I think they accepted the risks of harbouring us simply as being their patriotic duty. Thank God for people like the Blancs!

Pierre returned on the fifth evening, Amélie accompanying him. It was terrific to see a familiar face and we hugged and kissed in that peculiarly French way, while all trying to talk at once. Amélie was struggling for the right English words, Loki and I jabbering too quickly for her to understand properly. Eventually we overcame our excitement and Loki insisted on knowing how Freya was before we dealt with anything else.

'She is OK,' Amélie assured him. 'She can't wait to see you. Like the rest of us, she couldn't believe you stayed behind.'

'Well, I was hardly going to abandon her, was I?' Loki replied.

Amélie squeezed his arm and smiled. '*Non.*' I detected

an anxiety about her that set me on edge, especially when her smile quickly faded. 'We've been tipped off that the centre of town may be searched tonight. You have to be moved. At once.'

'Unfortunately your papers aren't ready yet,' Pierre added apologetically. 'Jacques said there was a delay. So, if you get stopped there'll be nothing we can do for you. Do you understand?'

'Yes, but wouldn't it be safer to be dressed as German soldiers again?' said Loki. 'We could pretend to be taking you somewhere, even under arrest if necessary.'

Pierre shrugged. 'If you wish. I have to meet up with my brothers this evening so Amélie will take you to our new safe house. It's across town, on the road towards the Château Rochefort. Good luck.' He nodded to Amélie, shook our hands and slipped out of the door into the night.

As we hastily changed back into the Nazi uniforms, Hélené went to fetch a suitable bag for us to carry our other clothes and gear in. Our emergency-supplies bag taken from the Heinkel was looking rather the worse for wear and might draw attention. I instructed Hélené to burn it.

'So Pierre has brothers,' I observed while buttoning my tunic.

'*Oui*, Finn,' said Amélie. 'Three of them. Pierre is the youngest. Their father owned a farm just a few miles outside Rochefort. Now the farm belongs to them and their mother. Monsieur Truffaut also led the largest of the local Resistance groups until his arrest. After a lot of arguing everyone's agreed that Jacques can take over. Pierre wanted his eldest brother, Alain, to be in charge, but Alain said it was better that Jacques was, especially as he has authority from London.' She looked troubled.

'What's wrong?' I asked.

'I am worried,' she confessed. 'The SS have caught twelve partisans in the last week alone. It will make our job much harder. We need many partisans for Operation Death Ray, to create a big enough diversion. Jacques is trying to persuade the communists to join us. They are trouble but we need them. So far Jacques has had little success. Yesterday he ordered Odette to radio London and tell them that maybe the operation should be delayed until we regroup.'

'And?' asked Loki.

'We're still waiting for a reply.'

'Any idea who's talking?'

She shook her head. 'Jacques told me he's given clear instructions to everyone that they must not carry out any acts of sabotage or raids or do anything to upset the Germans until after Operation Death Ray. That may help prevent anyone else being caught. The last thing we need is for the town to be on high alert. He told me that at least everyone's agreed to that, even the communists. So fingers crossed.'

We thanked Hélené and Henri Blanc profusely for all they'd done. Their smiles, firm embraces and handshakes told me they were both mighty glad to see the back of us. They'd breathe more easily and sleep better from now on. Amélie led us across town.

'Have you been home to see your mother?' I asked.

'*Non*, Finn. Jacques went one evening but said it was too dangerous to return. He said Mother was sure the Germans were keeping an eye on her.'

'Why? Is she involved with the Resistance too?' asked Loki.

Amélie laughed. '*Maman! Non.* She is, how we say, *faible*, erm, frail, fragile. I think it is because of Father's important work in Berlin.' She paused and looked around. '*Ah, bon!* We're almost there.'

The safe house was suitably unremarkable, situated midway along a street of identical detached villas. The front garden was overgrown with weeds and the windows were shuttered. Many houses looked similarly neglected, as if abandoned months ago. Amélie explained that ever since her country was overrun by the Nazis, and the French army had surrendered, tens of thousands of soldiers were being held as prisoners of war. Many other men and women had been shipped off to work in German factories too. And then there were the stories she'd heard of whole Jewish communities being rounded up and shipped off to labour camps in the east. It left streets half empty. We crept round to the back of the house and Amélie gave the signal – three heavy taps on the shabby wooden door, followed by two light ones and finally one thunderous one. Max, clutching a pistol, appeared and ushered us in. Grinning with delight, he slapped me heartily on the back. 'It's good to see you. Thank the Lord you made it safely. Believe me, the way things are looking, we need all the help we can get.'

He led us down a cramped set of stairs into a dimly lit basement that smelled of damp earth. Streaks of green mould decorated the walls. The place was a pigsty. An old tea chest served as a table and upturned crates as chairs. Straw and blankets were scattered round for sleeping on and there were piles of clothes and weapons strewn everywhere.

'Freya!' Loki ran and hugged her tightly.

'Odette! I'm Odette,' she replied, throwing her arms round him.

It was a joy to behold. I'd not seen them both looking so happy in ages. Finally, once they could be prised apart, I gave 'Odette' a hug too. Jacques, we were informed, had gone off for yet more clandestine meetings, trying to organize what was left of the fragmented group of local partisans into something resembling a fighting unit. He wouldn't return until the following day. Loki and I settled down and told our story before listening to what had happened to the others after the drop.

'An old baker's van was waiting for us on the road close to the river,' said Freya. 'We drove south, away from Rochefort, and then doubled back by train and on foot.'

'You were lucky, extremely lucky,' I noted. 'Had you hung around a few more minutes, I doubt you would have got away. Do you think Fritz knew we were coming?'

'Jacques says *non*,' Amélie replied, 'but I am not so sure. Why, what's the matter, Finn?'

I glanced to Loki and saw him peering at me expectantly. I explained what Nils had confided in me, and that we'd heard a Luftwaffe pilot refer to a 'Freya discovery' during our flight. Everybody frowned. Nobody could make sense of it.

'By the way, I informed London that you'd made contact with the Resistance and were safe,' said Freya. 'They were extremely relieved.' She brewed some fresh coffee on a small stove, handing me a piping-hot mug. It was real coffee, not the horrid chicory substitute used back in Britain.

Max, or should I say 'Luc', was keen to fill us in on the latest plans for Operation Death Ray. Removing some loose bricks from the cellar's wall, he seized a hidden map and spread it out on the upturned tea chest. It was extremely detailed, and many notes, lines, circles and arrows had been added to it by hand. 'As you weren't at the final briefings at Mulberry House, I suppose you don't know all the details about Operation Death Ray. I'll fill you in.'

Loki and I crowded round.

'Although the cliffs are tall, there is a gully,' he began, pointing out exactly where the break in the cliffs was located. 'The original plan was for our engineers to arrive by boat, move up the gully, unbolt the radar equipment and then carry it back down the same way. Thankfully, the narrow beach at the base of the cliffs hasn't been mined because it almost disappears at high tide. Unfortunately the plans have changed.'

'*Changed?*' I asked.

'Yes, Finn. We've just heard from London. Now their latest crackpot scheme is to send in paratroopers. They'll land on the south side of the château and fight their way north to the cliff edge and the radar site, dismantle the equipment, then carry it down to the beach to waiting boats.'

Loki looked up. 'Why the change?'

'Simple,' Max replied. 'A few machine guns on the top of the cliff could stop even a decent-sized force climbing up the gully. They might even prevent the boats from reaching the shore in the first place. Best if they're taken out by a ground force. Then the boats can approach safely for the pick-up.'

It made sense. 'So that's the radar site, is it?' I asked, pointing to a cluster of shapes marked in pencil very close to the edge of the cliffs.

'Yes. And close by are the laboratories the Moutons built before the war. The château is several hundred yards away. It's approached from the road between Rochefort and Le Havre via a mile-long private drive. There's dense woodland on both sides. The SS and Gestapo are using the château as their HQ. *Typisch!* They always commandeer the best places.' His finger danced about the map, pointing to another feature. 'See those? They are the barracks.'

'How many men?' I asked.

'Close to two hundred, Finn. And then there's probably another forty or so responsible for operating the radar equipment.'

I balked and nearly choked on my drink. '*Two hundred?* That's a small army.'

'Exactly! That's why the diversion we're responsible for setting up is so important,' Max continued. 'We must get as many soldiers away from there as possible. *And* keep them busy while the paratroopers drop in. If we fail, it will be a slaughter.'

'Has Jacques decided on what sort of diversion?'

'*Oui!*' Amélie answered. 'Erm, how you say, sabotage *un train des équipages.*'

I was a little unsure exactly what she meant but understood the words 'sabotage' and 'train'!

'There's a regular supply train once a week,' said Max, pointing to the snaking railway line. 'About six miles from Rochefort in the direction of Le Havre, the railway passes close to a fuel depot. That's where we'll strike for maximum effect. London's approved the plan. Fritz will need every man he can get to sort out the mayhem we've got in store for him.'

As I blew the steam from the top of my mug, it dawned on me that Operation Death Ray was one hell of a challenge. There was an awful lot that could go wrong. Timing seemed critical. Then I recalled that Amélie had said Jacques wanted the whole thing delayed. I was beginning to understand why. 'This is all assuming the raid goes ahead,' I commented. Max looked up at me and frowned.

'I told them Jacques wants the raid *retardé*,' Amélie confessed.

Loki was peering at the map over my shoulder. 'It's a

tough task. I mean, for our engineers to get in and out within an hour or two of parachuting in. Rather them than me.'

'How are the preparations for our diversion going?' I asked, despite guessing that with all the recent arrests it was an uphill struggle.

'We have everything planned,' said Max, inhaling sharply. 'Naturally, the fuel depot is heavily guarded. The only way we'll get in is dressed as soldiers.' He reached for one of the bags brought from Mulberry House. From it he took one of the German uniforms I'd seen delivered to the house the night we arrived. 'We're going to split into two groups. I will lead the team entering the depot. Our task is to set charges beside the fuel tanks. Jacques will deal with sabotaging the railway line. The idea is to blow the tracks as the train reaches the depot, derailing it. If we get our timing right, everything will happen at once. It'll be chaos.'

Freya added, 'Our biggest problem is convincing enough volunteers to take part. The communists will only join us if we promise to organize a series of supply drops for them by the RAF. Their list of demands is as long as my arm. Jacques is trying to negotiate.'

Loki laughed. 'He could promise them the world! Just to get them on board.'

Amélie cursed. 'Yes, but if we don't keep our promises, they'll be trouble. Fighting the Nazis is hard enough. We don't want the communists against us too.'

'What about your Resistance group? How many are left?' I asked.

Amélie looked away and shuddered. Freya replied, 'Barely a dozen, Finn. And most of them aren't too keen to act until things quieten down.'

'So it may be down to us then,' I said grimly.

Freya searched through a bag and handed me some printed leaflets. They were in French, so I struggled to make them out totally, but they looked like advertisements asking for volunteers to work at the local hospital. 'Jacques has asked us to deliver these tomorrow,' she said. Seeing my confused look, she grinned. 'They *appear* innocent enough, so if Fritz gets hold of one he won't be suspicious. But they're much more than they seem, Finn. There's a hidden message. You need to read every fifth word, working backwards from the end of the leaflet. It's a call to arms. We're targeting a few families who have helped Jacques out in the past. He believes that with a little persuading, they might . . .'

I handed them back. 'Bit of a long shot, if you ask me.'

'Perhaps, but we have to try. I'm distributing them tomorrow morning,' said Amélie. 'I wouldn't mind some help.' She looked at me expectantly. 'I have some shopping to do as well.'

I shrugged. 'Happy to help. Better than sitting around in this place all day.'

'And I have to contact London at midday,' Freya said. 'I'm going to use another safe house close to Rochefort's station to transmit from. Jacques is meeting me there. Loki, you and Luc can come with me. Keep a lookout from the end of the street. I'd feel safer.'

With tomorrow planned, we relaxed and set about eating our meagre rations of watery stew that tasted as if it had been reheated one time too many, accompanied by stale bread. 'You know, I was shocked to see Renard and Véronique the other day, here in Rochefort,' I said, idly thinking aloud.

No one looked surprised. 'Why?' said Amélie. 'After all, Renard, or rather Félix Mouton, has lived here most of his life.'

It dawned on me that they already knew he'd returned. 'True, but there was only a week between us following him around the streets of Bournemouth and spotting him back here in Rochefort. That's pretty impressive.'

Max stuffed an oversized wedge of bread into his mouth and tried to speak. 'Maybe he didn't go to Berlin.' He saw my puzzled look, chewed hurriedly and swallowed hard before offering his reasoning. 'Perhaps he came straight back to Rochefort. My theory is that he's brought the blueprints here, to the château, or rather to the laboratories there.'

That would make sense, I realized. 'Have you told London, Freya? That Renard and Véronique have been seen in Rochefort.'

'No need, according to Jacques. He said that everything was being taken care of.'

'What does that mean?' asked Loki, pulling a face.

Freya glanced to the ceiling as if to say, *God knows.*

Amélie shrugged. I felt uneasy. Just what did Jacques have planned? How come he knew Renard was back in Rochefort? All through our training at Mulberry House, Jacques seemed to know a lot of things, important things, that none of the rest of us did. And I'd had enough of being given just part of the picture. I made a mental note to challenge Jacques about exactly what he knew as soon as he showed his face. These were dangerous times and I didn't want any nasty surprises.

Chapter Twenty-five
Beware of Fat Men!

The next morning we all set off on our various tasks. I prayed we didn't get stopped without identity papers. If we did, it would be down to Amélie to do the talking. She instructed me to act dumb, stupid, or as she said, '*Un imbécile.*' She reckoned the Germans would soon grow tired of trying to question an idiot! I was happy to play along.

Elaborating on his plan to get into the fuel depot, Max thought it best that we complemented our German uniforms by making ourselves look a little older. Top of Amélie's shopping list was some talcum powder to grey our hair and a bottle of collodion to age our skin.

But first there were the leaflets to deliver. This took us across town and mercifully proved uneventful, until Amélie led me towards a smart street called the rue St Patrick. She stopped at the corner and grabbed my arm. 'Listen, Finn. Keep your eyes open. They may be watching number twelve.'

She hurried on past one large imposing stone house after another. I noticed her snatching brief glances at the tall ornate windows. '*Who* might be watching?' I asked repeatedly. She said nothing. My anxiety ratcheted up a notch when she stopped outside number twelve and peered at it over the top of a hedge.

'I think it is safe, Finn. Follow me.'

Hurrying up the path, she knocked briskly on the door while I scanned the road for suspicious-looking characters, and neighbouring houses for twitching curtains. There was no reply, despite her striking the door with her fist so hard I could hear the noise echoing through the inside hall.

'Just slip the leaflet under the door,' I suggested. 'Or wedge it somewhere in the frame.'

Ignoring me, she set about hunting beneath some flower pots.

'What are you doing?'

She stood up, clutching a key. It suddenly dawned on me. This was her house! I was scared – so much so I could hardly breathe. Jacques had said the house was being watched, that it was too dangerous to come here. 'Are you mad?' I whispered. 'What if . . . ?'

Unlocking the front door, she gave it a firm kick open and exclaimed, '*Voilà!*'

On her heels, I slammed the door behind me and leaned heavily against it. 'You had no right coming here,' I snapped. 'It's too dangerous.'

She spun round and our eyes locked together. 'I had to, Finn. Don't you understand? It might be the last . . . ' Her voice trailed off. '*Maman!*' she called out over her shoulder.

'There's no one here,' I said breathlessly, my heart pounding. 'We should go.'

'Maman!' she shouted repeatedly as she moved from room to room. Hands on hips, and rather confused, she added, '*Je ne comprend pas pourquoi?*'

Then it hit me. Something was terribly wrong. The house had that dusty, stale, musty odour of somewhere that had been shut up for a long time. The kitchen pantry had little food in it, and what there was had gone rotten. It was obvious that no one had been living here for some considerable time.

'But Jacques said that he'd been here and . . .' The perplexed expression on her face turned to one of alarm. 'What's going on, Finn?'

I had no idea. I wondered why Jacques had claimed to have visited the house and spoken to his mother if, in fact, he hadn't. The only explanation I could think of was that, like us, he had found it empty. Fearing something awful might have happened, maybe he decided to protect his sister by not telling her. Unsure how she might react, I chose not to share my thoughts with her either. 'We'll find out from your brother later,' I said, trying to sound casual, reassuring, as if there was undoubtedly a perfectly sensible explanation. 'Can we go now? *Please?*'

Heading for the centre of town, I tried to behave as if I'd lived in Rochefort all my life, born and bred here, stepping confidently along pavements as if I'd done so a million times already. It was easier said than done. Everything was so unfamiliar. My nerves were on edge, my stomach unsettled to the point where I felt nauseous. Amélie was still pondering what on earth could have happened to her mother.

Entering the vast square, I saw it was market day. Stalls had been set out in a huddle on the cobbles. Hurrying past them, it soon became apparent just how dreadfully scarce fresh food was. Nevertheless, the townsfolk of Rochefort had ventured out in numbers, no doubt keen to bask in the warmth of the spring sunshine. Cyclists weaved through the crowds ringing their bells and waving to neighbours and friends. Old men in threadbare jackets, worn leather boots and berets perched on walls or sat huddled together on benches. I guessed they were probably gossiping about the war, reminiscing about the good old days when France was a force to be reckoned with, and updating each other on the latest scandals unfolding behind closed doors.

Amélie walked briskly and with purpose. She did not want to get stopped, especially with me in tow, no matter how convincing an imbecile I was. What she didn't realize, however, was that if I was searched, my lack of papers wasn't the only potential problem. A German soldier might also wonder about the foot-long, slender metal tube hidden in the lining of my coat, accessible by a loop of string poking through a small hole in my inside pocket. It was a *welrod*. Good old Smithy had kindly thrown a few into the supplies along with all the Stens and explosives, and that morning I'd decided it was safer to carry than a revolver. The welrod contained a single bullet and came complete with silencer. As we hurried past the *hôtel de ville* with its swastika fluttering in the breeze, I began to wonder if I'd been wise to arm myself at all. Maybe I really was a bit of an *imbécile*. Maybe I didn't need to pretend.

Guards slouched in doorways, their faces blank with boredom, their rifles propped up against doors and windowsills. Others stood in small huddles, smoking and chatting. I recalled our training at Mulberry House. If there was trouble, if we needed to make a run for it, which way would I go? Could I weave between the stalls, hide beneath one, grab a bicycle and dash down a side street? My fear of capture made me look at everything with a very different eye.

Of the various items on our shopping list, the collodion was likely to pose the greatest difficulty. It wasn't something people purchased very often. When applied to the skin, the syrupy liquid dries rapidly, leaving a crinkly residue. Perfect, according to Stanley Briggs, for ageing the skin or faking wounds and scars. Because it was used in some medicines, a pharmacy seemed our best bet, although our enquiries at the first three shops were met by despairing shakes of the head. Amélie knew of one more shop worth trying. It was a small pharmacy tucked away in one corner of the town square. With luck we'd be able to get the talcum powder there too.

As Amélie pushed open the shop door, a small brass bell tinkled above her head. At the same moment I spotted something in the square. A tall, skinny young man stepped out of a telephone kiosk, looked upwards and gave a blatant signal to someone. My Special Ops training told me that his nod was no accident, no nervous tic. He peered across the square. The expression on his face was odd; sharp, I thought, definitely focused, and maybe a little vengeful. Curious, I turned and looked in the same direction.

Some distance away a large trestle table had been set out in the shelter of a stone archway. Two German Wehrmacht officers were sitting behind it. Armed guards stood beside them. A small queue of men and women began gathering to their left, stretching out along the pavement. The young man by the kiosk glanced at his watch and then, thrusting his hands into his trouser pockets, hurried off into a side street. Something was going on. I just knew it. I peered up to where he'd signalled – the church and its ornate bell tower. At first I was blinded by the low sunlight, but gradually my eyes adjusted to the brightness. It was then I realized there was someone up there, in the tower, crouching between the stone pillars. Seeing him made me swallow hard. Whoever it was had a rifle! He carefully, purposefully, raised it to his shoulder. Then I realized I recognized him. *Pierre!* I fizzed with panic. Something terrible was about to happen. And trouble was the last thing we needed.

I ran into the pharmacy and closed the door. The bell tinkled again. Amélie was standing by the cash register. The pharmacist, a woman of about forty with greying hair and thick glasses poised precariously on the very tip of her nose, had already put a tin of talc in a paper bag resting on the counter. Amélie took the opportunity to stock up on supplies, asking for five large crepe bandages which ended up in the bag too. The pharmacist scratched the back of her head thoughtfully, however, when Amélie enquired about the collodion. My heart sank. Then, raising a finger as if she'd suddenly remembered something, she said she'd take a look out the back of her shop, just in case there was an old bottle gathering dust. I waited for her to disappear before speaking. 'We've got to go,' I said quietly, tugging gently on Amélie's sleeve. 'There's going to be trouble here any minute.'

'What are you talking about, Finn?'

'Trust me,' I said. 'Pierre Truffaut's out there and he's about to do something he'll regret. Put the money on the counter and let's get out of here. Now!'

'*Ah, bon!*' came a shout from out the back of the shop. The pharmacist reappeared clutching a small brown bottle. '*Huit francs,*' she declared, placing the bottle carefully into the bag.

Amélie dug into her purse and slowly began counting out the money. *Hurry up!* I fretted. I went to the door and peered out. A clock above the entrance to the town hall struck eleven. On the last clang, a car appeared at speed from a side street, its tyres screeching as it swerved round the corner and entered the square. There were two young men inside. It was too late to do anything. All I could do was stand and watch.

The car, a rusting, mud-encrusted grey Citroën that looked as if it had spent its life crossing fields and trans-porting bales of straw, slowed down as it approached the table under the archway. A machine gun appeared out of the passenger's window. I heard someone scream. Five seconds later the gun's magazine was empty, walls had been peppered with bullets and the two Wehrmacht officers were dead. Everyone in the queue had thrown themselves to the ground. The Citroën revved and its tyres squealed. The car accelerated in our direction. I glanced up and realized it was Pierre's turn to act. His job was to give covering fire. As soldiers rushed into the road behind the car, lifted their rifles and took aim, Pierre tried picking them off, one by one. He was a cracking good shot, maybe even good enough to give Freya a run for her money. He didn't waste a single bullet, either. But there were simply too many soldiers. Several turned their weapons towards the bell tower.

Save yourself, Pierre. You've done what you can. Get the hell out of there before they trap you.

The Citroën, its engine howling in low gear, was still heading directly towards us. Everything was happening so fast. The car's windscreen shattered and the driver slumped forward. A horrible lump formed in my throat as I sensed what was about to unfold. 'Jesus! Run, Amélie!' I yelled. Grabbing her hand, I pulled her towards the shop counter. Throwing ourselves over it, we landed in a heap on the other side. I reached up and snatched up the paper bag, and then cowered, tensing my whole body in anticipation. The pharmacist, realizing what was about to happen too, stepped backwards, pressing herself against the shelves of neatly arranged glass jars. She let out a stifled cry. Her spectacles fell from her nose, revealing eyes that were wide open with terror.

I heard the soft thud of tyres mounting the kerb. The sound reached my ears a split second before the Citroën ploughed through the shop window. The noise was deafening. The floor shuddered beneath me. Tiles fell from the ceiling. Bottles toppled from the shelves and smashed all round us. Fainting, the pharmacist slid to the floor. I rose to my knees and dared to peer over the top of the counter. There was a loud hiss amid the dust. Smoke billowed from the crumpled front of the car. A young man lay on the bonnet, on his back, his arms outstretched, his head twisted at an unnatural angle. The other young man, the driver, sat slumped over the wheel. Neither moved a muscle. I spotted soldiers running towards us.

Amélie stood up, saw the bodies and shrieked. '*Non! Claude! Philippe!*'

'Pierre's other two brothers?' I asked.

'*Oui*, Finn.'

'Hell! Out the back way,' I said. 'Quickly. The Germans will arrest us otherwise. Just for being here.'

We crawled into the back of the shop and ran out through the rear door into a small yard. Once through a wooden gate at the end of the yard, we found ourselves in a narrow alley. We ran as fast as we dared. Amélie was limping slightly. There was a nasty shard of glass stuck in her right knee. Blood was dripping onto her shoe. 'Stop a second,' I said when I reckoned we were far enough away. 'Give me one of those bandages.'

I knelt down, gently picked out the lump of glass, wiped the blood away and then frantically set about wrapping the bandage tightly round her leg. 'There, that should hold until we get you back to the safe house,' I said breathlessly. 'Damn Pierre and his brothers. What were they thinking? They know their orders. No Resistance activities until Operation Death Ray has been completed.' I ran my fingers through my hair in exasperation.

'Can you really blame them, Finn?' Amélie replied, flexing her leg and adjusting the knot I'd made in the crepe. 'After what happened to their father.'

'Yes, I can blame them,' I snapped. 'There's a bigger picture, Amélie. More is at stake than one man's revenge against another. Those idiots may have just jeopardized everything. And at least two of them are dead. What a waste. And God knows whether Pierre will get away from the church alive.'

We walked briskly through the streets. Glancing at my watch, I realized it was after half-past eleven. Freya was due to contact London at midday. Jacques was meeting her at the safe house a stone's throw from the station. The Truffauts' personal vendetta had compli- cated things and I reckoned Jacques needed to be informed without delay. There would be reprisals. The town would be swarming with soldiers hammering on doors and searching everywhere. The people of Rochefort would be taught a harsh lesson and made to pay dearly. Suspects would be arrested and interrogated. I wondered just how many innocents would be rounded up, lined up against a wall and shot. My fears also made me anxious for Freya. 'Do you know the address of the safe house Freya's using?'

'*Oui*, Finn. It's in the rue de la Gare. But remember, her name is Odette!'

Approaching a busy junction, I came to a decision. 'We must go there. Jacques needs to know. We have to tell London the situation here is deteriorating.'

Many houses near the station had been boarded up. Breathless, we arrived at one end of the rue de la Gare. It was a long, arrow-straight road, the station visible at the far end, at least two hundred yards away. 'The house is about halfway down on the left-hand side, Finn,' said Amélie. 'The one with the dark-green door.'

We'd taken barely a dozen steps when I heard '*Pssst!*'

It was Max. Crouching behind a low wall to our right, he looked scared. He held a finger to his lips and beckoned us to join him. We hurried across the road. 'What's the matter?' I asked, dipping down behind the wall.

I began to explain what we'd just witnessed in the square but Max interrupted, his voice tense with anxiety, 'See that fat man, Finn? Far end of the street. See him?'

Walking in our direction there was indeed a fat man wearing a long dark raincoat and broad-brimmed hat. Two things struck me as suspicious. One, he walked extremely slowly, and two, he repeatedly peered at his watch.

'He's Abwehr,' Max whispered hatefully. 'German Intelligence. I'm sure of it. He's looking out for a transmitter.'

It was one minute before midday. Freya was meticulous. If her schedule, her *sked*, as it was known, required her to contact London at midday, she'd do her utmost to be right on time. 'What can we do?'

'Nothing except pray, Finn. Pray really hard,' Max replied.

'Where's Loki? Did he enter the safe house with Freya?'

My question was met with a shake of Max's head. He pointed across the road. Loki was pressed deep into a recessed doorway. I gasped in surprise. He was looking directly at me, frantically mouthing something. I couldn't make out what. I gestured to him, encouraging him to risk crossing the road to join us. But he refused to budge.

'And what about Jacques?' I asked Max. 'He was supposed to meet Freya here.'

'I've not seen him, Finn. Of course, he might have got here before us. He might be inside too.'

'Wait here. I'm going to talk to Loki.' Carefully I rose to my feet and innocently wandered across the road.

Reaching the recess, Loki grabbed me and said, 'It's a disaster, Finn. Is that bastard still heading this way?'

'Yes. Max thinks he's Abwehr. Any ideas?'

We both knew the Germans were good at tracking down wireless operators. Often they used unmarked vans with directional aerials. But they had other cunning methods too. The fat men were one of them. Of course, they weren't really fat at all. Beneath their raincoats, receivers were strapped to their stomachs. They walked the streets listening out, sometimes via headphones concealed beneath their hats, other times the signals registering on a dial disguised as a wristwatch. 'We should deal with him, Finn. Are you armed?'

'Maybe we should sit tight. Not make a move unless he goes inside the house. I've got a welrod and silencer. But it's only one shot and hopelessly inaccurate. How about you?'

'Colt revolver. No silencer though. We can't just wait here. *We can't!*'

'Listen,' I said. 'Let's slowly head towards him. If he goes inside the safe house, we'll follow him and nobble him.'

'Sounds good, Finn.'

It was the best plan I could think of in the panic of the moment. Gingerly we emerged from the recess and ambled along the pavement as casually as we could. If the fat man ventured into the house alone to make the arrest, we'd probably be able to save Freya. But the German Intelligence Services weren't stupid. They were many things, mostly unpleasant things, but they definitely weren't stupid. The fat man stopped outside the safe house, the house with the dark-green door. He took ten paces back, then five paces forward. *Shit!* I reached inside my coat, felt in the pocket for the loop of string connected to the welrod, grasped it tightly and prepared myself for the awful moment when I'd have to draw my weapon.

The fat man looked up at the house and studied the upstairs windows a moment, then lifted a whistle to his lips and blew on it long and hard. Troops appeared from side streets as if out of nowhere – I counted at least a dozen. *A trap!* My heart felt like it had stopped. My knees turned to jelly. We froze. In just seconds the house was surrounded. The door was battered down and soldiers rushed inside. Moments later Freya was dragged out and unceremoniously thrown down onto the pavement.

I pulled the string to raise the welrod, then grabbed its end and drew it out. Two soldiers roughly man-handled Freya to her feet. She looked dazed. Another thug emerged from the house carrying her suitcase containing the transmitter. Caught in the act! She had no defence, no way out. Interrogation and a death sentence awaited her. I wanted to call out, to shout that we were here, that we'd rescue her, but I didn't. She glanced briefly in our direction but didn't shout to us. Instead, she hurriedly looked the other way. I knew why. Despite her horror she wanted us to keep away, to abandon her, so we'd be safe.

Max and Amélie joined us. Loki drew his Colt revolver, hiding it beneath his coat. 'I'm not going to let them take her,' he snarled.

'Are you armed, Max?' I asked.

'No, Finn. I thought it too dangerous.'

Without a word, Loki set off in Freya's direction.

About fifty yards separated him from the huddle of soldiers surrounding her. I ran after him. 'This is suicide,' I whispered.

'I don't care, Finn. We stand or fall together. That's what we promised each other, and that's how it will be.'

Catching us up, Max appeared again at my shoulder, standing tall and flexing his muscles. 'I think I can take a couple on. Maybe if I can grab a gun or something. I'll do my best.'

The odds were worse than four to one. We had only surprise on our side. I knew it wasn't enough. I knew that we wouldn't succeed. But Loki was right. We'd stand or fall together. I removed the safety catch on my welrod and set about choosing my target.

Amélie raced past us, turned and stood in Loki's way. '*Non!*'

He tried pushing her to one side.

She threw her arms round him. '*Non! Arrête! Arrête! Arrête un instant. Reste là!* Stop! For God's sake, stop!'

Max hesitated and grabbed my arm. 'Maybe she's right.'

'A few more steps and we're all dead,' Amélie whispered. '*All dead!* Do you hear me? Put your guns away. Put them away.'

Loki tried to prise her off but her grip was tight. 'Let go of me, Amélie,' he snarled. 'I have to try. I won't let them take her.'

Sickening feelings of horror and helplessness welled up inside me as more soldiers arrived. A car appeared too, screeching to a halt beside the kerb. Its door swung open. Freya struggled, desperately trying to free herself. She swore, spat and kicked out at them. She wasn't going without a fight. Her spirit was strong, her strength suddenly doubled. She broke free. A soldier swung his rifle at her, catching her full in the ribs. She fell like a stone.

Tears streamed down Amélie's cheeks. '*Non*, Loki!' she cried softly. 'Walk away. We must walk away.'

Chapter Twenty-six
In the Midst of Treachery

Somehow we got back to the cellar of the safe house in one piece. Max hurriedly began gathering up our various weapons and equipment. It was too dangerous to stay there. We had to find somewhere else to hide out. If, or rather *when,* Freya talked we'd undoubtedly be raided. Loki was inconsolable and alternated between bouts of angst-ridden fury and crushed, despairing sobs. Finally his fury won over all his other emotions and he took out his frustration on the crates that had served as our chairs. Most soon lay in pieces. As I paced back and forth, giving Max a helping hand with the packing, my brain buzzed with questions. Was it pure coincidence that the fat man had been in the rue de la Gare at precisely midday, exactly when Freya was due to transmit? No. It had to be more than a coincidence, I realized. Soldiers were waiting to pounce. The whole thing smacked of betrayal. Someone had been talking. Someone we trusted.

'Probably Monsieur Truffaut,' said Max when I asked for ideas. 'After all, he was the leader of the Resistance. He knew all the contacts. And the location of the safe houses. Probably knew all about us coming too, and simply cracked under interrogation.'

It sounded plausible until Amélie threw a spanner in

the works. 'He may have betrayed some of the other partisans but not Odette. She only decided to use that particular safe house yesterday. And Monsieur Truffaut was arrested before we even arrived. So, no way could he have known her *sked* for contacting London.' She peered at her watch. 'Where is Jacques? It's unlike him to miss a rendezvous.' Biting her nails, she added, 'I think he must've been arrested too. *Désastre!*'

Loki slumped down onto the earth floor and buried his head in his hands. Rubbing his cheeks until they were red, he asked, 'Any idea where they'll take her?'

'Well,' Amélie replied, 'probably to the château. That's where the SS and Gestapo are. That's where they normally take people. There are large wine cellars beneath the building. Perfect for holding prisoners.'

Had there been any crates left to smash up I'd have happily kicked them into the middle of next week.

'Christ, we're in a mess! Freya's arrested, Jacques is missing, our plan's ruined, and Fritz has our wireless transmitter so we can't even call London.'

Amélie looked up at me. 'We have got another transmitter,' she revealed. 'It's not as powerful but we have used it before.'

'Where is it?'

'It's hidden in the woods not far from here along with the rest of our equipment. I suggest we go there as soon as it gets dark.'

Distant taps on the back door indicated we had a visitor. '*Jacques!*' Amélie said hopefully, jumping to her feet, her face lighting up. Max reached for a pistol and together we made our way up the stairs.

Pierre could barely stand. His right arm was draped across the shoulders of a taller, older boy I recognized from earlier that day. He'd been the one who'd signalled to Pierre from the telephone kiosk. I assumed he was the fourth of the Truffaut brothers. I was right. His name was Alain. We helped them inside. Pierre's jacket was soaked with blood. 'Get him downstairs,' Max ordered.

We managed to get Pierre down into the cellar. He was in great pain. Escaping from the church tower, he'd taken a bullet that had gone right through his left shoulder. While the others tried to get him comfortable, I sought out the first-aid kit we'd taken from the Heinkel. Popping open the lid, I fumbled with the syringes and small ampoules of morphine. 'Any idea how much we should give him?'

Max seized the tin from me. 'I'll do it.' Deftly he broke the top off one of the ampoules, filled a syringe and then stabbed the needle into Pierre's thigh. It didn't take long for Pierre's pain to dull and for him to cease groaning. Tearing off his shirt, Amélie used some antiseptic to clean up the wound and then set about bandaging it.

'He's lost a lot of blood. I'll do what I can but he needs a doctor.'

Only once Pierre had been left to sleep did we get properly acquainted with his brother, Alain.

'What you did today in Rochefort was crazy!' Amélie

spat angrily. 'Two of your brothers are dead, and the third is lying here. It was madness.'

Alain responded by looking at her coldly. In fact, I was struck by how icy his piercing pale-blue eyes were. I'd only ever seen eyes like his once before, many years ago on a hunting trip deep into the wilderness of my homeland. I was being watched by wolves lurking at the edge of a forest. I froze on seeing them. But it was their eyes that put the fear of God into me. They were eyes that wanted to kill.

'*Œil pour œil*, Amélie,' Alain hissed uncompromisingly.

'What does that mean?' I asked.

Loki managed to translate. 'An eye for an eye, Finn.'

'Revenge for your father?'

Alain's deadly gaze settled on me and he nodded. 'It had to be done.'

Amélie swore at him. 'You know what Jacques told you – no raids until our job here is complete. He told me everyone had given him their word. *Everyone*, including you.'

Alain pulled a face. 'You are mistaken. The raid in Rochefort's square had Jacques' full agreement. Of course, although we were desperate to avenge our father, we did question the timing. Your brother said it needed to be done, that a tough message had to be sent. He encouraged us.'

'You liar!'

Despite Amélie's disbelief, I reckoned Alain had little to gain by lying. I believed him. And that was troubling. Their raid would lead to reprisals, to heightened security, just what we didn't need. Why would Jacques encourage them to act now, at just the wrong moment?

Loki suddenly stood up and took a deep breath. 'All right,' he began. 'The way I see it, we've got to try and rescue Freya. And quickly too, before the Gestapo break her. Otherwise she'll meet the same fate as Alain's father and we can forget all about Operation Death Ray. The Germans will know all about it and we'll stand no chance.'

'Agreed,' I said. 'But we've got to get ourselves organized and come up with a plan to get her out of the château. Any ideas?'

Unfortunately my question was met by silence. Then Max tentatively raised a hand. 'Do we have anyone inside the château, anyone who might help us?'

'There is one person,' Alain declared.

'Who?'

'Monsieur Lefebvre, of course.'

To say Amélie was startled would be an understatement. 'But he's in Berlin,' she shouted at him incredulously.

'No he isn't,' Alain replied calmly. 'Your father returned to Rochefort weeks ago. He's working in the laboratories in the château.' He frowned. 'Surely you knew, Amélie?'

She sat down heavily on a blanket covering a bale of straw and shook her head. 'Non. I don't understand. Who told you?'

'He's been seen several times walking in the grounds of the château. I'm sure Jacques knows. It's odd that he didn't tell you.'

Bewildered, Amélie stared blankly into thin air. No one spoke for several minutes, during which the pieces began falling into place inside my head, like the puzzles I used to do back home on a rainy Sunday afternoon – joining up the dots with a pen to reveal a picture. There'd always be a point when, suddenly, enough dots had been linked that I could see what the final picture would look like. I'd reached that moment. The trouble was, it didn't make sense. I ran through it all again.

Too many things had gone wrong – someone was talking. A traitor lurked in our midst and whoever it was knew a great deal. Then there was all that confusing stuff Nils had told me about 'Freya detection' – I couldn't discount the possibility that Fritz knew we were heading for France. With so many partisans being rounded up, Operation Death Ray was crumbling before our eyes and our planned diversion seemed an impossible task. So much so Jacques was asking London for the whole operation to be put off. Pierre and Alain's escapade was the last thing we needed, yet they'd under-taken it with Jacques' blessing. Then there was the strange disappearance of Amélie's mother, despite Jacques saying he'd visited her. Why had he lied? Their house had been empty for ages. And why hadn't he told Amélie that their father was back from Berlin? Worst of all, there was Freya's capture. I was damn sure Fritz had been tipped off that she'd be there. I was faced with a horrible fact: only a handful of people knew she'd be using that particular safe house, and that she'd be transmitting at midday. Discounting Loki and me, that left Max, Amélie and Jacques. The fact that Max was German ought to have been enough to place him at the top of my list of suspects. But he'd stood shoulder to shoulder with us as we walked down the rue de la Gare. He was willing to die trying to save Freya. So I doubted it was him. What about Amélie? No, I thought, she just seemed increasingly bewildered by each additional twist and turn of events.

Jacques? Where was Jacques? He was supposed to meet Freya at the safe house. But he didn't. *Jacques!* I'd reached the same awful conclusion again. In my head it was simple: either Jacques had been captured and had talked, or he was a rotten egg. Had Freya's capture been the only disaster, I'd have bet my life that Jacques had been arrested and interrogated. But it was all the other stuff that, when added into the equation, pointed to him being the traitor. Then I remembered something else. Jacques had met with Renard back in England. Had Renard turned him into a double agent, like he had Véronique? Was Jacques' real mission to make sure Operation Death Ray failed? Although I'd convinced myself that I was right, there remained one thing I just couldn't fathom – *why*? Why would Jacques betray us?

Wondering how best to express my thoughts, I decided there was no easy way. I began by outlining all that had gone wrong. Loki was first to grasp what I was saying.

'Are you telling us you reckon Jacques is a double agent?'

Amélie shrieked. 'That's crazy! Jacques is no traitor.'

'I'm afraid Loki's right,' I said. 'Think about it, Amélie.'

'That's mad. I know Jacques better than anyone. He hates the Nazis. He'd never work for them. He'd never betray the Resistance, or anyone in Special Operations.'

'You may not know him as well as you believe you do,' I said. I began repeating the evidence for the prosecution.

'*Ferme la! Ferme ton bec!* Shut up! Shut up!' she shouted, covering her ears. Tears welled up and cascaded down her cheeks.

'But what clinches it for me,' I continued, 'was that he never made it to the rue de la Gare today.'

Loki's face darkened. 'If you're right about that, Finn, then he sent Freya into a death trap.'

All Amélie could do was shake her head in denial. She couldn't find the words to defend her brother, or the innocent explanations needed to explain his odd behaviour. In the end she just broke down into jerking sobs that, like hiccups, just wouldn't go away. Max took pity and tried comforting her. It was probably the worst moment of her life, not least because I think she knew it was all true.

Loki was seething. Grabbing my arm and dragging me aside, he whispered venomously into my ear, 'If I ever see Jacques again, Finn, *I'm going to kill him!*'

Chapter Twenty-seven
London Calling

While we continued packing, Loki hunted for a scrap of paper and a pencil. He handed it to me.

'What's this for?'

'Sending a message to London, Finn. As soon as we get to the woods. You're better than the rest of us at coding and Morse. Max and I decided it's best that you do it.'

Reluctantly I accepted the task. I wasn't a patch on Freya but knew that Loki was even more fingers and thumbs than me. I sat down with him and Max and worked out what we wanted to say, keeping in mind that our message had to be kept brief. It was important to spend as little time as possible on air to minimize the chances of Fritz intercepting us. Eventually we agreed on the following:

URGENT . . . ODETTE ARRESTED . . . WILL TRY RESCUE . . . SUSPECT JACQUES IS ENEMY SPY . . . DEATH RAY COMPROMISED . . . ADVISE NEXT STEPS

That was the easy bit. Before it could be sent it needed to be coded. I took a deep breath and got to work. I had to be meticulous: one tiny mistake could render the whole message gibberish. We'd been taught a method of coding called the Playfair Code. Every agent had to memorize a key phrase. Mine was *On a dark and stormy night.* Step one was to write out the key in rows of five letters, remembering to ignore any repetitions and then to add the remainder of the alphabet to complete a grid. Having created this, I took pairs of letters from our message, beginning with 'UR', and located them in the grid. Thinking of their positions as being the corners of a square or rectangle, I then made a note of the opposite corners. These were the letters I'd transmit. The code was virtually unbreakable unless you knew the agent's key phrase. When I'd finished, I double checked it and added my 'identifier' – a string of Fs – so London would be alerted to the fact it was me on the other end and not Freya. She used a string of Os.

'What shall we do with Pierre? He doesn't look too good,' said Loki, having inspected him at close quarters. 'We can't take him with us.'

'When it gets dark I'll try and get him to a doctor. I know one I can trust, but he's on the other side of town,' said Alain.

'You'll never manage to move him alone,' said Max, sizing up the task. 'I'll give you a hand.'

As the sun set and darkness fell, we gathered up the holdalls containing our supplies and swung them over our shoulders. Max and Alain dragged a weak and unsteady Pierre up the steps and to the back door of the safe house. 'All being well, we'll join you in the woods later, once Pierre's in safe hands. Good luck,' said Max. They disappeared into the night.

We gave them five minutes before heading off in the

opposite direction. Amélie led the way. She was still in a state of turmoil, stomping rather than walking, kicking out at invisible stones, incessantly muttering to herself and not bothering to look back to see whether Loki and I were managing to follow her all right. Having taken us through a gate to the rear of the property, she then guided us across a large area of wasteland, annoyingly overgrown and littered with rubble and refuse. Then we had to crawl through a smelly culvert close to the railway line for several hundred yards before finally taking a gravel track that brought us to the edge of the woods. Amélie headed deep into the trees. She moved quickly. I couldn't work out how she managed it. It was as if she could see in the dark. In the end I supposed it was simply that she knew the way off by heart. Loki and I struggled to keep up. It was too dangerous to risk using torch light, so progress was slow and hazardous, spiky branches and brambles prodding, slapping and scratching our faces without warning. We had to bat them back as best we could with our flailing arms. Eventually Amélie veered off through a narrow, almost imperceptible gap in the bushes. 'This way,' she whispered. Thorns clawed at my clothes as we scrambled through a tangle of briars and dense bushes. Crouching on all fours, Amélie suddenly announced, 'We are near. Stay here. I'm going to check everything is all right.'

It was a relief to finally crawl out of the undergrowth into a small clearing. Taking a pen torch from her pocket, Amélie hunted for a log partially hidden beneath a bush. Dragging it out, she then gave it a hefty kick. The end dropped out. '*Voilà!*'

The log was hollow. Inside was our spare transmitter, or rather the pieces of it. I helped her remove the various bits and began assembling it. 'Are you sure this is going to work?' I asked sceptically. 'It doesn't look very powerful. That battery is rather small.'

'It worked last time, Finn . . . Loki, can you give me a hand to drape the aerial up in those branches?'

Twenty minutes later, everything was set. I had my headphones on and a finger poised over the key pad that I'd balanced on top of the log. In my other hand I held the coded message. Amélie shone the pen torch over my shoulder. Loki knelt beside me, ready to hand me a pencil so I could scribble down London's reply. I took a deep breath and flicked a switch. My headphones hissed and crackled. Morse was a whole different language, comprising just dots and dashes. We'd practised it so many times that it should have become second nature, our tapping fluent and precise. But my confidence seemed to drain from me. I began tapping but quickly made a mistake, then another. I stopped, cursed, rubbed my hands together, flexed my fingers and began again.

'There. It's done.' I flipped another switch. 'Let's hope they're listening.'

An acknowledgement arrived almost immediately. The signal was poor, sounding distant. But I understood it without needing to write it down. It was one of many short, standard replies. Tearing off the headphones,

I said, 'We have to wait. They'll send their instructions in two hours.'

Amélie looked at her watch and then flicked the power switch on the transmitter. 'We must save the battery. It is the only one we've got.' She crawled to a tree and sat with her back against the trunk. Drawing up her legs tightly, she rested her chin on her knees and shivered in the cold night air. Loki and I settled down on either side of her. 'You're wrong about Jacques,' she said. 'Trust me. I know him.'

Nobody spoke for ages, and then Loki piped up. 'A truck. We need a German truck.'

'What for?' I asked.

'We'll drive right up to the château, fight our way inside, rescue Freya and then leg it. Smithy gave us enough gear to make quite a stand.'

I chewed it over for a few minutes. Loki's plans were often pretty simple and direct. Blaze in, knock a few heads together, do the business and then get the hell out of there. It might work, of course, but I wondered if a few modifications might make it a little less risky. 'I'd prefer to try and get in and out as Germans. I know! Maybe we could forge some papers – orders from their High Command. Pretend that Berlin wants Freya taken to Nazi HQ for interrogation and that we've come to transport her.'

'Idiots!' Amélie muttered under her breath. 'It sounds a stupid plan.'

'She's right, Finn. There's not enough time to forge anything. I reckon we've got twenty-four hours.

Forty-eight at the most. After that, everything is lost.'

In training at Mulberry House we'd learned a lot about the Gestapo's methods of interrogation. In all likelihood Freya's would begin slowly, gently, the Gestapo simply pointing out that spilling everything would be in her best interests. When that didn't work, they'd apply stress, depriving her of sleep, food and water, and repeatedly take her from her cell for bouts of questioning. If, after about a day, that didn't do the trick, they'd resort to other methods, the kind Monsieur Truffaut experienced. Even the most courageous couldn't be expected to resist for long. At Mulberry House we'd been taught to stall as best we could, try to hold out for forty-eight hours, enough time for others to make their escape. But the Gestapo weren't stupid. They knew that was precisely what agents were trained to do. I wondered how Freya would fare. At what point would she regret not accepting her L-pill from the brigadier? She was tough for a girl, not just physically, but in spirit too. She'd inherited that from her father, Heimar, a man who spent his life hunting in the great expanses of Norway's wilderness. Maybe seeing she was just a young woman, the Gestapo might be misled, I thought. They'd not be used to someone like her. *Or would they?*

'It's almost time, Finn,' Loki announced, peering at his watch. 'Let's hope X has some bright ideas.'

London's reply was long. They repeated it to make sure I got all of it down. Then I set about decoding the long string of letters. With Loki and Amélie peering over my shoulders, I slowly revealed our instructions.

'Jesus, Finn, that can't be right,' said a shocked Loki. 'You must've made a mistake.'

Unfortunately I'd not made any mistakes at all. I stared at our orders in utter disbelief.

MESSAGE UNDERSTOOD . . . OPERATION HAS BEEN BROUGHT FORWARD . . . DEATH RAY MUST PROCEED WITHOUT DELAY . . . WILL BEGIN TOMORROW NIGHT . . . AIR DROP AT 2300 HOURS . . . PICK UP ON BEACH AT 0030 HOURS . . . GET THERE IF YOU CAN . . . WARNING . . . CARPET LAYING BEGINS 0100 . . . IF CAN'T BE REMOVED FREYA MUST BE DESTROYED . . . GOOD LUCK

Loki was shaking his head adamantly. 'No! No way. Can't be.'

I read and re-read the message and then sent a quick reply requesting clarification. All I got in return was the message re-sent, without any alterations. In the end, fearing I'd already been transmitting for way too long, I signed off and removed my headphones.

'This is impossible,' said Amelie.

It was *all* impossible, I thought. Why did they want Freya destroyed? Did she know too much about Special Ops? Was that it? Did we have to either save her or make sure she was silenced for ever? For once in his life, Loki was dumbstruck.

Of course, I could understand why London, fearing

Freya would eventually buckle under interrogation, were bringing Operation Death Ray forward. They knew the train timetable. They knew that only one supply train came per week. And to wait another week was simply out of the question. But they also knew we were heavily compromised. How could we be expected to undertake such a major diversion? And what was all that about carpet laying?

We heard a noise. Someone was coming. We reached for our guns.

Chapter Twenty-eight
Impossible Choices

Max and Alain emerged from the bushes. Thankfully Pierre had made it into safe hands. According to the friendly doctor, he'd live. Loki showed them London's instructions. Max couldn't believe the bit about Freya either. About the rest he was philosophical, saying that we'd simply have to try our best in difficult circumstances.

'Does anyone know what they mean by "carpet laying"?' I asked.

Max nodded. 'I keep forgetting, you and Loki weren't at all of the briefing sessions back at Mulberry House, were you?'

'No,' I said. '*Enlighten us!*'

'Walker told us that they wanted to cause Fritz as much inconvenience as possible. Knowing a lot of research goes on at the laboratories, they reckon that destroying them will set Fritz back months, maybe years in his radar research. So, whether Operation Death Ray succeeds or fails, after the boats have left the beach the RAF is going to fly in and bomb the whole area. There'll be nothing left of the château or its laboratories.'

Loki raised his hands to his face and let out a groan of anguish. 'We've got to save her, Finn. We've got to.'

'Yes. But how?'

Max suddenly snatched up a Sten. 'Sssh! Someone else is coming,' he whispered.

In silence we listened to the cracks and snaps of twigs breaking underfoot and the rustling of bushes. When a shape finally emerged from the undergrowth on all fours, Amélie pressed the switch on her pen torch. We all gasped. *Jacques!*

'What the hell's been happening?' he said, shielding his face from the brightness of the torch light.

No one lowered their weapons. 'Are you alone?' Max asked.

'Of course. Can somebody tell me what's going on? Why did you abandon the safe house?'

'Where have you been?' I asked sternly.

Jacques tried to explain that he'd got delayed by German patrols a few miles outside of town and couldn't make the rendezvous with Freya, but I don't think anyone believed his story for one minute. Fearing Jacques had led the enemy to our hide-out, Max and Alain moved to the edge of the small clearing and listened out for a possible ambush. Amélie's torch remained fixed on her brother but I noticed the beam flicker strangely – her hand was shaking. As Jacques tried to scramble to his feet, Loki moved rapidly, knocking him back down onto his knees. 'Hands behind the back of your head, Jacques. Do it! Now.' Loki pressed the barrel of his revolver against Jacques' left temple.

'What are you doing?' he protested. 'Get off me, you idiot. And put that gun down.'

The accusations flew. 'You're a traitor. You've betrayed everyone.'

'What? Don't be stupid,' he replied.

'You're working for the enemy. Did Renard recruit you? What rewards did the Nazis offer you?'

'This is nonsense.'

'It's the truth, Jacques. We've worked it out,' I said. 'All along you've been trying to prevent Operation Death Ray from going ahead. That's why so many partisans have been arrested, why the Germans arrived so quickly after we landed, why Freya got caught.'

Jacques was suddenly fearful. '*Non!* Tell them, Amélie. I'd never betray anyone.'

We all looked at her but she said nothing. She did not defend her brother. Alain turned and marched across to where Jacques knelt. 'This is for my father,' he hissed. Turning his Sten gun round, he swung it viciously, the butt smacking the side of Jacques' head. His glasses flew off into the bushes and he rocked for a moment before falling forward like a felled tree. Had he not been wearing spectacles, had the thick arm not cushioned the blow, I think Alain's strike would have killed him there and then. But Alain wasn't done. He launched his right foot, the heavy boot sinking into Jacques' ribs. 'That is for Philippe.' He kicked him again. 'That is for Claude.' And he kicked him a third time. 'That is for Pierre, and all the others you've betrayed.'

'Finn, hand me one of those welrods. One with a silencer,' said Loki.

Amelie cried, '*Non!*'

'It has to be done,' Alain snarled.

Clutching his sore ribs, Jacques tried to lift himself up, and desperately began crawling towards the bushes where his glasses had landed. 'You don't understand,' he groaned. He was like a frightened, wounded animal, making a last desperate bid to escape. Alain's boot came down on him hard. Jacques wasn't going anywhere – except hell.

'*La vérité, Jacques*,' Amélie cried. 'The truth.'

'Yes, Jacques,' I said. 'The truth, the whole truth, and nothing but the truth. Let's hear it. Your last chance to speak.'

'*Oui, Jacques. La vérité, rien que la vérité, toute la vérité*,' Amélie sobbed.

His face bloodied, Jacques raised a hand to his mouth and removed a broken tooth. 'I did not betray your father, Alain. He must have just been unlucky, or careless. That is the truth. OK, so I did encourage you and your brothers to take revenge, but all I wanted was for the Germans to be placed on alert, to flood the town with extra soldiers. That way I could tell London it was simply too dangerous for Operation Death Ray to proceed.'

'Why don't you want the operation to go ahead?' I asked.

'Before our escape to England my father was in Berlin,' Jacques replied. 'A few weeks ago he returned to Rochefort. I learned that from Renard. It didn't seem that important until X informed me that the château and laboratories would be bombed immediately after Operation Death Ray.'

'*Papa!*' Then Amélie gasped as if she'd suddenly understood something devastating. '*Maman?*'

Wincing, Jacques spat out some blood and nodded to her. 'Yes, Amélie, *Maman* is being held at the château too. To make sure Father co-operates.' He summoned his strength and dragged himself up onto his knees. 'So you see, Amélie, if Operation Death Ray goes ahead, our parents will be killed! I am not proud of what I've done, but I had to try and save them. Please try to understand.'

'Oh, Jacques, why didn't you tell me?'

'This is all a pack of lies,' Loki snarled hatefully. 'Why didn't you simply tell X about your parents being inside the château?'

Grimacing with pain, Jacques spat out more blood and snorted with derision. 'You know X as well as I do, Loki. He sees only the big picture. Operation Death Ray is more important than my parents, your parents, anyone's parents, in fact. More important than me or you. If I'd told him, he would simply have found someone else to lead the raid. I wouldn't have been able to stop it.'

'And what about Freya?' said Loki. 'Did you betray her?'

Jacques lowered his head and nodded. 'I'm sorry, Loki. I will never forgive myself. But London kept insisting that the raid proceed despite all my efforts. It was my last resort. I couldn't think of anything else. I figured that if our group was compromised, they'd *have* to reconsider.'

'You bastard! I hope you rot in hell.' Loki pressed the welrod against the back of Jacques' head. Through clenched teeth, he hissed, '*Goodbye, Jacques!*'

'*Non!*' Amélie screamed.

Chapter Twenty-nine
Taking a Chance

'Wait!' I shouted.

Loki hesitated and looked round at me. Amélie's feeble torch light caught his eyes. They looked wild, full of bloodlust.

'Killing Jacques won't solve anything,' I said.

'*Justice!*' he hissed. 'It's like Alain said, "An eye for an eye."'

Amélie ran and threw her arms around her brother. Loki ordered her to move away. She refused, clinging to him tightly.

'Do it,' Alain called out. 'Kill him.'

'No!' I shouted. 'Put your gun down, Loki. I believe Jacques' story. And what would you do in his position? If it was your mother and father? You'd stop at nothing to save them.'

'I wouldn't betray you, Finn. I'd rather die.'

'I know, but what about the others? Think about it. We've only known them for a matter of weeks. Given the choice, who would you save?'

'No. They're Special Ops, Finn, like us. I'd not betray them.'

'Really? Supposing you faced a stark choice. Either they die, or your parents die. You have to decide. There are no other options . . . Well, which would it be? Do you betray your fellow agents or do you effectively sign your parents' death warrants?'

Loki's hand, gripping the welrod, began to shake. 'That's not fair, Finn.'

'No, it's not. But it's real.'

I could sense Loki struggling inside. 'But he betrayed Freya.' With renewed conviction he pressed the end of the welrod hard against Jacques's head.

'Listen, maybe not all is lost,' I said hurriedly. 'Maybe there is a way out of this, a way to save everyone *and* get the job done. But it'll need all of us. Jacques, you know the inside of the château, don't you?'

He nodded. 'Yes, Finn, we've been there several times in the past when our family celebrated special occasions with the Moutons.'

'So you know the layout inside.'

'Some of it.'

'Ever been down into the cellars?'

'*Oui!* We used to play down there while our parents talked,' Amélie interrupted.

'Excellent. Then I've got a plan that might just salvage something from this God-awful mess. So, put down the gun, Loki.'

He didn't budge. 'Let's hear this plan first.'

'Like you suggested earlier, we need a truck,' I said. 'We already have enough German uniforms. We'll set up the diversion and then head back to the château. We'll pretend Amélie and Jacques are our prisoners and that we're taking them to the château for questioning. That'll get us inside. Once there, we find

Freya *and* Jacques and Amélie's parents, then head for the beach.'

Max rubbed his chin thoughtfully. 'Not a bad idea, Finn, but will we really have time to set off the diversion *and* get back to the château before the paratroopers drop in?'

'No you will not,' interrupted Alain. 'There is too much to do.' He sounded very sure of himself. 'Unless . . . Listen, I have an idea. I know most of my father's old contacts in the Resistance *and* I know the area like the back of my hand. Although many have been arrested, I can get enough partisans together to handle sabotaging the railway line. All I need from you are the explosives and pressure switches. I'm afraid you'll have to place the charges in the fuel depot, but if you set the delay correctly you can give yourselves sufficient time to get back to the château before all hell breaks loose.'

'Are you sure you can do it?' I asked. Alain nodded. Somehow I knew he'd not let us down. I reached out and shook his hand firmly.

'Timing will be everything,' observed Max. 'The fuel depot is about six miles from the château. We'll still need that truck.'

Again Alain came to our rescue. 'That's easy enough. There are always trucks on the road between Rochefort and Le Havre. If you are all in uniform, flag one down and then ambush it. As there are woods all along that road, it will be easy to park up in the trees until it is time to make your move. All we need to decide is the exact timing.'

'Then we have a plan,' I said. 'Everybody agreed?'

With great reluctance Loki nodded and lowered his gun.

Everyone settled and tried to get comfortable for our long wait through the night. I noticed that only Amélie sat close to her brother. It was as if treachery was some kind of contagious disease and no one else wanted to risk being infected by it. Loki took me to one side. 'Are you sure we can trust Jacques, Finn?'

'We have to,' I replied. 'We'll have very little time once inside the château. We need someone who knows the layout. We just have to take a chance on him.'

'Can't Amélie show us the way? She's been there too.'

'Maybe, but she's that much younger than Jacques. She might not recall the layout as clearly as him.' I sensed Loki remained unconvinced. 'Listen, we'll watch him like a hawk. One wrong move and we'll deal with him. Permanently!'

Loki settled beneath a tree some ten feet from Jacques and Amélie, and stared at them through the darkness. Jacques chain-smoked, the tip of his cigarette glowing red, a pinpoint of light that told us he was still sitting there and hadn't tried to make off.

Like me, I think Loki spent the next hour or two recalling all that had happened since our arrival at Mulberry House and just what other instances pointed to Jacques' guilt. I remembered that on our last night together, when we were introduced to *Luc* and *Odette*, Amélie had spotted the MADE IN ENGLAND label in Freya's glove and Max had later said that he'd seen

Jacques, not Madame Dupuis, checking over the gloves. Even then Jacques had been planning ahead!

'It was a bit risky, wasn't it, Jacques?' Loki suddenly piped up. 'Letting Fritz know we were flying in. I mean, had there been a firefight, you might have been killed along with the rest of us.'

'What are you talking about? I didn't tell anyone about the drop.'

'Lies, lies, lies . . .' Loki tutted. 'Tell him, Finn, about all the references to Freya that have been picked up over the airwaves. We even heard a Luftwaffe pilot mention it during our flight in.'

I recounted everything starting from the afternoon Nils had told me about the intercepted radio message mentioning *Freya detection*.

Jacques' reaction was unexpected. He began to laugh. Loki scrambled to his feet, clearly intent on rushing Jacques and making him pay dearly for his outburst. I managed to restrain my friend and calm him. 'Explain yourself, Jacques,' I ordered.

'What you overheard has nothing to do with *your* Freya, Loki. The Germans have codenames for many things, just like we do. *Freya* is the name they have given to their new long-range radar system.'

'Yeah, right. That's rather a neat coincidence,' Loki responded disbelievingly. 'Can't you do better than that?'

'It's true. An unfortunate coincidence. Of course, the Germans should really have called the device *Heimdall*, but that would have been far too obvious.'

Something clicked inside my head. Like all

Norwegian children I'd grown up reading the many Norse myths and legends. Heimdall was one of the gods, a watchman, who possessed great stamina and acute senses. It was said he could hear grass grow and see a hundred miles by day as well as by night . . . Exactly like radar! And Heimdall was often portrayed as the champion of the beautiful Freya, the goddess of love. I recalled the odd wording of the intercepts . . . *Freya Meldung – Freya detection*. They suddenly made sense. That's exactly how Luftwaffe pilots would talk about an enemy aircraft having been picked up by their new radar system. Jacques was telling the truth. Then something else clicked inside my head. *Of course!* I reached for London's decoded reply. 'Now I get it,' I said, waving it under Loki's nose. 'When London says *If can't be removed Freya must be destroyed*, they mean the radar equipment, not *our* Freya!'

My unravelling of the true meaning of London's reply offered Loki a little much-needed cheer. To pass the time, we got Jacques to tell us what he knew about Fritz's radar systems. Being so into engineering and having gleaned much from contacts with his father, Renard and some of the British scientists from Worth Matravers who attended the briefings at Mulberry House, Jacques appeared to know a great deal. More than Nils had explained to me during our flight over.

Fritz was fiendishly clever. Although their Freya system was rubbish at accurately locating British planes, it had such a long reach, it enabled their early detection.

This was vital as it gave the Luftwaffe loads of time to get airborne and into the right sector. Then, as our aircraft got close, a different German system – Jacques called them *Giant Würzburgs* – tracked them precisely. The really clever bit was that they used two Würzburgs alongside one another, one tracking our planes, the other the intercepting Luftwaffe fighters. Knowing the exact positions of both, the ground operators were able to guide their pilots to intercept our bombers. Now I knew why British losses had become so horrendous. I also understood why our experimental cockpit version of radar was so important – our pilots would see the enemy coming, despite the darkness and cloud. It might give them the edge.

'If you manage to steal this Freya device, what use will it be to you?' asked Alain.

Jacques stubbed out his cigarette on the ground before replying. 'If we can discover how it works, then we can come up with a way of *brouillage* . . . erm, how you say, *jamming it*.'

'If we all get out of this alive, maybe your father can help our experts,' I added.

'Yes, Finn, if we succeed I doubt X will have much trouble convincing him.'

We took it in turns to stand watch and then get some sleep. An hour before dawn we sorted through our gear, selecting the items Alain needed for sabotaging the railway line – several hefty lumps of plastic explosive, a handful of detonators and a couple of pressure switches that would be placed beneath the rails, the weight of the train activating them when the wheels passed over. We ran through our plan and timings once more. The supply train would be passing the fuel depot at ten-thirty that evening. When it derailed, mayhem would break out. We'd set the charges inside the fuel depot to go off five minutes later, doubling the panic. By the time it all kicked off, we'd need to be back close to the château, ready to drive inside as soon as the local garrison's soldiers had left for the depot. With the parachute drop scheduled for eleven, it would all be hellishly tight. If the slightest thing went wrong, our grand plan would unravel and Operation Death Ray would be in tatters.

We said our goodbyes. Max, Loki and I shook Alain's hand firmly and we wished each other luck. Alain cast Jacques a cool look and muttered to me, 'Keep a close eye on him, Finn.' Swinging the bags over his shoulders, he slipped away into the trees.

'Right,' said Max. 'We'd better figure out precisely where we're going to ambush the truck, and just how exactly we're going to get in and out of the depot in one piece!'

Chapter Thirty
Unexpected Visitors

I shall never forget the looks on the faces of those two corporals. We flagged down their truck in the middle of nowhere, about a mile from the château. Initially our German uniforms reassured the driver and his passenger. That is, until we lifted our weapons, ordered them out of their cab, frogmarched them into the woods, bound and gagged them, and ordered them to lie face down in a ditch and not move until dawn. The younger of the two shook like a leaf and promptly wet himself.

The back of the truck was full of boxes, mostly food, wine and brandy destined for the dining tables of the SS and Gestapo at the château. We'd already decided that whatever the truck was carrying, we would 'deliver it' to the depot – that was our ruse to get past the sentries at the gates. Max's face lit up on inspecting our cargo. 'Toll!' he exclaimed. 'Leave it to me,' he said. 'I know exactly how to talk our way inside.'

By nine o'clock we were half a mile from the depot's entrance and almost ready. We just had one thing left to do, and it wasn't the nicest of tasks. Since only Max, Loki and I were going in, Jacques and Amélie had to be kept somewhere safe. We agreed to drop them off near the depot and pick them up again on our return – only there was more to it.

It was Loki's idea but Max and I went along with it. Loki feared Jacques might have second thoughts about our plan; that he might scarper and dash to the château to alert everyone, hoping that his parents might be evacuated before the raid began. Whether Loki was right or not, it simply wasn't the time to take unnecessary risks. So we tied up both Jacques and Amélie and hid them in the trees close to the road. Accepting their fate, they didn't protest, but in the beam of the truck's feeble headlight I saw the sorrow on Amélie's face. After all we'd been through together, it had come down to this – fear and distrust.

I sat in front with Max, who drove us to the entrance of the depot where we were flagged down. I felt the hairs rise on the back of my neck. *Stay calm!* I kept telling myself. *Act confident. Act normal!* Loki remained in the back of the truck, hiding behind the boxes and guarding the bags containing the explosives, time pencils and the tape he intended to use to strap the devices to the fuel tanks.

A rather lazy sentry approached, rifle slung over his shoulder. Max leaned out of the window and waved some papers we'd found in the cab under the sentry's nose. Cheerfully he announced that by order of German High Command all troops were to be given extra rations to celebrate the recent victories of the glorious Third Reich, and we had the honour of making the deliveries. It did the trick. The barrier lifted without further ado, and we drove inside.

A straight road stretched out before us, lit by a string

of hooded lamps. Massive circular steel tanks, at least twenty feet high and fifty feet in diameter, lay in the darkness on both sides of us amid a mass of pipes, ladders and gantries. The air was thick with fumes. Thankfully there were few soldiers wandering about now we were inside.

'Slow down,' I said to Max. 'And keep to the right.' I turned, banged a fist on the back of the cab, slid open a small hatch and called to Loki, 'There's a place up ahead without lights. It's pitch black. Jump out there. We'll pick you up again in ten minutes on our way out. Same place. OK?'

'Understood, Finn.'

'Good luck.' I slid the hatch shut and glanced at Max. 'Time to start praying.'

Loki dropped from the back of the truck and disappeared among the fuel tanks. Max and I made for the main building, a dull flat-roofed brick block, two storeys high. A worker in overalls kindly directed us to the 'stores' at one side of the building. Having parked up, we climbed out, casually ambled to the back of the truck, lifted the canvas awning and began unloading the boxes.

'*Hey! Was machen Sie da?*'

We paused and looked over our shoulders. A rather short, stern-looking Wehrmacht officer was peering at us from a doorway. We put down the box, snapped to attention, saluted, then Max set about explaining what we were doing here. The nature of our delivery was sufficiently interesting for the officer to want a closer look. He approached and gestured for us to show him. We opened a box and stood patiently while he peered inside and examined a few bottles. He seemed pleased.

'*Neunzehn hundert, fünf und dreissig! Ein besonderes gutes Jahr für Burgunder. Wunderbar!*' he enthused. '*Weitermachen.*' He waved in the direction of a covered store area and then wandered off clutching a bottle. I looked at Max and grinned.

Grabbing the last of the boxes, I saw our supply bags hidden at the back of the truck. I had an idea. Rummaging inside, I felt for the telltale furriness that could mean only one thing – one of Smithy's stuffed rats. Locating one, I grabbed a time pencil. They were clever delaying devices containing a detonator set off by a spring-loaded plunger. A piece of copper wire held the spring under tension. By bending one end of the pencil, it broke a glass ampoule inside containing strong acid that would eat through the wire. Eventually the wire would break and the device would go off. How long this took depended on the strength of the acid and the thickness of the wire. I bent the pencil to activate it, and then inserted it into the poor beast's backside. I stuffed *Herr Ratte* between the bottles, resealed the box and lugged it into the store area, where I hid it at the back of the pile. The time pencil had a one-hour delay – *wunderbar!*

Loki was waiting for us in the shadows and leaped aboard as we trundled past. No sooner had we exited the main gate than I slid open the small hatch and called out to him. He shoved an arm through and gave me a thumbs-up. Everything was set. I just prayed Alain would be equally successful in dealing with the railway line. We picked up Jacques and Amélie and headed for the château. It was all going so smoothly, so well. Somehow I just knew that the rest of our mission wasn't going to prove quite so easy.

At ten-fifteen we were in position, parked fifty yards along a gravel track in the forest, a stone's throw from the entrance to Château Rochefort. I peered up at the night sky. The weather was fine, with just a little broken cloud and a light wind – perfect for the parachute drop.

Max whistled nervously while picking at crinkly bits of dried collodion on his face. He'd applied the solution that afternoon in an attempt to make himself appear much older. The shoulders of his uniform looked like they were covered in dandruff – it was the dusting of talc he'd applied liberally to his hair. Seeing the results of his efforts, the rest of us had abandoned the idea!

The wait began to get to me too. Loki remained in the back of the truck with our *prisoners*. Amélie and Jacques complained bitterly when Loki refused to loosen their bindings. He insisted they should remain tied up – at least until we were inside the château – in case the guards at the gate decided to take a close look at them. Only once there – with no chance of turning back – would Loki untie them and return their weapons.

Max drummed his fingers on the steering wheel. 'I

hate this part, Finn. The waiting. The lull before the storm. I just want to get on with it. All this hanging around drives me crazy.'

At ten thirty-five I climbed down from the cab and walked a little way into the trees. I needed a pee before we set off and all hell broke loose. Loki joined me. 'Well, it's almost time, Finn,' he said.

'Uh-huh. Damn this blasted zip!'

Beneath our uniforms we were wearing dark civilian clothes. At the right moment we'd discard the uniforms. That way I hoped to avoid being shot by the British paratroopers. Unfortunately, taking a pee with two pairs of trousers on and two zips to negotiate wasn't easy. It was the sort of problem encountered by Special Ops agents that wasn't covered in any of our lessons back at Mulberry House. I'd barely sorted myself out when we heard an explosion that sounded like distant thunder and there was a shimmering flash on the horizon. It was rapidly followed by an orange glow in the sky. I peered at my watch – ten-forty. It had begun!

'Best get back to the truck, Finn.'

Within minutes, a convoy of trucks and motorcycles shot past us, speeding in the direction of Le Havre and the fuel depot. We counted them. Every truck meant fewer soldiers to deal with at the barracks. Five trucks – that probably equated to at least a hundred men, half the total garrisoned at the château. But it meant there were still a hundred for us to overcome. 'Come on,' I muttered under my breath. 'More please.' A minute later another two trucks hurtled past.

I turned and banged a fist on the rear wall of the cabin to let the others know we were off. Max fired up the engine and slipped into gear, then turned off the gravel track and onto the road. Accelerating, he ground through the gears. I reached into my coat pocket and removed two hefty lumps of plastic explosive. Then, glancing out of the windscreen, I held my breath as two German motorcycles shot past us, heading in the other direction, the drivers raising their hands to say hello as they whizzed by. If only they knew!

Max took his foot off the accelerator and slowed. Just a few hundred yards separated us from the entrance to the château. Both sides of the road were bordered by woodland, and to my left a string of telegraph poles stretched into the night. 'Stop here,' I said.

Max applied the brakes. I jumped from the cab, ran to the nearest telegraph pole and taped a lump of explosive to it. Then, fumbling in my pocket, I took out a time pencil, bent it, gave it a shake and pressed it into the explosive. These particular time pencils had a ten-minute delay. I ran to the next telegraph pole and repeated the exercise, then rushed to clamber back into the cab. 'All done,' I said with relief. 'With any luck they'll knock out Fritz's communications and stop them calling for reinforcements.'

Max pulled off again. Rounding a gentle bend, he suddenly stiffened and took a sharp intake of breath. 'There it is, Finn. Château Rochefort.'

I banged on the cab again. 'This is it!' I yelled.

Max turned off the road and approached the heavily fortified gates. Sentries shone their torches at us and waved for us to pull over. 'Let me do the talking, Finn,' said Max. He opened his window and poked his head out. '*Wozu die ganze Aufregung?*' he shouted.

He was asking what all the excitement was about. One of the guards called back that there'd been a major raid by the Resistance at the fuel depot and that there were reports of fierce fighting. I thought of Alain and said a quick prayer for him. His mother had already lost a husband and two sons. That was a big enough sacrifice, wasn't it?

The guard approached the cab and shone his torch at Max and then at me. Max explained that we had two prisoners in the back. The guard signalled to a colleague who was in charge of a hungry-looking Alsatian and ordered him to take a look. This he duly did, calling out that everything was in order. A few cheerful words later and the gates were swung open: we were on our way again. Max wiped the sweat from his brow, looking extremely pleased. I peered at my watch – ten minutes to eleven. We had so little time.

The driveway up to the entrance of Château Rochefort was wide, as straight as the barrel of my gun, and a mile long. My mouth grew dry. I knew the hardest part of our mission lay right in front of us. Max leaned forward, peered up at the sky and whistled. '*Ach du meine Fresse!* Look at that, Finn. What a sight!'

The night sky was peppered with parachutes, dozens of them, some little more than specks, others already large enough to see the men dangling from their cords. Most were drifting slightly to the south of us. A few would miss their landing mark, a handful probably ending up in the trees. It was an amazing, heartening sight. But it also meant we needed to get a move on. 'Put your foot down, Max!'

The château was an equally incredible spectacle. It was vast, with row upon row of shuttered windows, towers at each corner, and was constructed in stone that looked solid enough to withstand a howitzer. The facade was lit by the feeble light of a waning moon. A broad set of stone steps led up to the main entrance, above which hung the obligatory swastikas. Two guards flanked the heavy wooden doors. Clutching their rifles in front of them, they gazed up at the parachutes in astonishment. Distracted, the soldiers hardly noticed our arrival. Max stopped opposite the entrance and we climbed out, ran to the rear of the truck and lifted the awning.

''Raus! 'Raus!' I shouted, waving the barrel of my machine gun. Jacques and Amélie hesitated and then jumped down. They looked terrified.

Loki climbed out too, handed me a bag from the back of the truck and gave me the faintest of nods. I slung the bag over my shoulder and together we marched our prisoners towards the main entrance, Max leading the way, his pistol drawn, barking various orders at us in German. The two sentries had overcome their surprise and raised their rifles, aiming them into the sky.

Anyone who was a half-decent shot could probably hit a parachutist as they drifted slowly down and came in to land. Realizing this, Loki duly dealt with them using a short burst of his Sten.

Throwing open the door to the château, Max strode inside with an air of authority. A middle-aged Nazi official sitting behind a desk in the hallway slammed down a telephone, rose abruptly to his feet, snapped to attention and saluted. '*Heil Hitler!*' His eyes flashed at each of us in turn. '*Das Telefon – die Leitung ist tot. Was ist los?*' he stammered. He was trying to tell us there was something wrong with the telephone. I hid my delight.

Max walked up to the guard's table, lifted the phone and listened. Banging it down, he turned to me and said, 'Well done, Finn, the lines are down.' His sudden switch to English caused the blood to drain from the German official's face and he raised his arms above his head.

The inside of the château was even more jaw-droppingly splendid than it looked from the outside. Fancy furniture, gilded paintings and mirrors surrounded a large staircase that led up to a galleried landing. The place stank of wealth once belonging to the Moutons, now the property of the Third Reich.

Alarm bells began ringing throughout the building. There was one in the hall, right above the official's desk. It was deafening. I couldn't even hear myself think. A few rounds from my Sten silenced it and punched a nasty hole in the plaster of the wall. The official began to shake from head to foot.

From elsewhere in the building panic-stricken shouts

reached our ears. We didn't have much time. Loki loosened Amélie and Jacques' bindings, and I handed them
Stens and clips of ammunition. With his revolver pressed
into the official's neck, Max took delight in leaning over
the desk and politely asking where Odette Ravoir was
being held and where in the château the Lefebvres were
located. Alone and hopelessly outnumbered, the official
was soon spilling the beans. Monsieur and Madame
Lefebvre's room, he informed us, was on the third floor
in the east wing.

'I know the way,' said Jacques. 'I'll go and get them.'
He turned and charged up the stairs.

Gunfire broke out in the grounds of the château. The
paratroopers had begun landing and were fighting their
way to the cliff top, the location of the radar installation.
We had to move fast. 'The cellars are that way!' Amélie
shouted, pointing to a side door. 'Through there. It's a,
erm, a servants' hall. At the end there are steps.'

Two soldiers appeared on the other side of the
entrance hall. Loki and I opened fire and dealt
with them.

'Go and get Freya!' Max shouted. 'Amélie and I will
stay here and keep our escape route clear. Well, don't just
stand there, Finn, get a move on!'

Together, Loki and I rushed through the side door
and pounded down the inner hallway. There were lots of
doors to choose from. 'Amélie said the one at the end!'
I shouted breathlessly. Reaching it, Loki pressed himself
up against the wall and held his Sten in readiness as I
reached for the handle. I flung open the door and was

confronted by a spiral stone staircase. Hurrying as fast as we could, we twisted downwards. I began to feel giddy and had to reach out for the handrail to steady myself. At the bottom we burst through another door and found ourselves entering the château's cellars. They were vast, comprising long passageways with whitewashed walls and arched ceilings lit by a string of lamps. On both sides lay cavernous recesses, many of which stored thousands of dusty, cobweb-laden bottles of wine on tall racks. I saw the four guards immediately. They were crouching, weapons poised and ready for trouble. They'd undoubtedly heard the alarms.

Had we not been in German uniform I think they would have opened fire without hesitation. But they did hesitate, thinking we were on their side. '*Schnell!*' Loki yelled. '*Odette Ravoir. Wo ist sie?*'

Though clearly confused, the guards relaxed slightly, one gesturing towards a series of heavy iron doors behind them. The others appeared to be looking past us, as if expecting partisans to arrive on our heels. '*Was ist los?*' one asked nervously. They hadn't figured out that a whole heap of trouble had already arrived and was standing before them. Together, Loki and I lifted our Stens and let them have it. The loud *rat-a-tat-tats* echoed and reverberated in the confined space. Wayward bullets pinged as they ricocheted. Dozens of bottles shattered, shards of glass flying in all directions, and gallons of red wine spraying into the air. It looked as if there was blood everywhere, but mostly it was 1934 Château Rochefort burgundy.

Lifting a bunch of heavy keys from a hook on the wall, Loki called out to Freya and we heard her muffled replies from inside a cell. The third key we tried turned in the lock and Loki shoved open the door. '*Freya!*'

She was in a wretched state, her clothes torn, her face bruised, but it was her eyes that captured and held my attention. They were defiant, full of fire and determination. I knew she'd resisted, that she'd said nothing, that she'd managed to hold out. Loki seized her tightly and they hugged.

'Are you all right?' I asked.

Over Loki's shoulder she nodded to me. 'Yes, Finn. I'm all right. I knew you'd come.'

'Well you two can save it for later,' I said. 'Right now we've got to get the hell out of here.' I prised them apart and handed Freya my Sten, removing another from my shoulder bag as we ran back through the cellar.

'Wait,' Freya called out. 'There are others here. We can't leave them to die.' Grabbing the bunch of keys from Loki, she fumbled desperately with them as she hurried to unlock the other cells. The ragged, beaten and broken prisoners slowly emerged from their dark holes, all unsure quite what was happening.

There were four of them, three men and a woman. I berated myself for my unkind thoughts – that in their state they'd slow us down. I remembered Amélie saying that a dozen partisans had been arrested in the last week alone. About to ask where the others might be, I stopped myself. I think I already knew the answer – in the woods to the east of Rochefort with bullets in their heads. 'We'll have to get them to the boats somehow,' I said.

We made our way back to the entrance hall. The others were waiting for us; Amélie was hugging a middle-aged woman – Madame Lefebvre, I presumed. Wearing a sickly yellow dressing gown, her hair dishevelled from sleep, she looked frail and bewildered.

'Where's your father, Jacques?' Loki asked.

'Mother says he's working late in his laboratory.'

'Do you know where?'

'Yes. We'll have to fetch him.' Jacques studied the four partisans we'd just released, nodding hello to two of them. Evidently he knew them, and I wondered if he'd been responsible for their capture. If he had, then it must have been a strange moment for him to see them reappear before his eyes, like ghosts returning to haunt him.

Deciding now was the time to dispense with our uniforms, Max, Loki and I put down our weapons and hurriedly began tearing them off. We could still hear gunfire. Jacques and Amélie slipped outside to see what was happening. Freya covered the other doorways in the hall with her Sten while we changed.

I was midway through yanking my outer trousers off when I caught a whiff of something odd and strangely familiar – *strawberries*! Someone behind me cleared their throat extremely loudly, almost theatrically. Instinctively I looked round and then up the sweeping staircase. *Renard!* He was pointing his pistol at me. To his left was

Véronique. Her pistol was trained on Freya. I froze, as did Loki on spotting them. Freya was willing to have a go at shooting but I shook my head at her. Véronique would have beaten her to the trigger.

'So what do we have here?' Renard began, casting his eyes over the partisans. 'A rescue attempt? I must congratulate you on getting this far. *Bravo!* Unfortunately this is as far as you go.'

Jacques and Amélie came back in through the front door, spotted Renard and stopped dead in their tracks. I don't know who appeared more surprised, Jacques or Renard. But it was Renard who reacted quickest, bringing his pistol to bear and forcing Jacques and Amélie to drop their weapons.

Renard was also first to speak. 'Jacques, I'm most disappointed. I was hoping to recruit you, but I see you've already made up your mind about which side you're on. Still, never mind. I must admit, I did think it was a little strange bumping into you back in London. A bit *too* much of a coincidence. I should have realized you were on to me. What are you, SIS?'

'No. Special Operations.'

Renard looked blank. 'Never heard of them,' he declared. Then he sighed. 'I'm sorry, Jacques, but you do realize this is the end of the road for you. For old time's sake I wish I could let you go, but alas my work in England isn't yet finished. I'm afraid I'm going to have to shoot you along with everyone else.'

I noticed Véronique squinting at me. I think she suddenly recognized me from The Melksham hotel incident. Because of it, I resigned myself to being second on Renard's list for execution.

'Cover me, Véronique,' Renard ordered. He strode down the steps towards Jacques. When he was three feet from him, he stopped and held his pistol at arm's length, the barrel almost touching Jacques' head. '*Adieu, Jacques!*'

Madame Lefebvre and Amélie screamed, and the other partisans shielded their faces in horror.

A single shot rang out.

Chapter Thirty-one
The Great Escape

A tiny wisp of smoke wafted from the end of the pistol's barrel. Only it wasn't the barrel of Renard's gun, but Véronique's!

Renard slumped to the floor. Véronique's shot had struck him in the temple. From a distance of about thirty feet it was a tricky shot with no room for error. It was by far the best shot I'd ever seen with a handgun. Madame Lefebvre ran and embraced Jacques, sobbing hysterically.

I looked at Véronique as she descended the rest of the stairs. She smiled at me. 'Hello, Finn,' she said coolly. 'I had a feeling we'd meet again.'

Jacques prised himself from his mother's grasp and called out angrily, 'Why did you leave it to the last possible second? That was far too close for comfort. Supposing you'd missed. I'd be dead!'

'I never miss,' she replied. 'Now, shouldn't we get out of here?'

Filing out of the door, we took up defensive positions at the top of the steps behind low walls. I scanned the scene. Our truck remained where we'd left it. Straight ahead of us the mile-long drive stretched off into the night and towards the road to Rochefort and Le Havre. The restricted area and our route to the beach lay to our right. The sounds of gunfire came from that direction too. This wasn't going to be easy. 'We should use the truck,' Max suggested. 'Ram our way through the gates to the restricted area. It's got to be better than risking going across several hundred yards of open ground. The other partisans are in no fit state to fight or run that distance.'

'Good idea,' I said. 'Load everyone up. Get them to lie down on the floor. Freya, Amélie and Véronique, you three offer covering fire out the back. Loki and Jacques, you two hang onto the doors of the cab. Max, drop us off at the entrance to the laboratories.'

Once we'd climbed into the truck Max revved fiercely and wasted little time in driving towards the barbed-wire fencing and the arc lights bordering the restricted area. I could see flat-roofed, single-storey, partially buried buildings beyond – the laboratories. The gate had already been blown open, the twisted remains dangling on bent hinges. Soldiers from both sides lay dead in our path. Max swerved to avoid them. Small fires – the aftermath of the explosions – lit the night with a flickering orange glow. 'Stop here!' Jacques shouted, pointing to a doorway.

Max slammed on the brakes. Jacques and Loki jumped down and I tumbled out of the cab. 'Don't hang around, Max. Try and get as close to the cliff top as you can!' I swung the door shut.

The entrance to the Mouton laboratories was closed but the lock proved no match for the drilling burst of fire from my Sten. Loki kicked the door in and the three of us advanced down one whitewashed corridor after another, alarm bells ringing in our ears, our guns poised, our hearts in our mouths.

Jacques knew the way and led us through labs containing long benches piled high with amazing equipment that hummed and buzzed, and lines of radio valves that glowed like weak light bulbs. Vacuum pumps clacked and snorted. Bright-green dots tracked their way across the screens of cathode-ray tubes and the needles of a hundred dials flicked back and forth while tiny lights winked at us from the depths of a bird's-nest tangle of wiring. The place was deserted.

Jacques reached another door. 'This is Father's office – at least it was before they took him to Berlin.' He grabbed the handle, twisted it and threw the door open.

Inside we found a frightened Monsieur Lefebvre with a handful of his fellow scientists and technicians huddled together in one corner. At the sight of Jacques, he looked astonished; holding out his arms, he ran and hugged his son. Jacques spoke quickly to his father and I struggled to understand what he was saying, although I think he mentioned something about rescuing him and about fulfilling promises he'd made a long time ago. Monsieur Lefebvre was overcome with emotion.

Loki ordered the others to lie on the floor. There simply wasn't time to work out whose side they were on.

Still grasped in a bear hug, Jacques informed his father that he was taking the family on a very long holiday to England, a prospect that was greeted favourably by Monsieur Lefebvre, especially when he was told that within about half an hour the whole site was going to be blown to smithereens.

'The blueprints,' I shouted. 'Where are the blueprints for the magnetron?'

Jacques tore himself free and repeated my question to his father in French. Excitedly Monsieur Lefebvre rummaged through a filing cabinet, yanked out the stolen documents and handed them to Jacques, who hurriedly stuffed them inside his jacket.

'Can we get the hell out of here now, please?' Loki pleaded. 'The boats are due to leave in twenty minutes.'

Outside the laboratories the gunfire had grown louder and was interspersed with the flashes and thunderous cracks of grenades and mortar fire. I feared the worst. Our paratroopers were engaged in a ferocious firefight with German troops from the barracks. They had to hold them off. They needed to keep the gully to the beach open or everyone would be trapped on the cliff top.

Monsieur Lefebvre showed us a short cut between the laboratory buildings. Zigzagging from one area of moon shadow to the next, we hurried as fast as Monsieur Lefebvre could run. He was out of shape and quickly began gasping for breath.

Approaching the edge of the laboratory complex, I took the lead, racing on ahead, slamming myself up against the wall, ready to risk taking a peek towards the radar installation and cliff top. I could hear an engine, and voices too. As the others reached my shoulder, I glanced round the corner and let out a cry of fright.

Our truck stood thirty feet in front of me. Its engine was running but its windscreen was shattered and the canvas awning was on fire. The driver's door was off its hinges and Max was kneeling on the ground beside it, his face splattered with blood. 'Don't shoot,' he cried. 'We're Special Ops. We're on your side. *Don't shoot!*'

He wasn't talking to me!

I suddenly realized that everyone else had jumped from the truck and were standing, sitting and lying in a bewildered state on the other side of it.

'Jesus, Finn!' said Loki, brushing past me. 'They must have been hit by a grenade or something.'

We rushed forward to help them. The next few seconds were the scariest of my life. No sooner had I reached Max than soldiers emerged from the gloom, British soldiers, their faces blackened with burned cork, their Tommy guns raised. And they were shouting at us, at one another, at anything and nothing. We were in the midst of the confusion, panic and bloodlust of a fierce battle. Their hearts would be pumping as quickly as ours, their nerves as strained, their fingers as horribly trigger happy. One wrong move and we'd all be dead. I dropped my Sten, fell to my knees, placed my hands on my head and yelled to the others to do the same. And then I joined in with Max's chorus: 'We're Special Ops. We're on your side!'

They seized our weapons and surrounded us. The barrel of a Tommy gun was pressed against the back of my head. There was so much shouting and yelling and deafening gunfire that I couldn't even think straight enough to say a last prayer. Max was kneeling three feet in front of me. Shards of glass from the shattered windscreen were embedded in his cheeks and forehead, and rivulets of blood were trickling and dripping from his chin. I turned my head. Loki had a barrel held inches from his left temple. For one agonizing moment nothing seemed to happen. It was as if time had stopped. And then came a voice out of the night.

'All right, lads?'

Startled, I gasped. 'Smithy? Is that you?'

'Most certainly is, Mr Gunnersen. I was told we might bump into each other.'

His ugly face emerged from the gloom. There was a huge grin on it. He hauled me to my feet, shook my hand firmly and then began bellowing orders. Medics were summoned to help Max and the others. Three more paratroopers were ordered to escort everyone to the gully and down to the waiting boats.

Reunited with Madame Lefebvre and having surveyed what was going on all round us, Jacques' father suddenly understood the objective of our mission – to steal the Freya radar device. He grabbed Jacques' arm and spoke quickly to him. Jacques nodded and hurried to where I was standing next to Smithy and Loki. 'My father says that we must take the Freya equipment from inside the control bunker. The rest of it, all the aerials and stuff out here, will be useless without it. He says it's vital.'

'Ruddy hell, that's a tricky one,' Smithy said, rubbing his chin and peering at his watch. 'They're defending the bunker with machine guns. We haven't got much time to break through. It's already after twelve. We've got to be out of here in fifteen minutes. So far the lads have managed to maintain our position by keeping most of Jerry pinned down at the edge of the woods. But we can't hold out for long, and no doubt their reinforcements will be here at any minute.'

'I know what to look for!' Jacques shouted. 'Father described it to me. But I'll need some help.' He glanced towards me expectantly.

Small-arms fire erupted close by, making us all flinch and duck as wayward bullets whizzed past our heads and pinged into the wall of the laboratories. We had to decide what to do – now! There was no time to think about it. I looked to Loki and he nodded to me. 'We'll come with you, Jacques.'

'Oh, bugger,' Smithy swore. 'The brigadier will kick my backside all the way from Land's End to John o' Groats if I let anything happen to you under my watch. Suppose I'd better tag along then, hadn't I?'

'We'll come too,' said Amélie and Freya simultaneously.

Smithy shook his head. 'The four of us will suffice. Now get the hell out of here, ladies. My decision is final.'

As we re-armed ourselves, I was glad to see the others being led towards the gully, the beach – and safety.

'Right, lads, now I'm in charge of this one,' Smithy

said as we crouched in a huddle. 'Listen, do what I tell you, and for Christ's sake keep your heads down. Follow me, stay close, and don't dare make a ruddy sound. If I hear as much as a fart I'll have you all booted out of Special Ops and you'll spend the rest of the war knitting scarves for the WAAFs. Have I made myself clear?'

Smithy led us along the cliff path in single file. We encountered a constant stream of sappers and soldiers heading in the opposite direction. All were carrying strange pieces of equipment. We had to give way when a team of four passed us struggling to roll a large metal dish along the path. Jacques gasped. 'That's a Giant Würzburg aerial,' he said in astonishment. 'Be careful not to bend the dipoles,' he called out after them. More men appeared out of the gloom, lugging sections of a huge rectangular metal grid strung with wires. 'See that?' Jacques pointed. 'That's part of the new Freya system. My God, they're really going to get away with this.'

The gunfire grew louder as we approached the radar installation. In the darkness I could just make out men clambering over structures, hammering and levering bits off with crowbars. There was much shouting, chivvying and yells of encouragement. Reaching a small raised embankment, Smithy dropped down on one knee and waved us to do the same. He pointed to a low concrete structure some forty yards ahead of us and partially buried. It was located right in the middle of the whole radar site. 'See the slits in the concrete walls, lads?' he whispered. 'They've got machine guns inside them.

Ruddy great big ones. And the bastards have got every direction covered. If we simply charge them, we'll get mown down. So, first things first. At least one position has to be neutralized.' He removed a grenade from his pocket. 'Now, here's the plan. I'm going to count to three and then make a dash for it. I'd appreciate it if you gave me some covering fire.'

He didn't wait for us to question his plan. Counting to three quickly, he leaped up and made a zigzagging dash across the exposed ground. The three of us let rip with our machine guns. Unfortunately so did the Germans, forcing Smithy to take cover by throwing himself flat on the ground about midway to his objective. He was pinned down in the open.

We set about reloading while trying to figure out a way to help him. While we dithered, the sound of hurried footsteps behind us heralded the arrival of Freya. Clutching a rifle, she threw herself down beside us. 'What's happening?' she asked.

'I thought you were heading for the boats with everyone else,' I whispered.

'I was, but then I remembered.'

'Remembered what?'

'That we promised to stick together, no matter what. So here I am. Where's Smithy?'

I pointed and explained the problem. Jacques lifted his Sten above the top of the embankment and emptied another magazine, but as soon as Smithy tried to move he got pinned down again. Freya lifted her rifle and rested it on top of the grassy mound. I immediately understood what she was thinking. 'Do you think you can you hit whoever's manning the machine gun behind that narrow slit?' I asked.

'I think so.' She positioned herself carefully and seemed to take for ever to line up her sight. Her concentration was intense despite Jacques' impatient muttering. For a moment I think Freya was imagining she was back home, out in the wilderness with her father, hunting an elusive deer hidden deep in the woods. Gently she squeezed the trigger, a shot rang out, the butt recoiled into her shoulder and she let out a small cry of '*Ja!*' like she always did when she knew she'd shot well.

Loki let rip again with his machine gun and Smithy crawled forward. This time no return fire came from the enemy's position.

Out of the darkness Smithy shouted, 'Bloody good shot!'

Freya really had done it! We scrambled over the embankment and hurried to the wall of the bunker, where Smithy was waiting. 'For once I'm glad you disobeyed orders, miss,' he said, looking relieved.

Together we jumped down into a deep concrete-lined trench that led to the entrance of the control bunker. Smithy's grenade blew the door. He led us inside, dispatching all resistance with short bursts of his Tommy gun. A corridor led us to the heart of the facility and the control room.

I cast my eyes over all the equipment. There was tons of it – banks of dials, and screens that were used to observe the return radar pulses. There was so much gear it would take a month of Sundays to remove it all. And we didn't have one Sunday, let alone a month of them. Jacques scanned the room and quickly pointed out the key items he was pretty sure were associated with the Freya device and, despite his calls for us to be careful, the rest of us set about levering the equipment out of the racks and consoles, using the butts of our weapons. Carrying as much as we could manage, we headed out, Freya covering our backs.

Pursued by enemy small-arms fire, we trailed back along the cliff-top path. The gear was heavy and sharp metal edges bit deep into my hands. As we groaned and cursed, lugging our treasure as best we could, it dawned on me that we were pretty much on our own. The paratroopers had already evacuated, heading for the beach. We were the last ones remaining on the cliff top, and our time was up. It was past 0030 hours. I prayed one boat had stayed long enough to pick us up. I puffed and panted, my muscles burning from the weight of the equipment held agonizingly against my chest.

'Not far now!' Smithy shouted.

We reached the gully, right on the edge of the cliffs. I peered down at the churning, foaming sea that glistened in the moonlight, and saw a landing craft. They'd waited for us! I felt euphoric. We were going to make it. About to begin my descent towards the beach, I heard a single burst of machine-gun fire. It sounded close. *Very close.* I turned round. Some twenty yards behind me Jacques lay face down, motionless.

Returning fire, Smithy appeared at my shoulder. 'Christ! It's too late. Leave him. Down to the beach. Now! All of you.'

Ignoring the order, I dropped my equipment and ran to where Jacques lay. Freya arrived beside me. We turned him over. His eyes were open but held a lifeless stare. Freya looked up at me and shook her head. 'He's dead, Finn.'

I reached inside his coat and pulled out the folded blueprints.

As our landing craft motored through the swell and headed out to sea, Loki and Freya huddled together in the bottom of the boat to avoid the worst of the spray. I couldn't bring myself to look at the grieving Lefebvre family, so instead I gazed back at the slowly vanishing cliffs of Normandy. Jacques, I realized, had accomplished what he set out to do – rescue his mother and father. In doing so he had paid the ultimate price. In spite of him, in the end Operation Death Ray had been completed successfully. I decided I'd talk to the others as soon as we got back to Mulberry House *before* any debriefings. I wasn't sure if they'd see things my way. I saw little point in shouting from the rooftops that Jacques had betrayed us. That wouldn't solve anything. In his parents' eyes Jacques was a hero. Perhaps that was for the best. After all, he'd faced one of the hardest dilemmas imaginable. Who the hell was I to judge him? My thoughts turned to home, to Mother and Anna. Wherever they were, I prayed they were still alive and not suffering at the hands of the Nazis. Home suddenly seemed far, far away, and yet I desperately wanted to be back there.

Véronique appeared at my shoulder and put her arm round me. 'Quite an adventure, don't you think?'

'A nightmare, more like,' I replied. 'I was convinced you were a double agent.'

She laughed sarcastically. 'Sometimes even I'm not sure whose side I'm on.'

I looked at her in astonishment.

'In our line of work we have to do things we don't like, Finn. Things that we don't want to do, that seem wrong, all to keep one step ahead. Our job's certainly a hellish one, but the prize is precious and worth the sacrifice. Freedom is priceless, but you already know that, don't you?'

I thought for a moment and then said, 'Do you mean like killing that man at the hotel and then running back to Renard to make sure your cover wasn't blown? Like me, I guess you didn't know the waiter was a member of the SIS, one of your own.'

'No, I didn't know,' she replied. 'But I didn't kill him, Finn. You did, albeit unintentionally. He never recovered from banging his head against the table when he fell.'

The boat rocked viciously in the swell. I suddenly felt sick. The world seemed to spin. I closed my eyes. When I opened them again, Véronique had gone from beside me. The drone of aircraft engines drew my attention to the sky. There were dozens of planes passing overhead and they were sweeping in low towards the French coast. Minutes later powerful explosions, sounding like claps of distant rumbling thunder, reached our ears and flashes lit up the horizon. It wasn't long before it seemed like the whole of France was on fire. I reckoned Rochefort was getting a pounding too. I thought back to the London Blitz and the carnage wreaked by the Luftwaffe. Now we were returning the ghastly favour and I had no doubt civilians would suffer hellishly. Would it ever end?

Smithy appeared beside me. 'Our lads in Bomber Command are putting on quite a show, aren't they? When we get back I expect you'll appreciate a few days' rest. Recharge those batteries.'

I yanked the folded blueprints from inside my coat. 'Here – a present for X and the brigadier.'

'Well done, Mr Gunnersen.' He cheerfully gave me a hearty slap on my back. 'Good work. I knew you lot would turn out all right. Could feel it in my guts from the first day we met.'

Yawning, I suddenly felt woozy with exhaustion. 'I feel like I could sleep for a month!'

'A week will have to do, I'm afraid. According to the brigadier, X is planning another job for you.' He laughed in a manner I didn't much care for. 'Consider what you've just been through as a taster, a gentle intro-duction. Your work has barely begun, Mr Gunnersen, barely begun!'

Postscript

In the years leading up to the Second World War rumours abounded that a horrific death ray had been invented which could blast aircraft out of the sky. Although the rumours proved false, scientists in Britain's Air Ministry worried whether building a death ray was technically possible. The question arrived on the desk of Robert Watson-Watt at the National Physics Laboratory. His assistant (Wilkins) set to work on the problem. The answer was rather surprising. He calculated that in theory radio waves could be used to create such a device but it would require an incredibly powerful beam, far more powerful than they were presently able to produce. However, he reckoned it ought to be possible to test the idea out by seeing if they could detect ordinary radio waves reflected from an aircraft. Their experiments proved successful. Radio direction finding (RDF) was demonstrated for the first time. Today we call it radar!

Because of their work, by the time war broke out Britain had a defensive chain of coastal radar stations providing our fighter squadrons with a vital early warning system. Had we not had radar, maybe the outcome of the Battle of Britain would have been different, and maybe Hitler would have given the green light for Operation Sealion, the full-scale invasion of

Britain!

The Nazis developed radar too, but their version appeared different and so the British set out to discover how it worked. It resulted in one of the most daring raids of the war. During the night of 27–28 February 1942 British paratroopers landed close to the coast of Normandy and a village called Bruneval. They fought their way to the tall cliffs, and the location of a German radar station comprising the Giant Würzburg and Freya installations which lay at the heart of the enemy's defences. Under fire, they dismantled the equipment and carried the pieces down the cliffs to waiting landing craft belonging to the Royal Navy. The mission, code-named Operation Biting, was hugely successful. The local French Resistance also played their part, providing important information about the strength of German forces and the extent of defensive positions. Capturing this vital equipment led to a method of radar jamming being perfected, thus protecting the pilots and aircraft of Bomber Command. This amazing true story inspired *Special Operations: Death Ray*.

Eventually, aircraft were fitted with a form of radar as well, enabling pilots to detect the enemy at night and in thick cloud. A vital component in this system was the magnetron. You may not have heard of a magnetron before but it is very likely that you have one at home – in your kitchen – because a magnetron is also used to generate the microwaves in your microwave oven!

Although *Death Ray* is a work of fiction, Finn Gunnersen's clandestine world of Special Operations is also firmly rooted in real events. A dozen houses in the beautiful New Forest in southern England were requisitioned during the war and, along with other locations, including Arisaig in the Scottish Highlands, formed part of a training school for secret agents. The organization was called the Special Operations Executive (SOE). In total secrecy about three thousand men and women of more than fifteen different nationalities passed through the school during the course of the war. Many were subsequently sent behind enemy lines on dangerous missions. Most of these volunteers were ordinary people, not highly trained military personnel. The heroism and sacrifice of numerous agents is well documented and we owe them a great debt of gratitude for the work they did. The training Finn and his friends received at Mulberry House and at Arisaig has been based on true accounts of the skills taught to agents at the time. Lying on the foot plate and rolling off really was considered the safest way of getting off a fast-moving train! Of course, it is so dangerous that it's not something that should ever be attempted. Unless, that is, your country is at war and you are running for your life!

The Playfair Code

In the early years of the Second World War both the SIS and the SOE used the same method of enciphering their Morse-code messages. Each agent was given a unique keyword or phrase to memorize. It was a closely guarded secret. In *Death Ray* Finn's key phrase was: *On a dark and stormy night.* The Playfair code worked as follows:

The first thing Finn did was write out his key phrase in lines of five letters, each line directly underneath the previous one, to form the beginnings of a grid. Importantly, no letter gets repeated, so, for example, although the letter O appears twice in his key phrase it only appears once in the grid.

So Finn's grid looked like this:

```
O   N   A   D   R
K   S   T   M   Y
I   G   H
```

Finn then added all the unused letters of the alphabet in the right order to complete a 5 x 5 grid. As the alphabet contains 26 letters and only 25 are needed, the letters I and J are both treated as I. This is what Finn's completed grid looked like:

```
O   N   A   D   R
K   S   T   M   Y
I   G   H   B   C
E   F   L   P   Q
U   V   W   X   Z
```

The message Finn sent to London in *Death Ray* was:

URGENT . . . ODETTE ARRESTED . . . WILL TRY
RESCUE . . . SUSPECT JACQUES IS ENEMY SPY . . . DEATH
RAY COMPROMISED . . . ADVISE NEXT STEPS

Finn divided his message into pairs of letters (called bigrams):

UR . . . GE . . . NT . . . OD . . . ET . . . TE . . . etc.

Taking each pair in turn, Finn located their positions in his grid. So, for the first pair, 'UR', their positions are:

O	N	A	D	**R**
K	S	T	M	Y
I	G	H	B	C
E	F	L	P	Q
U	V	W	X	Z

Now comes the clever bit! Finn had to think of these letters forming the opposite corners of a square or rectangle (in this case the square, **ORUZ**). He then wrote down the opposite corners to **UR** – that is, **OZ**. These are the letters he transmitted to London (there they'd do the operation in reverse to decode it).

If you try out the Playfair code, you will soon discover several complications. Quite often pairs of letters fall in the same row or column and hence don't form a square or rectangle. For example, the fourth pair of letters (or fourth *bigram*) in Finn's message is **OD**; both letters are in the top row of his grid. Finn would get round this by shifting the second letter one space (either left or right, or up or down). In the case of **OD**, Finn would shift down. So the pair **OD** becomes **OM**, enabling him to form the rectangle **ODKM**. Taking the opposite corners, he can now code **OD** as **DK**. Worse still, sometimes he would be faced with coding an identical pair of letters, for example **DD**. To make a square out of these Finn would have to shift the second letter in both directions; that is, *diagonally* – so **DD** would become **DY**, thus creating the square **DRMY**. His coded letters for **DD** would thus be **RM**.

These complications can make decoding a message quite a challenge because the person receiving Finn's message doesn't know that he's had to make the above adjustments. So they would simply decode each pair of letters and try to form proper words from them. What would look like bad spelling mistakes would alert them and they'd then try out various options until the message made sense.

As you can imagine, coding and decoding was a hard task for an agent working in the field, demanding great concentration and attention to detail while always fearing possible discovery and arrest. Try and see if you can work out the rest of the coding. Then imagine you've received the message and have a go at decoding it using the same approach, or invent your own key phrase and grid.

The Playfair code was extremely hard for the enemy to break, although it had one major drawback. If captured, an agent might reveal his key phrase under interrogation. The enemy could then use it to send false messages.

A series of 'security checks' were often included, e.g. deliberate mistakes – their presence or absence alerting London that the agent had probably been compromised. Eventually the SOE developed its own coding methods, including what were called *WOCs* (Worked Out Codes) printed on silk. The agent could easily destroy them if he or she feared capture, and with no secret key to remember, there was nothing the agent could divulge under interrogation. These later evolved into what were called *One Time Pads*, in which a *WOC* was used just once and then destroyed.

Finn has sent you an urgent message. Can you decode it?

DH FU RK OZ OL RM NI GE HF YH KL

O	N	A	D	R
K	S	T	M	Y
I	G	H	B	C
E	F	L	P	Q
U	V	W	X	Z

TIPS:

1. First use the above grid to decode each pair of letters in turn and write your answers in the boxes below, underneath Finn's coded version. The first pair is tricky to fully decode so I've got you started and helped you out by solving the three other really difficult pairs.

DH	FU	RK	OZ	OL	RM	NI	GE	HF	YH	KL
HA					DD			GH		TY

2. *Now look at your results and see if you can read the message. If you can't, it is because one or more of your pairs needs to be reversed (there are two ways of writing down each pair). For example, when you decode Finn's second pair, FU, you will find that it forms the square EFUV. You can write down the opposite corners as either EV or VE. You can't be sure which is correct until you try and read the message. So work along your decoding from left to right, and see if by switching round your pairs of letters you can make sense of the message.*

Good luck.

(Note: Those I've already solved for you are in the right order.)

3. *Still having problems? Hint: Finn's message contains five words (4, 3, 4, 8 and 3 letters respectively).*

SOLUTION:

Finn's message: Have you read Dogfight yet?